"WEST OF FAMOUS is a terrifically smart, strong thriller from Joni Fisher, whose crime novels get better with each entry in the series."

—Linda Fairstein, New York Times Bestselling Author of the Alexandra Cooper novels and winner of the Nero Award

"SOUTH OF JUSTICE is a multilayered, intricate, and suspenseful page-turner you'll want to read in one sitting."

—Diane Capri, New York Times and USA Today bestselling author of the Hunt for Jack Reacher thrillers

"Combining the elements of a police procedural and a suspenseful thriller, Fisher tics all the boxes for a compelling crime novel that will keep readers turning pages to the satisfying conclusion."

—Recommended by the US Review

BOOKS BY JONI M. FISHER

North of the Killing Hand

South of Justice

West of Famous

EAST OF EVIL

JONI M. FISHER

ISBN-13: 978-0-9972575-8-8 (Trade paperback)
ISBN-13: 978-0-9972575-9-5 (eBook)

Edited by Victoria Curran and Boswell Professional Writing Services
Original Cover Design and Formatting by Damonza.com

To loved ones lost.

ACKNOWLEDGMENTS

Special thanks to Victoria Curran and Cynthia A. Boswell of Boswell Professional Writing Services for their editorial wisdom and sharp minds. Warm thanks to J David Ivester, Literary Publicist and Marketing Specialist of Author Guide, for directing this book's path to readers and translating terms like pitch blurb, branding, metadata, digital rights management, and SEO into plain English.

Deep thanks to Damonza.com for the gorgeous cover art and internal formatting.

Many blessings go to authors Jamie Beckett, Donna Kelly, Terri Johnson, Carol J. Post, and C. J. Sweet for their blunt and specific advice on that first ugly draft.

Profound thanks to brilliant beta readers: John M. Esser, Maury L. Fisher, M.D., Caryn Frink, D'Ann Jirovec, Audrey Nettlow, Carol Speyerer, and Martha Walker for taking my long journey toward publication seriously.

EAST OF EVIL

· 1 ·

Monday, April 19, 2010

NEFI'S LIFE-CHANGING DAY started ordinary and turned peculiar on the way to morning classes.

A tingle ran up her neck. The sensation heightened her senses, akin to hearing a distant scream. While other Harvard students hunched over cell phones, Nefi scanned the shop-lined street at the edge of campus. On a van's rear window, she spotted the reflection of a broad-shouldered man half a block behind who was taking awkwardly long strides. Unlike other students trudging to campus, this man had no backpack straps on his shoulders. With his face shadowed by a ball cap, he kept his hands in his jacket pockets.

Nefi unzipped her raincoat to access her cell phone. April weather in Boston could bring rain, snow, or cold wind, and this morning's damp breeze in the low forties shot through her open jacket. The wind also carried car exhaust fumes and the hum of traffic. Her thick neck scarf kept her warm enough to prevent shivering.

She pulled her trusty old cell phone from the inner pocket of her coat and flipped it open. After pressing the camera icon, she held the phone up to her ear, stopped, and turned sideways on the sidewalk, aiming the lens at the stranger. She took a few photos. Feigning conversation, she checked her watch, nodded, and glanced at the man.

The stranger immediately looked down, further obscuring his face with his Red Sox cap while he slowed his pace. Clean-shaven, he was about five feet eight inches tall in dark blue jeans, brown hiking boots, and a plain navy-colored zip-up jacket. His athletic gait and posture suggested sports or military training.

Her Advanced Abnormal Psychology class started promptly at 8 a.m. She had overdue homework to turn in and despised being late to class. After turning toward the path to William James Hall, she tucked her phone away and elongated her stride to the stark white boxy four-teen-story building. Of all the buildings on campus, Nefi ranked it the second ugliest structure after the Science Center. William James Hall towered over the surrounding older, stately red brick buildings like a giant cheese grater.

She decided to test if the man was following her. Once inside the building and on familiar ground, she dashed into a recessed doorway where the overhead floodlight had burned out. She remembered it because the shadowy area had spooked her last week. Standing in the darkness, she watched students pass by in groups and couples in animated conversations. Others, absorbed by the small screens of their cell phones, marched at a zombie's pace while people maneuvered around them.

The stranger charged through the corridor, dodging around slow-moving students, his head pivoting at open doorways. He glanced at the dark doorway where Nefi stood but continued to the elevators. At the elevators, he stopped, removed his hat, and combed his fingers through his short hair. He scowled and tugged his hat on.

Nefi's curiosity turned to alarm and then anger.

The man was retracing his steps in the hallway when Nefi stepped into the light.

He flinched and halted two paces from her.

The stranger flashed through three emotional reactions—surprise, fear, and disgust. It was his last reaction that piqued Nefi's curiosity. Why would a stalker feel disgusted? Was he following the wrong person?

"There you are," he said.

Nefi loosened her arms, reached into her left sleeve, and grasped her knife handle.

Carrying a weapon on campus violated Harvard University policies. Having a double-edged knife on campus was punishable by a fine of up to $1,000 and two years in prison. Still, Nefi weighed the probable legal punishment for carrying her knife against the permanent consequences of being beaten, raped, or killed and decided in favor of self-defense. With campus violence becoming more common, she believed waiting to be rescued by campus security could be a fatal mistake.

Students passed behind the stranger. If she cried out for help, would they take action or take pictures to share on social media? She assumed she was on her own. At five feet eleven inches tall, Nefi had a height advantage over him, but he looked strong.

His attention shot to Nefi's hands while he eased his

hands from his pockets and spread his fingers in front of his waist. "I'm a friend of Ruis Ramos."

She recognized his voice, then his face. His hair was slightly longer than at Ruis's wedding. Ruis was her best friend's older brother. At the wedding, Ruis had called this man by a nickname. "Repo?"

He smiled and extended his hand. "Hello, Miss Jenkins. My real name's Arlo."

Leaving her knife in its sheath, she shook his hand.

In the time it took to blink twice, he had looked her over from hat to boots. Guys often did that. When men looked at Nefi's best friend Martina, they flirted, and their pupils expanded. When they noticed Nefi, they reacted to her height. Arlo showed no pupil response of arousal or fear.

Nefi sighed. "Did Ruis send you to protect me?"

Arlo smiled at two women passing by, and one smiled back. He chuckled and faced Nefi. "The way I hear it, Martina finds trouble, and trouble finds you."

Nefi nodded. "And here you are stalking me."

"I told Ruis I was moving to Boston, and he said I should stop by to see how you're doing." His half-shrug and glance away suggested a trace of deception.

"You could have called." Nefi stilled her body and studied his face.

He rolled his eyes. "Okay. We had a little wager. I bet I could sneak up close enough to touch your shoulder before you spotted me. He bet I couldn't."

The male ego mystified her. Was this just a bet, or was Ruis's friend practicing stealth for another reason? She weighed his ego against his safety and favored his safety. "I spotted you two blocks ago."

"No way." He flashed straight white teeth. The smell of coffee wafted from him when he spoke.

She showed him the photo on her phone. It was worth being late to class to observe his reaction—the moment expectation collided with reality.

His eyebrows rose. "Huh. I saw you stop and answer your phone. Very tricky. What gave me away?"

"No backpack. Military posture. But the real tell was when I looked at you on the street. You immediately turned away."

"I didn't want you to see my face." He raised one shoulder.

Though his behavior made sense to him, Nefi wanted him to understand why it didn't work. "Which is exactly how a stalker behaves. How do you normally react when a woman catches you looking at her?" Nefi shrugged off her backpack and dangled it by a strap at her side to remind him she needed to go to class.

Arlo blinked a few times then his eyelids closed half-way. He worked his jaw. "I wasn't looking at you like that."

Funny how being on the receiving end of honesty could hurt. Nefi planted her free hand on her hip.

"I mean, I know you're engaged." Sweat beaded on his face.

Ruis had probably told him. Ruis treated Nefi like a spare sister. Had Arlo taken the information about Nefi's engagement as a warning? She nodded as if accepting his excuse. "What do you normally do if a woman catches you watching her?"

His shoulders relaxed. "I smile. But if I'm shadowing someone, I don't want to interact. I don't want to be noticed."

Nefi drew from a criminology lesson. "It doesn't matter if the subject sees you. Did you know eyewitness accounts are the least reliable evidence in court?"

Arlo's eyebrows furrowed as he pulled his head slightly back.

Nefi said, "People are generally not observant. I'll prove it. Close your eyes."

He did. His eyelashes were dark and long. He'd missed shaving a spot along his left jawline. Woody, sensual cologne emanated from him in heatwaves.

She had been close enough for him to see her at Ruis's wedding and today. He considered her an acquaintance, a friend of a friend, but did he really *see* her? Most people stared once they noticed her eyes. Amber is the rarest eye color in humans. During a freshman year party, a drunk frat boy pointed and backed away, calling her a vampire. Hollywood has its standard for monsters, one of which is to mimic the eye color of predators like the eagle, the tiger, and the wolf. "What color are my eyes?"

"Light blue."

"I rest my case."

Arlo opened his brown eyes. "Whoa. Are those colored contact lenses?"

Nefi shook her head.

He continued to stare. "Ruis said you're the only person who could sneak up on him."

Nefi smiled. For whatever it was worth, she could sneak up on a Navy SEAL who now worked for the U.S. Marshals Service. "Did you serve with Ruis?"

Arlo leaned closer to Nefi and lowered his voice to a whisper. "I flew a Sikorsky Seahawk. Can't tell you where, when, or why, but that's how I met Ruis."

Nefi nodded. All Ruis's military friends kept secrets.

"I'm joining my brother's business as a private investigator." He dug a business card from his jacket and handed it to her.

Nefi tucked the card into the top pocket of her backpack. "How much was the bet?"

"Two hundred dollars." He waggled his eyebrows. "If I give you half, will you say I won?"

"Ruis says, 'Don't lie to someone who trusts you and don't trust someone who lies to you.'"

He nodded slowly and smiled without showing his teeth.

Of course, Arlo was testing her. Ruis's friends shared his honor code.

"Thanks for letting me practice."

Alone in the corridor with Arlo, Nefi said, "You're welcome to try again. Don't grab me from behind because that won't end well."

His eyes widened. "Noted."

Nefi carried her backpack to the elevator and pressed the button. When she glanced down the hall, she noticed Arlo had stepped into the shadowed doorway where she had hidden.

"Arlo, I can see your hat."

Once he pulled off his ball cap, darkness enveloped him. "Perfect."

The elevator opened, so Nefi rode it up to her floor and sneaked into the back row of the classroom. After muting her phone and checking for new text messages, she dug out her pen and notebook while the professor spoke.

"Narcissistic personality disorder. One percent of the population exhibits this cluster B personality disorder, often caused by trauma that results in low self-esteem. A narcissist will do almost anything to be the center of attention, including playing the victim, twisting situations through reverse projection, blaming others when caught doing inappropriate or cruel things, and interrupting others' conversations. Naturally, they are attracted to high-profile jobs such as politics and entertainment to feed their egos. Rejection and criticism, in turn, tend to harden them emotionally."

These characteristics fit an uncomfortable number of politicians Nefi had met through her uncle, Senator Hamilton Jenkins. Fortunately, her uncle had a servant's heart with a sharp eye for spotting narcissists and liars. He also excelled at handling people diplomatically.

In the margin of her notes during the lecture, Nefi penciled in the initials of celebrities who fit the profile characteristics. She had watched the evening news all semester to identify abnormal personality traits like the ones described in the textbook. The class taught the basics. Watching for people who fit the various abnormal personality traits was simply fieldwork.

Last week, at a friend's trial, she helped the defense team with her observations.

Her friend, Blake Clayton, had been charged with a capital offense, so Nefi skipped classes to attend the trial. She would have testified as a character witness if asked. After all, Blake was one of three men who had risked their lives to find her in the Amazon jungle after her parents were murdered. She could never fully repay Blake, Ruis, or Vincent for their journey to find her and bring her to the United States.

She longed to use her talents at the FBI, but the bureau's

age requirement meant she'd have to wait two more years to apply to the agent training program.

This was the last semester of her bachelor's degree in psychology. She needed to turn in overdue homework and catch up on her studies before final exams.

Her roommates would be no help because Mutt and Cassie were sports fanatics, and April was the busiest sports month of the year.

"Miss Jenkins."

Nefi looked up from her notebook at her bearded professor. "Yes, sir?"

"See me after class."

A collective "ooooh" sounded from her seventy classmates.

The professor eyed the students over his wire-framed glasses. "Miss Jenkins attended a felony trial last week, and her homework was to write a field report to identify and analyze abnormal behavior in one person."

"Was it the accused?" one student shouted.

"It was a witness," Nefi answered.

"How many would like to hear her report now?" The professor opened his arms.

All hands shot up. Nefi tugged the report from her notebook. After the professor nodded, Nefi stood and delivered her findings to the psychology majors she had come to know and respect over four years. The class spent the rest of the session debating the report.

·2·

THAT EVENING IN her room, Nefi reviewed her psychology textbook and lecture notes. Voices from the common room carried through the door, disrupting her studies. She checked her phone for messages from her best friend and found none. Her roommates, Marines studying on the G.I. Bill, didn't worry about upcoming exams as much as they did about which sport to watch at night. Nefi envied their early morning discipline for studying, which gave them free time in the evenings. April held the convergence of the end of the regular season for the National Basketball League and the National Hockey League, the NCAA basketball championship, the National Football League draft, and the opening day of major league baseball.

Nefi didn't care which major sporting event was on tonight. She planned to spend the evening wearing earplugs. After rereading a paragraph on the McNaughten rule and its use in an insanity defense, she rubbed her eyes.

Bang. Bang. Bang. Her door rattled under the impact, identifying it as Mutt's knock.

"Enter." Nefi turned away from her desk and removed her earplugs.

The door swung open. A broad-chested man filled the doorway with muscles and charm. "Hey, sorry to bother you, but apparently, it's my turn for kitchen duty. As usual, someone had a cooking frenzy." Mutt grimaced. "I'll give you five bucks." His black T-shirt announced, "Gun control means using both hands" in bold white letters.

Accepting his offer, Nefi stood and approached the doorway.

Grinning, Mutt backed out of the way.

On her way through the apartment's living room, Nefi smiled at her other roommate. When stressed, Cassie baked brownies and cookies, filling the room with scents of cinnamon, chocolate, and calories.

Cassie James peered over a *Sports Illustrated* magazine from her nest of pillows on the sofa. "She's not your maid." Her brown skin blended with the leather sofa. She wore her hair cropped an inch off her scalp. It wasn't the same Marine high-and-tight style Mutt wore, but close.

"I notice your favorite cooking days are my kitchen duty days," Mutt muttered.

Cassie raised the magazine, blocking her grin from her accuser but not Nefi.

The large television screen flickered silently through the news. Mutt picked up the remote in one hand, a brownie in the other.

Nefi plucked a bite-size warm brownie from the counter between the living room and the kitchen. How had she survived childhood without tasting chocolate? It was one of many experiences she missed growing up in a remote village in Brazil. After that first taste of chocolate in high school in the U.S., Nefi understood addiction's power. "I need a break from abnormal psych."

Cassie snorted, opening her hand toward Mutt. "Looking for a case study? I present Corporal Michael Ulysses Trace the Third, better known as Mutt, who served as an Explosive Ordnance Disposal Specialist."

Cassie and Nefi agreed that taking a job defusing bombs was insane. They watched Mutt's favorite movie, *The Hurt Locker*, so often they could recite lines from it. Mutt suffered bouts of post-traumatic stress disorder, which gave him nightmares and made him hyper-alert in crowds.

Nefi avoided mentioning Mutt's PTSD to focus on his dislike of handling dirty dishes. "Would you say his avoidance behavior indicates an obsessive-compulsive disorder or a phobia?" Nefi chewed the brownie while leaning her hip against the counter's edge. The dishes stunk of sour milk and the green protein slime Mutt consumed for breakfast.

Cassie laughed.

Mutt crossed his arms and stood his ground in the center of the common room. He was an intimidating figure in his black t-shirt and sweatpants, but Nefi had never witnessed him angry or heard him raise his voice. He opened his mouth at the exact moment the door buzzer sounded. He set down the remote, strode to the condo's entrance door, and pulled it open.

"I'm, uh, looking for Miss Nefi Jenkins?" The question squeaked through taut vocal cords.

"You are?" Mutt's voice rumbled.

"I'm Ronald Lancaster. Are you perhaps Miss Jenkins' fiancé?"

Mutt snorted. "Do I look crazy?"

Nefi and Cassie shouted in unison. "Yes."

Mutt turned toward the kitchen and Nefi. "Miss Jenkins, are you expecting a well-dressed gentleman?"

Nefi cleared gooey chocolate from her teeth with her tongue and swallowed. After stepping around Mutt, she looked down at a man in his forties who wore an impeccable navy pin-striped suit, a white shirt, and a red power tie. The stranger had the build of a man who spent long hours at a desk and dined at the finest restaurants. The thick lenses of his black-framed glasses magnified his eyes.

"Good evening. I'm Ronald Lancaster, and I'm here to discuss your trust fund."

Nefi said, "No, thank you," and closed the door.

Mutt raised his eyebrows. "You have a trust fund?"

Nefi shook her head as the door buzzed again. She opened the door.

"Miss Nefi Jenkins, I have important paperwork regarding your trust fund."

"I don't have one."

"You do, and I am shocked you don't know about it." Ronald didn't flinch or display any signs of deception. "Senator Hamilton Jenkins gave me your address."

Her uncle didn't easily give out her address or phone number, so Nefi decided to listen to Mr. Lancaster.

"May I come in? I have spent significant time trying to reach you."

Nefi put a hand on Mutt's chest and gently pushed him out of the guest's way. Remembering her aunt's lessons on manners, she decided to make the stranger feel welcome. "Michael Trace and Cassie James, I introduce Mr. Ronald Lancaster."

Ronald shook hands with Mutt, then crossed the room toward Cassie with his hand out.

Cassie rose from the sofa and towered over him. She shook his hand. "So, where do you work, Mr. Lancaster?" She released his hand.

"I'm with Attucks, Bird, and Copley. We're an investment company with offices in six major cities. I'm from the Boston group."

Mutt plucked his cell phone from his pocket and started typing with his thumbs. Next, he held his phone to his ear. "Hello, I'm looking for Attucks, Bird, and Copley?"

Ronald pivoted toward Mutt. "What are you doing?"

Mutt placed his phone against his chest. "Checking your credentials. You don't mind, do you?"

Ronald sighed. A black leather briefcase hung from his left hand.

Nefi waved toward the dining table. "Would you like coffee and a brownie?"

He narrowed his eyes at the tray of brownies. "No brownie, but I'd like coffee. The strongest you have, please, no sugar." Ronald set his black leather briefcase at the head of the six-place table, then pulled back one of the sturdy wooden chairs and sat.

Mutt stood near the table and the guest. "Hello, I'm looking for Mr. Ronald Lancaster. Sure, I'll hold." He looked down at the guest's feet. "Nice shoes."

Ronald did not seem amused.

Nefi planted a mug emblazoned with Semper Fi in large letters under the spout of the Keurig machine. She stuck a Green Mountain Bold coffee pod in the machine and pressed the button for a 6-ounce cup. The machine hummed as it drew water into the heating mechanism. Nefi checked her phone for new messages and, finding none, she sighed.

Meanwhile, Cassie seated herself at the table. Assuming her poker-playing expression, she addressed Mr. Lancaster, "How challenging was it to locate Nefi all the way from Boston?"

Boston was the twenty-fourth largest city in the country, and the greater Boston area had thirty-five colleges, universities, and community colleges. The Harvard campus, where Mutt, Cassie, and she studied, sat across the Charles River in Cambridge, north of downtown Boston.

Ronald sat back in his chair. His brow furrowed for a moment. "To clarify, I'm not the agent of record. My colleague in Washington, D.C., handled the account." He folded his hands on the tabletop. "According to our company files, Miss Jenkins' last permanent address was in McLean, Virginia."

Cassie and Mutt turned toward Nefi. The Keurig gurgled black wakefulness into the Semper Fi cup.

Nefi took a deep breath while waiting for the cup to fill. "Let me guess. All mail was returned undeliverable."

Ronald cleared his throat. "Why didn't you submit a change of address?"

Nefi carried the steaming cup to Ronald and set it before him. "About the trust fund I didn't know existed?" She took a seat across from Cassie, so they bookended their guest.

A voice on Mutt's phone confirmed that Ronald Lancaster was away from the office. The voice offered to take a message.

"No, that's all right. I'll catch up with him later." Mutt pocketed his phone. He sat beside Cassie, across the dining table from Nefi. "The company confirmed they have someone by that name. May we see your identification?"

Nefi didn't mind her roommate's persistence. Her fiancé Vincent would have done the same thing. As an FBI Special Agent, Vincent tended to do background checks on people as though everyone lived under assumed aliases. When Vincent first heard about Nefi's roommates, he seemed surprised at the co-ed arrangement, but he relaxed once he learned Mutt and Cassie were Marines. Vincent said on active duty or not; they were never to be called ex-Marines. Once a Marine, always a Marine.

Ronald displayed his Massachusetts driver's license to all. "Normally, discussions with financial clients are conducted privately." His glance bounced from Cassie to Mutt and back again.

No one moved.

Nefi folded her hands on the table, mirroring her guest to show agreement or empathy. She'd learned the technique in psych class. "Mr. Lancaster, I trust my roommates with my life."

"Semper Fi," Cassie and Mutt said.

Ronald downed a third of his coffee with his eyes closed. When he opened them, he nodded at the cup.

Cassie and Mutt exchanged a grin. They, too, liked their coffee strong.

After setting his cup to the side of his briefcase, Ronald eyed Nefi. "As you wish. My colleague in Washington, D.C., drove to your McLean, Virginia address to see why the mail was returned." He raised his eyebrows at Nefi.

Nefi nodded.

"He found an empty lot." Ronald pushed his glasses up the bridge of his nose as if focusing would clear up the mystery of how a house and mailbox would vanish.

"Someone firebombed the house last summer," Nefi said. "It was in the news."

Ronald's mouth fell open. He turned toward Cassie, who nodded.

Nefi added, "I had an enemy."

The corner of Mutt's mouth briefly lifted. He leaned back in his chair.

Ronald closed his mouth and blinked rapidly. "Oh, yes. I read about that. The news made it sound like a political attack on the senator over a drug bill he sponsored."

Nefi shrugged.

He opened his briefcase, removed a manila folder, and withdrew a form he placed on the table in front of Nefi. "This trust was activated weeks after your parents passed away."

"They were murdered," Cassie said.

After a long blink, Ronald leaned back in his chair. "I didn't know how they," he looked at the papers, "passed. I'm so sorry. Uh, the trust was funded by life insurance and your mother's existing trust fund. Our firm managed the investments in the combined trust." He took another gulp of coffee. "I have a copy of the agreement for you. Here." He tapped the file folder. "You have the option to choose another investment firm, but the financial advisor who managed your holdings was a respected senior part-ner, one of the finest in the field. He retired in October." He rested his open hand on the file.

Questions swirled in her mind.

Ronald pulled a gorgeous pen from his suit jacket, uncapped it, and set it near the form. Her uncle had a pen just like it—a Montblanc Meisterstruck. The burgun-dy-stained wood casing gleamed with gold accents. A man who managed other people's money relied on such status symbols to instill confidence in clients. Still, spending as much on a pen as Nefi's share of the rent seemed extravagant. Nefi bought pens by the box and considered retractable pens a luxury.

"When you reached age twenty-one last October," Ronald said, "You should have gained full ownership of the trust. Unfortunately, your birthday coincided with the senior partner's retirement. A new partner in D.C. was reviewing all the trusts when he noticed your birthday had passed. Last week, your file came to me. And now here we are. This form turns the ownership of the trust over to you."

Nefi picked up the pen and admired its heft and balance the way she examined a good knife. "What does that mean?"

"Your parents designed the trust to distribute monthly income. A clause allows extra drawdowns for medical care and other expenses. I recommend maintaining the basic structure of the trust."

"Can I do whatever I want with the money?" She balanced the pen on the side of her index finger at the joint near her nail bed. Holding it there, she glanced up at Ronald for his answer.

His attention was on the pen. He pressed the middle of his glasses, sliding them closer to his brow. "The trust is funded by investments, stocks, bonds, and real estate holdings, not cash. It isn't immediately liquid, and there are tax consequences to consider."

Though Nefi meant to ask if she could do whatever she wanted with the monthly payout, it was interesting to learn about the trust.

He exhaled slowly through his nose. "Do you know how many lottery winners end up bankrupt?"

"No, sir."

"Most." His eyes met Nefi's.

Cassie scowled. "What?"

"Really?" Mutt leaned forward and straightened his back.

Ronald continued, "If people don't know how to manage money, it doesn't matter how much they have." His eyebrows drew inward. His lips thinned in a tight line, and their corners pulled down for a fleeting moment.

Nefi read his expression. Ronald shared a truth borne from experience. She wondered if the experience was personal or witnessed. Either way, she appreciated the advice. It reminded her of something she read as a child in Brazil, where she learned English from her parents' Bible. A verse in Luke said that whoever can be trusted with little can be trusted with much. Ronald Lancaster was someone trained to manage fortunes. He'd taken the time to handle the paperwork on her account.

"I've seen people squander fortunes," Ronald added. "Sports figures, celebrities—"

"So, how much money are we talking about?" Cassie said.

Ronald drew in a deep breath and let it out. After clenching and unclenching his jaw, he answered Cassie while staring at Nefi, "This kind of money changes lives."

Nefi welcomed a change from her current financial state. Hundreds would replenish her savings, and thousands would reduce her student loans. She rolled the pen down her finger into her writing grip and signed the form.

"Would you please sign as witnesses?" Ronald slid

the form toward Mutt. "And I'll need to see your driver's licenses." The corners of his mouth pulled upward.

Nefi pushed back her chair and marched to her room. She grabbed her satchel from the hook on the back of her door and returned to the table. There, she pulled out her wallet and removed her driver's license. She handed the license to Ronald and noticed how soft his hand looked compared to Mutt's.

Mutt and Cassie confirmed their identities by holding up their licenses until Ronald nodded. The form and the pen traveled to Mutt, whose giant, scarred hands steadied the paper while he signed. He slid the paper and pen over the tabletop to Cassie. She signed and returned the form and pen to the guest. Ronald notarized the paper with a special stamp from his briefcase.

Nefi said, "Thank you for taking care of this. May I get records of the trust balance and what's in it year by year?" She needed more information so she could consult with her aunt and uncle when they visited at graduation.

Ronald seemed pleased. "Where would you like the monthly payment to be deposited?"

Nefi dug into the satchel for her checkbook. She tore off a deposit slip and handed it to her guest.

"I'll get that set up by the end of the week. The next deposit will be in your account by the fifteenth of May. Each monthly check will arrive on or before the fifteenth of the month." He clipped the deposit ticket to the signed paper and placed it in his briefcase. He capped his pen, tucked it inside his jacket, and handed a separate manila folder to Nefi. "This is a copy of your trust agreement." He looked at his hands.

The subtle tensing of Ronald Lancaster's forehead and

mouth could be interpreted as awkwardness or indecision to the untrained observer. To Nefi, these expressions revealed internal conflict. File in hand, Nefi waited. Perhaps her roommates expected her to respond because they, too, sat uncharacteristically still and quiet.

"I suggest you read it privately," the guest said softly. "Sitting down."

Nefi set the inch-deep file on the table. *The kind of money that changes lives*. The kind of money that caused a stranger to come in person to handle the paperwork. It must be at least a few thousand dollars, maybe tens of thousands from life insurance. Death was a dreadful way to gain money, but the trust meant her parents had planned to provide for her. Nefi settled that loving thought in her heart.

Lancaster eased his chair back and stood. Cassie and Mutt rose from their chairs.

Nefi used the back of her knees to scoot back her chair, and then she held out her hand. "Thank you, Mr. Lancaster."

Ronald shook her hand firmly and smiled at her. "My pleasure."

His warm hand was as soft as it looked.

Ronald released her hand and grabbed the handle of his black leather briefcase. He glanced at Mutt and Cassie. "It was an experience meeting you, Miss James, and Mr. Trace."

Nefi walked him to the door. After the guest left, Nefi returned to the table. Like she didn't already have more reading to do than she could fit in her long days, she decided she could sacrifice another hour of sleep to read this file, given enough caffeine.

Mutt eased around the table and peered at the file. "Does this mean you won't clean the kitchen for me?"

Cassie swatted his shoulder and turned toward Nefi. "You look like you just got bad news. What's with that?"

Nefi picked up the file. "How much money is enough to change a life?"

"In your case or in general?" Mutt crossed his arms and grinned.

Cassie closed her eyes, rolling them under her lids before speaking to Nefi. "Money can change your life for the better. Maybe you could buy a fourth pair of shoes." Cassie widened her eyes and opened her arms. "Or a car."

"I had a car once," Nefi said wistfully.

"I don't see a downside to having a trust fund dropped in your lap." Cassie emphasized her comment with her hands raised and her fingers spread.

Mutt tilted his head. "Are you thinking money is the root of all evil?"

"My parents were murdered over money."

Mutt dropped his arms and laced his fingers together. "There's nothing inherently noble in poverty or wealth. And yes, I have read the Bible." He side-eyed Cassie as if continuing a previous argument. "It doesn't say money is evil. It says the *love* of money is the root of all evil."

Nefi nodded. She carried the file to her room and shut the door. With her back against the door, she took a few deep, calming breaths. Of course, she couldn't concentrate on psychology with the trust agreement waiting to be read. How much was it worth? She paged through the agreement for a total and found only paragraph-long sentences laden with legal terms.

She didn't love money. Theirs was a fleeting relationship. It came. It went. She tithed just as her devout Baptist aunt and uncle taught her, and she tucked an extra ten percent of her income away in a savings account for emergencies.

She could certainly use a windfall to repay her aunt and uncle and to pay for her wedding whenever that was going to be. She believed she could handle the responsibility of managing more money because God always stretched her meager funds to cover her needs. She understood how to live within a budget and fully appreciated the difference between want and need.

However, it would be nice to pay for a few wants and travel by car instead of the bus. It would have been wonderful to fly to Oxford, England, to visit Martina over spring break.

She picked up her phone. Still no word from Martina. Her best friend must have been studying harder than ever because Martina hadn't returned a text or a call since Saturday. Martina had been her first friend when she arrived in the United States. Ruis Ramos, who had led the mission to bring Nefi from the Amazon to Uncle Hamilton Jenkins, introduced Nefi to his youngest sister. The Ramos family lived close to Senator and Mrs. Jenkins, so naturally, Nefi and Martina became classmates in high school. The distance between them felt as vast as the Atlantic Ocean, greater than the five-hour time zone difference. Days without a word from her best friend felt like a chasm of silence. Though they were the same age, Martina had overlapped graduate school classes with undergraduate courses while Nefi was about to finish her bachelor's degree.

Perhaps they would have earned master's degrees simultaneously if English had been Nefi's first language.

English was more challenging to learn than Portuguese and Spanish or the tribal languages of Tupi and Arawak. Nonetheless, Martina was truly as brilliant as Nefi believed her to be. Completing a graduate degree at twenty-one years old was the proof. Martina always was an overachiever.

Nefi crossed the room to her desk and set the trust file on her psych class notes. She sank into her desk chair. If there came a day when Martina no longer felt as close to Nefi as Nefi felt toward her, Nefi vowed to be gracious about it, though it would leave a massive hole in her heart.

The sudden, overwhelming dread that struck her last Friday had grown deeper. She'd had a nightmare about Martina. She'd even left a message on Martina's phone. Though that message felt embarrassingly strange and silly today, leaving it Friday had comforted her enough to go back to sleep. If only she could hear Martina's voice, she'd sleep better. It was useless to reason with feelings. Finally, she dismissed the fear of loss as projecting her anxiety about exams toward her friend.

The television blared from the common room.

Nefi rechecked her cell phone for a message from her best friend. No text. No voice mail message. No email. She tossed the device onto her desk. It skittered across the wood and stopped against the side of the psych textbook.

She longed to earn her graduate degree so she could join the FBI. She needed to study, but life interrupted her plans. Everyone else was busy doing important things. Her eyes darted from the textbook to the trust agreement file and back.

Her cell phone buzzed. The name Ruis popped up on the screen, so she immediately answered the call. He rarely called. Maybe he wanted to know about the bet with his pal Arlo.

"When was the last time you spoke with Martina?" Ruis's voice sounded strained, and he spoke slower than usual as if parsing his words.

So, Martina was on his mind, too. A twinge of alarm came over Nefi. "Friday."

"How did she sound?"

The odd question put Nefi off balance. Ruis always wanted to know what his baby sister was doing, but this seemed like an intervention probe. "She sounded normal. I told her I was just as sad as Oscar that she wasn't coming back during the school break."

"When did her school break start?"

"Mid-March." Why wasn't he asking his parents? They kept track of all their children.

"So...she's back in school?"

"No. She gets six weeks. Plenty of time to study for exams." Nefi envied Martina for being on Oxford University's trimester system. Each term lasted eight weeks, with long breaks in between. "What's this about?"

"I'm just trying to confirm where she is. When are her exams?"

"I think she said April twenty-fifth."

"Has she texted or emailed you since Friday?"

"No."

"Thanks."

"Exams for a master's degree must be tough, right?" After a moment of silence, Nefi glanced at her phone. Ruis had disconnected the call. He was a busy man, but why was his call so abrupt? She didn't get to tell him about Arlo or the bet. Why did he sound urgent? *Uh oh.* Did Ruis suspect Oscar was meeting up with Martina without telling anyone?

Martina would confide in me, wouldn't she?

Nefi felt a pang of doubt about her best friend spending weeks alone studying. Martina was such a social creature. It felt more believable that Martina wanted to spend time with her fiancé without the whole family watching. Certainly, Martina would be honest with her best friend—unless she wanted to allow for plausible deniability.

Nefi sighed and glanced at the trust document.

Going to New York City to visit Vincent for a weekend would be fantastic. As always, her fiancé was working. Responsibility was a burden he'd taken on most of his life. After his father died in the line of duty with the New York Police Department, Vincent joined the Marines so the family's savings could send his younger brother, Oscar, to college. After the Marines, Vincent earned a Bachelor of Science in criminal justice and joined the FBI. According to FBI policies, Vincent and Nefi could never work as partners, but Nefi wanted to follow in his footsteps and become his equal.

She glared at her phone. Martina was out of touch, that was all. They were best friends engaged to brothers, Martina to Oscar, and Nefi to Vincent. Even if Martina's friendship waned, they would one day be sisters-in-law. They were destined to be close for life.

Unable to shake off a creeping uneasiness about Martina, Nefi turned her chair away from her desk.

She texted a message to Ruis, *Are you worried about her?*

A reply popped up on the screen. *Always.*

Unloading and loading the dishwasher would give her time to clear her head. After that, she'd call Vincent.

VINCENT STARED AT a vending machine while deciding between sugar and salt. He tugged a dollar bill from his wallet and fed it into the machine. Because he had a soda on his desk, he opted to balance his diet with salt. He poked the combination of numbers and letters in the keypad for a bag of chips and watched the bag fall partway down the vending machine. Hung up on a candy bar, the bag pressed against the plastic window out of reach.

Of course, his entire day had staggered from one horrible event to another. The worst news was that Martina had been kidnapped. She was his brother's fiancé and Nefi's best friend. The stress left him emotionally drained. She'd been abducted in Miami while posing as a body double for a pop singer. It was the kind of trouble only Martina could manage to get into.

This went far beyond her usual boundary-pushing behavior. Now, her life expectancy had an expiration date. Even if the kidnappers didn't know they had the wrong girl, the ransom was due on Friday. Who would pay for their mistake?

After gaining permission from the FBI Director, Vincent sent a copy of the ransom recording to Ruis and asked him to join the investigation with the Miami FBI. Ruis understood the need for secrecy because Martina's life was at stake. Since Blake was no longer an FBI agent, he also volunteered to help Ruis.

Vincent was pounding the vending machine window with his fist until his pinkie finger tingled when his cell phone chimed. Nefi's photo popped up on the screen. His fiancée had an uncanny intuition, a trait that would make her an ideal FBI profiler one day. He often suspected she was psychic—if such a thing was real. His chest tightened. He bit his lip. There was no way she knew about Martina unless Ruis told her. Ruis wouldn't. He absolutely wouldn't. Ruis was a U.S. Marshal. He lived in a world of secrecy.

After a deep cleansing breath, he answered. "Hey, Nefi."

"I've got the weirdest news."

Vincent closed his eyes and leaned against the vending machine.

"I just met with a man from an investment company. He said my parents set up a trust fund."

Opening his eyes, Vincent took a breath. Nefi's parents had been dead for seven years. Why did it take so long to learn about the trust fund? "That is weird news."

"Apparently, the company has been trying to reach me since my twenty-first birthday. I signed the papers, and it's mine."

He eased his weight off the vending machine and glared at the bag of chips. "Congratulations."

The bag fell to the bottom of the machine.

"I haven't read through the whole agreement yet. It's about thirty pages of eye-watering legalese, and I need to study for exams."

Vincent retrieved the chips from the machine and walked to his desk. It warmed his heart to hear good news from Nefi. She'd lost everything she owned twice, so she didn't spend much on possessions. She didn't even own a bicycle. He wondered how she'd handle having money of her own. He knew she'd give the entire trust fund toward Martina's ransom, but he couldn't let her in on the investigation. She would take extreme risks, and she wasn't trained for this. Not yet, anyway.

"And I got a weird call from Ruis."

"Oh?" Vincent froze.

"He wanted to know about the last time I spoke with Martina."

He couldn't talk about an active case, and eventually, Nefi could discover he knew about Martina's kidnapping and said nothing. It was a no-win dilemma. Vincent held his breath.

"Do you think she's meeting up with Oscar instead of studying? Wait, don't tell me. If Oscar told you something in confidence, then don't tell me. She's a big girl. She can take care of herself."

Vincent dropped his face into his hand and exhaled. Martina was in over her head this time. The odds of survival for a twenty-one-year-old against hardened criminals were too pathetic to dwell on.

"Are you okay?"

"It's been a horrible day. I'm still at work."

"Oh, I'm sorry. I'll let you go."

"Never."

Nefi's laugh rang like music, lifting his spirit. "I love you, Vincent."

"I love you, Nefi."

With that, the call ended, and Vincent was grateful he didn't have to lie to the human lie detector. Earlier today, Oscar had called for advice. Vincent's younger brother Oscar said he couldn't remember doing or saying anything to make Martina mad, but she wasn't answering phone calls, text messages, or even emails. While Oscar talked, Vincent remained silent. Finally, Oscar concluded Martina was busy studying for exams. Although Vincent hadn't lied to his brother, he felt guilty about the sin of omission. He'd compounded the sin of omission by not telling Nefi about Martina.

Martina. Martina. *If you die, it will destroy Oscar and Nefi. Your whole family will mourn. How could you be so careless with your life?*

He bowed his head and prayed.

·4·

Friday, April 23, 2010

As THE ELEVATOR opened onto the lobby of the Grand Hyatt, Jane Wright automatically pulled her shoulders back and straightened her spine so her gown would drape properly and billow just so. Reaching her jeweled hand around Ted's forearm, she held on. Together they strolled from the hotel to the conference area. She tugged gently on her husband's arm to slow his long-legged gait.

It simply wouldn't do for a woman in her sixties to tumble off three-inch heels in a ball gown. "If you plan to run, let's trade shoes."

Ted chuckled and patted her hand. "Yes, dear."

April in Tampa, Florida, was humid and overcast in the high 80s. As the evening temperatures dropped and the sky cleared, Jane felt chilled. She wore a muted black and gold paisley-designed pashmina shoulder wrap over the sheerer of the two black gowns she'd brought. The fitted brocade bodice lifted her chest, and the chiffon skirt floated slightly in her wake. Thinner than most women her age, she liked to flaunt her figure. Why else suffer through endless salads and Pilates?

Steady in her heels, the toes of her designer shoes popped out below the gown's hem as she walked. Her diamond and sapphire earrings swayed gently with each step. Her gold Byzantine choker was narrow at the clasp and thickened at the hollow of her throat. The jewelry had been anniversary gifts from Ted and the shawl, a recent birthday gift.

Ted waved to the photographer whose work had earned a nomination at this year's National Journalism Awards hosted by the Scripps Howard Foundation. Though not as well-known as the Pulitzer Awards, the National Journalism Awards were prestigious. Thankfully, the cameraman had found a tuxedo that fit. *A rental, no doubt.* He'd even tamed his thick curls into a ponytail tied at his collar instead of his usual man-bun. His thick beard carpeted the bottom half of his face.

The photographer crossed the corridor. "Wow. Isn't this something?"

Ted nodded. "Marty, this is my wife, Jane."

Jane sighed. Ted often bungled simple etiquette. As the older and more important person, she should have been introduced to Marty. How could such a brilliant man not remember this? Maybe Ted didn't care. Or, maybe, this was his way of showing who was important in his life. And what was Marty's last name? She'd have to listen all night to catch it in conversation or find it on the evening's printed program. She nodded at the photographer rather than offer to shake his sweating hand. Poor Marty no-last-name might soak through his rented tux by the time the photography award was announced.

"Is Sandy here?" Ted asked.

"She didn't want to leave the baby with a sitter."

Immediately, an image came to Jane of a disheveled woman with a squalling child in her arms. Some women chose parenthood as a career, and some had parenthood thrust upon them. To Jane, parenthood meant a commitment of years of diapers and mess, noise, and chaos. No woman fully appreciated the vast commitment until it was too late.

Hundreds of voices in animated conversation thundered down the corridor. Walking toward the sound, the three of them funneled through a doorway into the multitude of journalists and publishers pouring into the cavernous ballroom.

The Audubon Ballroom had 10,000 square feet filled with banquet tables and two sets of long tables at the front flanking a large podium. The 22-foot-high ceilings featured a grid of beams. Inside the center of each square, multi-faceted funnel-shaped chandeliers sparkled. Floor-to-ceiling windows adorned one wall. According to Ted, nine hundred people had registered for the ceremony.

Stationed at the ballroom doors were college-age journalists with clipboards.

Ted approached one of them. "Good evening. I'm Ted Wright, and this is my wife, Jane, and one of the finalists, Marty Sholgrin. We're with *The Sentinel-Times* of Richmond, Virginia."

The young woman scanned the list on her clipboard and made three checkmarks. "You're at table twenty."

Ted led the way through the crowd, looking over people's heads, tugging Jane's hand. Marty trailed behind. Their table, situated in the center of the room, had excellent views of the speaker's table. Ted pulled out a chair and smiled.

Jane gathered her skirt to her legs and sat. She would spend the night twisted sideways to see the stage, but it would do. Ted claimed the chair with the most direct view of the front by tipping it on its front legs against the table.

"Would you like a drink?"

"Chardonnay, please." Jane lowered her shawl off her toned shoulders to reveal the brocade bodice of her gown.

Marty parked himself to the right of Ted's seat. He gulped water from a glass goblet.

The editor and his wife arrived, followed by the investigative reporter and her husband. The investigative reporter's husband pulled out his wife's chair, smiled at the others at the table, and sat beside his wife. None of them introduced themselves. Perhaps Ted would remember his manners when he returned with the drinks.

Servers streamed between tables to deliver covered plates to the tables closest to the podium. Buttery scents flowed from their wake.

Ted returned with wine in one hand and a whiskey on ice in the other. After placing the wine glass in front of Jane's plate, he raised his glass to his colleagues. "Ladies and gentlemen, I'm proud to be here in honor of two award nominees from Richmond's own Sentinel-Times."

Their happy crew cheered and clinked glasses. *Fine. Never mind our names. We are The Richmond Sentinel-Times gang.* Jane took a sip at the exact moment she was bumped from behind, splashing wine down onto her front.

"Oh, excuse me." The server hefted a giant tray of plates behind Jane.

After setting her glass down, Jane plucked her napkin from her plate to dab the cold, wet spot. Good thing it was a white wine and not red.

Ted smiled over Jane's head. "No problem. It'll wash out, right dear?"

Jane sighed, dabbing the black silk brocade. Her husband believed everything was wash-and-wear except his suits.

"I better get out of the way." Ted took his seat.

The female, a thirty-something investigative journalist, stared across the table. Jane had blotted up as much wine as she could from her dress. Was the woman staring at the stain? Jane leaned forward in case another server tried to squeeze between the tables. She cautiously took a second sip of her wine, spilling none.

"Where did you get your shawl?"

"It was a gift." Jane inclined her head toward Ted.

The woman pivoted her head toward Ted. "Excuse me, Mr. Wright? Where did you buy your wife's shawl?"

"I picked it up in New York. At Macy's, I think." He smiled at Jane and placed a hand on her shoulder.

His big hand warmed Jane's skin through the shawl.

"It's not a Shahtoosh, is it?" Her shrill voice cut through the civility of small talk as if the garment had been created through child labor.

"The clerk called it a pashmina." Ted tipped his drink to his lips.

"Shahtoosh shawls are made from chiru, a Tibetan antelope. They're becoming an endangered species because of the demand."

Ted set his glass on the table slowly and gently. The room lights dimmed, warning people to take their seats. "Well, I doubt Macy's deals in black-market goods."

"How much did you pay for it?"

The reporter's self-righteous tone irritated Jane. Demanding to know the price of a gift crossed the line of decency. *Who does this woman think she is talking to her boss like that?* Jane eyed her. Ted was not one of her interview subjects to be brow-beaten into a confession.

Trapped between the publisher and his rude colleague, Marty moved his water glass toward the center of the table. The investigative reporter's husband avoided eye contact and picked at his salad. The editor and his wife sat perfectly still as if willing the woman to shut up. Was this young woman raised by parents who refused to spank her? Clearly, she didn't understand boundaries or manners.

"Why would you ask that?" Ted's voice was quieter than usual.

An intelligent person would have heeded the warning and apologized. The investigative reporter blundered on. "Well, a *real* Shahtoosh shawl costs over two-thousand dollars."

Jane leaned back into her cushioned chair. Trained as a lawyer, she recognized the false dichotomy the reporter had crafted. The reporter's hubris and self-righteousness had possibly led her to believe she had cornered the great Ted Wright. *Oh, here we go.*

Ted's direct gaze was legendary for freezing employees in their tracks. He was a tall man with an even larger presence. As a publisher, he rarely raised his voice to get things done the way he wanted. His whisper carried across the table. "Just to be clear, are you trying to shame me for unknowingly killing Tibetan antelope or spending less than two grand on a gift for my wife?"

Jane picked up her chardonnay while the reporter's mouth opened and closed like a fish out of water.

Silence spread from the center table to the ends of the ballroom. The room lights flashed, and all heads turned toward the podium except two. Jane raised her glass to the investigative reporter, who blinked and turned away.

Servers delivered covered plates to *The Sentinel-Times* table. When the table was served, the staff lifted the covers at once for the reveal. Glazed salmon, linguine alfredo, and buttery steamed asparagus filled the table with mouthwatering scents. The servers withdrew as the guests dug into their food.

The evening wore on from elation to disappointment as each category award was announced. Jane's purse buzzed just as the spot news award finalists were named. She pulled out her cell phone to identify the caller. Mr. Jones. Thankfully, she'd set the phone to vibrate, but the buzzing attracted Ted's attention.

He raised his eyebrows.

"It's nothing," Jane whispered. She jammed her phone back into her purse. Whatever Jones wanted could wait until she returned home from Tampa. She'd check her messages then. This weekend with Ted was a business trip for him, a vacation for her. Holding her phone in her lap, she smothered the vibrations and turned her face toward the master of ceremonies.

Ted was curious whenever Jane received calls from men. He was a trusting husband, but he paid attention to things. If he had seen the caller's name, he'd remember it. She would change Jones' listing on her cell phone to electrician or plumber, something dull and household related. She didn't know if Ted checked her phone like she often checked his, but she decided to be safe.

Marty elbowed Ted and whispered something as he pointed to the group from the *Denver Post*. The Associated Press also had two finalists, according to the program Ted plucked from under the floral centerpiece. Ted nodded.

The master of ceremonies continued with award after award. A few people left. The program showed three awards remained. Watching the photos of the finalists in the Photojournalism award, Jane recognized Marty. When the master of ceremonies called Marty's name, everyone at the table cheered. Marty wiped his beard and pushed back his chair. He shook hands with Ted and the editor before he dashed between tables to the podium. Ted's chest expanded as he applauded.

On stage, Marty received a trophy and an envelope with a $10,000 check while his photos flashed on two large screens flanking the podium.

After a brief thank-you speech, Marty returned to the table and planted the award beside the centerpiece.

Ted beamed at Marty, turning his back to Jane.

Jane felt a twinge of envy.

One team of servers cleared plates from the table. Immediately behind them, others placed servings of white chocolate mousse topped with a sliced strawberry.

The awards continued, leaving the most coveted award for the last—the investigative reporting award. Jane could not remember the name of the investigative reporter across the table. Had she taken life-threatening risks to gather and report on a scandal or corruption? Jane remembered a reporter from *The Oakland Post* she'd met at the 2007 awards ceremony. Chauncey Bailey investigated corruption in his community. He was murdered on his way to work in August of 2007 by the target of his reporting.

The master of ceremonies introduced last year's winner of the investigative reporting award. He then named the finalists in the category and the media companies they worked for while the crowd applauded each in response.

The young woman seated between Marty and the editor checked her lipstick with her phone. Of course, she used a camera app to see herself. She was of the generation that photographed themselves for social media whenever they brushed their teeth. She probably owned a selfie stick.

The master of ceremonies announced the finalists of the $15,000 Ursula and Gilbert Farfel Prize for Investigative Reporting. The woman across the table from Jane smiled and nodded as her name was read. The third and second place winners were announced, and then the master of ceremonies mentioned that the winner wrote an eye-opening series on child abuse in the foster care system. The reporter across the table covered her mouth with both hands while her husband slung an arm around her. She gave her husband a quick kiss. She strode to the podium while the crowd gave a standing ovation. She accepted her award on behalf of Richmond's finest newspaper, *The Sentinel-Times*, praising the editor and publisher for believing in her.

Ted and the editor glowed with pride. Ted looked as proud as if he'd won the award himself.

Well, well. Someone finally ascended to Ted's lofty expectations.

The woman carried the $15,000 check and the obelisk-shaped award to the table.

Jane could have caught fire unnoticed.

While everyone else at the table gushed their congratulations, Jane struggled through memories year by year to identify a moment when Ted had demonstrated the same level of genuine pride in her. Sure, he thanked her for cooking every time she served a meal. He thanked her for picking up the dry cleaning and the groceries. He thanked her for little things out of habit and good manners.

But, five years earlier, when Jane had redesigned the garden after weeks of digging, planting, and weeding, he pointed out a bush of pink roses among the bank of reds. After she planned the retirement party of the previous editor, Ted complained about the pasta and the dessert. It seemed that no matter how much effort, time, or planning she put into projects, he'd find a speck of imperfection. Her projects didn't earn money. Her projects didn't earn awards. When had Ted been proud of his wife?

Ted's heart was in his business. Running a media corporation took up most of his energy and time. He built what began as a mid-size newspaper into a local television station, a magazine, and an online news feed. With the advent of social media, the company's reach extended far beyond local news, connecting people to the community through special interests, tourism, business, hobbies, and family. Twice, larger media empires had offered to buy them out. They had tempted Ted with enough money to retire in comfort for four lifetimes, but he wasn't in the business just for money. He loved being an influencer. He said he loved nurturing talented people even though they'd abandon him at the first offer to work at a larger media company.

He even called his employees his family. Being the publisher made him the father of two-hundred unruly, demanding, and sometimes brilliant children. They were always on his mind. Ted agonized over firings even though the editor conducted the terminations. Occasionally, he bailed out a journalist who participated in a protest or refused to name a source in court.

Lately, Jane believed they should have switched roles. Ted should have stayed home to raise Marta. He would have thrived at it. He had the patience and temperament for the chaos and relentless demands of parenting. If her husband had stayed at home, she would have been free to pursue her law career and possibly a judgeship. She had a clear, objective, practical mind for order and details the law required. He was the sentimental one.

Ted remained standing and shook hands with the investigative reporter. "Congratulations. I knew you could do it."

His words struck Jane like hot spikes to the heart. In forty years of marriage, he had spoken those words twice—once after she graduated from law school and once again when Marta was born. Now, neither of those accomplishments mattered.

∽

Meanwhile, at her apartment near the Harvard campus, Nefi began her daily voicemail message to Martina, saying she was praying for her. She continued, "And I got the invitation to your graduation. I couldn't be there even if you had enough room for your entire family and me. The FBI internship starts on June seventh. I'm so sorry."

She drew a deep breath.

"Call me when you get a chance. Vincent and Oscar expect us to pick dates for our weddings."

Nefi caressed a beautiful, sturdy leather purse. Using her savings, Nefi had bought the iconic Louis Vuitton bucket purse Martina had been pining for since high school. Nefi wanted to "go big" on the gift because this was one of the most important days of her best friend's life.

"I also apologize for the bizarre message I sent last Friday. No, I'm not on drugs or drinking. I just had the worst vivid nightmare. You can tease me about it for the rest of our lives, but I had to send it to get back to sleep. There's more news, but I'd rather talk to you. Call me, okay?"

She spotted the clock by her bed and gasped. "Oh, yikes! I forgot about the time zone. Sorry. You will ace your exams. Goodnight, Martina."

Even though she had not heard from her best friend all week, Nefi felt a deep peace about her. She could not explain why, but she trusted her intuition. Certainly, if Martina were sick or hurt, Ruis would have called.

Tomorrow, she'd mail the gift. Nefi's aunt told her that it's tradition to put something inside a purse or suitcase given as a gift, so Nefi put a $20 bill in the graduation card inside the designer purse before she wrapped the gift in enough bubble wrap to protect it from falling off a moving truck.

·5·

Saturday, May 15, 2010

NEFI RETURNED TO her apartment after the last semester exam with an armload of mail. After she dumped it on the dining table, she spotted a hand-scrawled message from Mutt with forty dollars in cash.

Order pizzas to celebrate. Cassie wants Hawaiian, and I'll take my usual. See you at three.

At 2:30, Nefi ordered the food from their favorite pub. While she waited for the delivery, she nabbed a cold Dr Pepper from the refrigerator and sank into a chair to sort the mail into three piles. She opened the plastic bottle and took a long, satisfying caffeine and sugar hit. At the end of the table, Mutt's boxes of nutritional supplements piled up with his gun magazines. Cassie's mail included a few bills, two fashion magazines, and fifteen personal letters. Nefi received twenty personal letters, a few assorted bills, and a package from Oxford, England.

"Martina!"

Nefi hugged the package and gave a tearful prayer of thanks. She joyfully tore open the parcel to find a letter and something wrapped in thin paper, sealed with a sticker. She read the letter.

"The purse of my dreams!! Thank you. Thank you. I'm so sorry I haven't answered your messages. I lost my phone for a while and just got it back. The exams went well. Don't worry about my graduation because I can't attend yours. I have to pack the stuff I want to bring back to the states.

I have job interviews lined up. One is in Washington, D.C., so when I get the date for that one, I'll let you know. We have to get together. I have so much to tell you, but I want to tell you in person. Sorry for being mysterious, but you will understand why later.

Thank you for all your prayers. You are the best friend anyone could ask for.

Love,

Martina"

She pressed the note over her heart because she had not spoken with her best friend in a month. It felt like a test.

Digging into the box, she pulled out hefty black fabric that slipped out the sides of the paper wrapping. Nefi tore off the paper and held up the large cloth. It felt silky and substantial. She turned it over and over to find the top end of it. It was a hooded robe with two patches on the chest. One patch had the crest of Harvard University, and the other had the crest of Hogwarts School of Witchcraft and Wizardry. Nefi squealed with joy.

She had devoured the Harry Potter book series and dragged Martina to each movie as they premiered. The final book, *Harry Potter and the Deathly Hallows* was divided into two movies. The first half was scheduled to premiere in November. Nefi hoped Martina would take a job close enough for them to attend the movie together.

November felt like a lifetime away. Who knew what would happen between now and then? It wouldn't be the same to go to the movie with Vincent. *Did he even like the series?*

Nefi donned the robe and twirled in the center of the common room. She decided to wear it to graduation with her mortarboard. It was a perfect gift to tie Harvard and Oxford together because some of the scenes of Hogwarts were filmed on the Oxford campus.

The doorbell rang. Nefi plucked the cash from the table and answered the door.

The pizza delivery guy handed over three medium pizzas.

Nefi traded the pizzas for the cash. "Thank you."

He grinned as he dug a wad of small bills from his pocket.

"Keep the change."

"Hogwarts, eh?" He squinted at the patch. "*Draco Dormiens Nunquam Titillandus.*" Pocketing his cash, he added, "Do you know what it means?"

The city was full of students working part-time to pay for college. "Do you?"

He nodded and held his hand out, palm up. "I studied Latin in high school."

With her curiosity aroused, Nefi pulled a five-dollar

bill from her jeans pocket and set it on his palm. The scent of pepperoni and cheese awakened her appetite.

"Never tickle a sleeping dragon."

Nefi held out her hand, palm up.

He slapped his right hand over his heart. "I kid you not." His face confirmed his belief.

Nefi dropped her hand to her side. "Thank you for enlightening me." She smiled and wished she knew Latin. Though she only heard it spoken during Mass, it was the root language for many other languages.

The delivery man bowed dramatically and walked away.

Nefi closed the door. She set the pizza boxes in the oven and then walked to her room to read the last few pages of the trust agreement. After putting off the task in favor of studying for exams, the time had come to finish reading the document she'd fallen asleep on every night. Thick with legal jargon strung into forty-word sentences, the agreement wasn't as confusing as it was boring.

Because her parents had created it for her, the trust represented their love and legacy. Nefi longed to be a good steward of the money, whether a thousand dollars or a billion. She resumed reading.

"C. Descendants. References to 'descendant' or 'Descendants' mean lineal blood descendants of the first, second, or any other degree of ancestor designated; provided, however, that such references shall include, with respect to any provision of this Trust Agreement, descendants who have been conceived at any specific point in time relevant to such provision and who thereafter survive birth; and provided, further, except as hereinafter provided in this Section, an adopted child and such adopted child's lineal descendants by blood or adoption...."

As the only living descendant of Marta and Herman Jenkins, Nefi was their sole heir. Part D referred to the Internal Revenue Code, E to the Power of Appointment of the trustee, F to Governing Law, and then G Per Stirpes, a term she had to look up in the dictionary.

Latin again, of course. The pizza delivery man would have known it. It referred to "by roots" or "by branch" of a people in a family tree. The G clause explained how to divide distributions based on descendants of the living relatives of Marta and Herman, which Nefi understood to mean her, then equally to Nefi's living children, and then to her living grandchildren in the event of her death. In the event of all heirs being deceased, the trust would revert to the previous trustee or an assigned third-party trustee.

The last page was signed by her parents, a notary public, and two witnesses. She caressed their signatures, sensing their personalities in each line and slant of their cursive. Her mother's broad, loopy writing suited her open, optimistic spirit. Her father's scrawl resembled Uncle Hamilton's. As twins, they were so much alike in personality, habits, and appearance that they had blended into a single, loving father figure.

A fresh stab of grief reminded her of loss and death. Nefi had learned from her uncle that her mother had miscarried between high school and college. Nefi mourned the lost life. What if her parents had wanted more children? How wonderful it would have been to journey through life with a brother or sister!

They had signed the trust agreement the month before her birth.

They loved me before my first breath.

Comforted by that truth, she closed the document and

slid it into the file where she kept her bank statements. She heard the condo door close, followed by voices.

Her cell phone beeped with a text message from Vincent. *I'd like to come to Boston on the 19th to deliver your graduation gifts. Will you be in town?*

Nefi texted, *Yes!*

Great! I'll book a hotel. Have to leave early on the 20th.

Nefi hopped around her room in her hooded robe.

Mutt and Cassie called from the common room, "Where's the pizza?"

Nefi dashed from her room to the oven. The pizza boxes were still warm as she carried them to the dining table while Cassie and Mutt moved their piles of mail to empty chairs. Nefi placed the pizza boxes side by side on the table.

Mutt delivered two Dr Peppers and a beer to the table. Cassie set out paper plates and napkins. Each person sat in their usual chair. They bowed heads long enough for Nefi to give a quick prayer of thanks, and then they ate.

Mutt twisted the top off his bottle of Budweiser. "To graduation!"

They toasted with raised cans and a bottle.

After consuming a few slices of pizza, they sorted through their separate stacks of mail and boxes. Nefi opened more graduation cards and letters, carefully saving the checks and gift cards in a separate pile.

Mutt pointed a meat-heavy slice of pizza at Nefi. "What's with the cloak? Did you join a coven?"

"Martina sent it. I'm wearing it to graduation."

Cassie shook her head and set down her drink. "Might as well. Lots of people are decorating their mortarboards. I might do that next year." She was scheduled to finish her master's degree in engineering in a year. Men dominated engineering classes, so Cassie joked about being in the minority.

Nefi imagined a steam-punk theme mortarboard with moving parts.

Mutt washed down his fifth slice of pizza with a gulp of beer. After wiping his mouth with a napkin, he turned toward Nefi. "Will you be keeping your room this summer?"

The FBI internship at Quantico ran from June 7th to August 13th. She had applied to graduate programs at Harvard and CUNY Hunter College in New York City. Until she knew where she was going, she needed to live somewhere. "I'm coming back after the internship. I hope the trust fund pays enough for rent here and at Quantico."

Mutt set down his beer. "Today is the fifteenth."

Nefi raised her eyebrows at him. Mutt's statement seemed to be directed at her. Rent wasn't due until the first of the month. The fifteenth was the last day of exams for the semester. Was he waiting for an "amen"?

Mutt and Cassie traded a look of disappointment as they shook their heads.

Cassie closed her eyes and spoke as if to a child. "Mr. Lancaster said your first deposit would be made by the fifteenth of May."

"Oh!" Nefi raced to her room and dug her checkbook out of her purse. She called her bank on her way back to the table. After she identified herself by the account number, confirmed her address, and recited the last four digits of her Social Security Number, the automated voice recited the account balance. The number rang like a bell in her head. She set her phone on the table and took a deep breath as she subtracted the vast difference between the balance written in her checkbook with the balance she heard.

Cassie elbowed her. "Speak."

"The trust fund paid eight thousand dollars."

Cassie and Mutt leaned back in their chairs, and only the chair backs prevented them from falling to the floor.

Nefi strode to her desk for the trust agreement. She returned to the table and keyed the mobile number shown on Mr. Ronald Lancaster's business card into her phone.

He answered on the third ring. "Hello, this is Ron Lancaster. How may I help you?"

"Mr. Lancaster, this is Nefi Jenkins."

"What can I do for you, Miss Jenkins?"

"Sorry to bother you. I just received an eight-thousand-dollar deposit in my checking account."

"That's your monthly distribution. I mailed the report you asked for. Do you want to discuss it?"

Nefi sifted through her pile of mail and found a thick letter-size envelope from Attucks, Bird, and Copley. "Yes, just a moment." She tore it open and unfolded the papers.

Cassie leaned close to Nefi.

The numbers were far longer than Nefi dreamed they'd be. Columns of numbers filled the pages with headings like the number of shares, price per share, cost basis, value per year, unrealized gain or loss, investment return, holding period, accrued interest, and dividend value. She found a total at the bottom right corner of the last page. *Whoa.* It took her a moment to find her voice. "Um, so the trust is worth ten million dollars?"

Cassie covered her mouth with both hands, muffling her squeal. Mutt's jaw dropped, leaving his mouth open.

"Yes." Lancaster's voice rose from the phone.

"I'm going to get eight-thousand dollars every month?"

"If you need more to cover tuition and living expenses, you'll need to meet with the—"

"This is plenty, really. I didn't expect this much for the first payout of the trust."

"This isn't the first payout. Go to the second page of the report."

Nefi flipped to that page. There, under monthly distributions, was a list dating back to 2002 when the trust received the life insurance settlements. "I see it. Oh. Where did these distributions go?"

"They were paid to the trustee. See page three."

Nefi turned the page and read the name of the Trustee. Jane Wright.

Grandmother?

Ronald Lancaster's voice sounded far away. "Was there anything else?"

Nefi pulled her cell phone up to her ear. "No, sir. Thank you."

Cassie and Mutt gaped at her with slack-jawed shock. Cassie recovered first and hugged Nefi.

"You're rich! You're rich!" Cassie released Nefi and collapsed in her chair.

Mutt nodded. "Are you sure you want to do that internship at the FBI?"

"Of course, I do."

Mutt shrugged. "Why? You're going to make ninety-six-thousand dollars a year for breathing."

The trust fund lifted a great weight of debt from Nefi's shoulders. She could repay her aunt and uncle, pay off student loans, and afford a great place near Quantico.

"I'd run off to travel the world." Cassie gazed out the window.

Nefi drank the last of her soft drink while numbers danced and multiplied in her brain. She struggled to grasp the concept of a million of anything. Converting the dollars into something else might help. What if time was money? If one dollar equaled one second of life, then a million seconds would be twelve days! And ten million seconds would add up to one hundred twenty days. *Whoa.*

She wanted to call Martina, but Martina wrote that she didn't want to talk on the phone until they could meet face to face. Nefi wanted to share the news about her trust fund. She considered calling Vincent, but he'd be at work. Her attention drifted back to the report. The monthly payout began a few months after her parents died. The paperwork of filing their life insurance and activating the trust probably took that long.

Once the paperwork was sorted, grandmother became the trustee and started getting monthly payouts of eight thousand dollars. Nefi moved in with her aunt and uncle because all agreed Jane and Ted Wright were unsuited to take in a traumatized teenager. Perhaps grandmother sent money every month to Aunt Louise and Uncle Hamilton. The private school in McLean, Virginia, cost a fortune.

"She's got that weird look again," Cassie said. "I can almost hear gears turning in her head."

Mutt replied with an "uh-huh."

Cassie held up the last slice of Hawaiian pizza. "My momma always says rich people think different. Maybe that's her brain rearranging itself."

Nefi snorted. "I just realized the checks my grandmother sent every month were from the trust fund not from her."

Cassie's eyes widened. "Your grandma sends you eight thousand dollars a month? My grandmother sends me cookies."

Mutt cleared his throat. He glared at Cassie as if to remind her of social boundaries. Living with two women wasn't easy.

Cassie shrugged.

"She sends me two-thousand dollars a month." Tuition ate most of it.

Mutt rubbed his scarred hand over his mouth. He often did that when he weighed whether to speak.

Nefi leaned her elbows on the table and eyed Mutt. "Are you thinking what I'm thinking?"

Mutt raised his eyebrows while the rest of his face flashed expressions of awkwardness and contempt. "Where did six thousand a month go?"

Nefi nodded. "My aunt and uncle send me enough to cover the rest of my expenses. Maybe grandmother sends them money."

"Could be, but why? Does that make sense to send money to them to send to you?" Mutt raised an eyebrow.

Nefi slumped against the back of her chair. Why send part of the money so indirectly? "Maybe she sent it to them because she thought I'd squander it?"

Mutt's eyelids closed halfway, and his face relaxed.

The air conditioner kicked on, blowing cool air from the ceiling vents into the room.

Mutt was right. *It didn't make sense. At. All.* "I should ask her."

Cassie squirmed and angled her body toward Nefi. "Is

there a polite way to say, Hey, Grandma, what did you do with seventy-two-thousand dollars a year from my trust fund?"

Nefi grimaced. Seventy-two-thousand dollars! "Maybe she reinvested it."

"Read the report." Cassie waved her hand over the papers.

After scanning a report page, Nefi read a page titled long-term capital gains and losses. "I don't know where the money went, and the report is confusing. So, what does this mean?" She held up the page and read aloud, "There's a column named Method, and under that is FIFO. The other columns are Quantity or Face Value, Purchase Date, Sale Date, and Wash Sale Cost Basis Adjustment."

"Why not ask Mr. Lancaster?" Mutt crossed his arms.

"Or your FBI fiancé, perhaps?" Cassie batted her eyelashes.

"Oh, no. No. Vincent would probably start investigating and treat my grandmother as a suspect. What if I'm mistaken and the money is all there? Grandmother Wright is family. She would do what was best for me. I need to find someone to examine the trust fund to explain it to me." The staggering size of the trust felt like a mammoth responsibility. Nefi needed to understand it to manage it.

Cassie cleared the late lunch from the table. Mutt picked up his boxes and letters and headed toward his room. Having spoken their minds, they left Nefi to stew over her decision. She found herself in uncharted territory. The most challenging financial information Nefi ever had to learn was negotiating student grants and balancing her checking account. Investments, trust funds? Too complex.

Nefi toyed with her mail. A light blue envelope slid

out from the rest with a return address from North Carolina. She placed it on top of her stack of mail, scooped her mail into her arms, and carried it to her room. There, she opened the envelope on top. In it, Blake and Terri Clayton wrote that they sent a gift for Vincent to deliver. Blake added he would soon interview at the Tampa FBI field office. Terri, a large-animal veterinarian, would take the Florida licensing exam if Blake got the job in Tampa.

Blake Clayton spoke with a southern drawl. He had worked at the FBI with Vincent until his arrest concerning a cold case murder. She trusted Blake in a big brother kind of way. His family ran a horse breeding farm in North Carolina and owned a large plot of land. Maybe he had a trust fund. After finding his phone number on her cell phone contact list, she called him.

"Blake here."

"Nefi here. Thanks for the card."

"Hey, girl! How are you?"

"Took my last undergrad exam this morning."

"Nice."

"Thank you for the gift, whatever it is. I start the summer internship in Quantico in June."

"Vincent bragged about it. Congratulations."

"I hope you get the job at the Tampa field office. I hear a lot of old people move to Florida."

Blake chuckled. "And we have Disney World and Universal Studios, so you can come visit, kiddo."

"Deal. I'm calling because I need someone who understands finance and investments."

"Are you in trouble?"

"I inherited a trust fund. It's been managed for seven years by a trustee. I want someone to look over the whole thing to make sure there weren't any mistakes or bad investments made. Something doesn't add up, but I'm not educated in this kind of thing."

Silence dominated the call for about a minute. Nefi checked that the call had not dropped.

"I know someone who can do that. She's freak-ishly brilliant with computers and financial stuff, but she's expensive."

"Do you have a name and phone number?"

"I do. You can say I recommended her, but you might not want to mention you're engaged to Vincent."

Nefi immediately thought of Vincent's ex-girlfriend. "Rose?"

Blake burst into laughter that gradually decreased to snorting and gasping breaths. "Thanks. I needed a good laugh. Please, let's forget she-who-can't-be-named. No, the lady I recommend was in FBI training with us. She had to drop out because, in one of the training exercises, Vincent broke her arm."

Nefi gasped.

"It was an accident, but yeah. Her name is Helen Cho. The company she works for is Strategic Solutions based in Maryville, Tennessee."

"Thank you. Please don't mention this to Vincent. I don't want him to ask probing questions about the trust fund at graduation. My grandmother has a bit of an ego. She would probably make a scene if he questioned her. The financial discrepancies might be nothing or a misunderstanding. I don't know. That's why I need an outside opinion."

"Cho will find answers. Hey, have you and Vincent set a wedding date?"

"We haven't had much time to talk."

Terri's voice sounded in the background. Blake's wife and Nefi became fast friends during Blake's trial.

"It's Nefi," Blake announced. "Hey, Terri wants to talk to you."

"Hello!"

"Thanks for the card." Nefi recognized Terri's handwriting on it.

"Thank you again for your help during the trial. Now I understand what Blake's been saying about your skills at reading people."

"Your instincts about Blake were correct."

"Yeah, he's one of the good guys. Hug Vincent for me."

"Next time I see him."

Nefi's next call went to Strategic Solutions to speak with Helen Cho. After the second transfer, a voice answered.

"Hello, how may I help you?"

"I'm Nefi Jenkins. Blake Clayton recommended you."

"He's so kind. What can I do for you, Nefi Jenkins?"

Nefi explained the situation in detail, emphasizing that she didn't understand trust funds or investments, but from what little she knew, it seemed that something didn't add up. She asked Helen Cho if she could discreetly review the trust account and how it has been handled. As Nefi spoke, she heard the clicking of keys in the background.

"I'll be glad to. Email me all the documents you have along with the contact information of the person handling the account. I'll need a consent form to access the financial transactions. I'll email it to you. Sign as the owner of the trust fund. If anyone asks, I'll tell them I'm counseling you on money management."

"Thank you." Nefi gave Ms. Cho her email address and mobile phone number.

Helen Cho instructed Nefi where to email the documents, then she said, "I might need about a week turnaround after I get your papers and the consent form. Will that work for you?"

"Can you give me an estimate of your fees?"

"The maximum would be a thousand dollars a day, but this could take less than a week."

Nefi weighed the cost of knowledge against the cost of ignorance. Certainly, the unused thousands from each month's payout were reinvested in the trust, but she could stare at the columns on the report all day without understanding what she was reading. "Do you need a deposit?"

"Normally, yes, but I admire your uncle, Senator Jenkins. I did some work for his office. Are we a go?"

Nefi took a deep breath and mentally surrendered her first monthly trust fund payout. "Yes, Miss Cho."

"Call me Helen. I'll call you when my report is ready. I am texting my email address."

The call ended, and Nefi exhaled. She relaxed, confident Helen Cho would explain the complexities of investments and trust fund management in plain English. It was worth the first payout to have peace of mind. Tomorrow at church, she would donate ten percent of her trust fund payment to give thanks for it. Freed to focus on graduation and her upcoming internship, Nefi packed for her trip to the Brazilian Embassy in Washington, D.C.

·6·

Monday, May 17, 2010

AT THE END of a flight and a cab ride, Nefi arrived at the Chancery Building of the Embassy of Brazil in Washington, D.C. The building resembled a blue glass cube supported by recessed white cement columns connected by clear glass. The Brazilian flag flapped gently at the top of a pole in the center of a patch of grass in front of the cube. A huge section of the cube extended over the entrance, creating a shaded area.

Nefi adjusted the leather satchel strap that crossed her body. The satchel contained the paperwork for her appointment and a change of clothes in case she needed more time to complete her business with the Embassy.

Inside, she introduced herself to the receptionist while a uniformed guard stood nearby. The receptionist asked for her passport.

While Nefi dug her Brazilian passport out of her satchel, the receptionist spoke into her phone.

"Sir, she's here."

Nefi handed over her passport, which was quickly read and handed back.

"Please have a seat."

Nefi eased into the nearest cushioned chair. Behind the receptionist, a painting of the *Cristo Redentor* statue dominated the wall. The 30-meter-tall statue atop Mount Corcovado held out his arms as if to embrace the city of Rio de Janeiro. Nefi and Martina took a panoramic escalator and climbed over 200 steps to see it up close on vacation. Using Nefi's Portuguese and Martina's Spanish, they blended in better than most tourists.

A glossy brochure on the end table showed statistics on Brazil as a growing economic superpower. It credited President Luiz Inácio Lula da Silva's policies for lifting twenty-nine million people from poverty into the middle class. The brochure reported that Brazil ranked seventh in the world with the highest concentration of natural resources. It was on its way to becoming the third-largest producer of oil and gas and the seventh-largest market for automobiles.

Nefi smiled at the need for so many cars. True, Brazil was the fifth largest country in the world, but vast sections of the country were in the great Amazon rainforest, inaccessible to cars. In the rainforest, people travel by boat or on foot. Her parents never owned a car in Brazil.

The glass entryway opened, and a man in a deep blue suit entered, his face shadowed. He walked toward Nefi, so she stood to introduce herself. Then the man stepped under a light.

His Excellency, the Brazilian Ambassador, Alfonso Morales, opened his arms.

Nefi hugged him and felt fourteen years old again, even though she stood almost a head taller than her godfather, the man who had attended Harvard with her parents and uncle. Surprised to see him, she exclaimed, "What are you doing here?"

He chuckled.

"I mean, I wasn't expecting—"

"Your paperwork crossed my desk." He released her, introduced his secretary to Nefi by her full name, and added, "And this is my goddaughter, Nefi Jenkins."

The woman stood and offered her hand. "I'm pleased to meet you, Miss Jenkins."

Nefi reached over the desk and shook her hand. "I'm honored to meet you."

The Ambassador aimed his hand toward the door. "Join me for lunch at the residence so we can discuss things."

Nefi followed him outside to a pathway that led to a stately rectangular white stone building with four pillars at the entrance. Ambassador Alfonso Morales led the way and opened doors for her into an elegant lobby with a stunning curved granite stairway adorned with an ornate wrought-iron railing. The walls featured bold paintings marked with small plaques naming the artist and title of each work. She gaped at the majestic splendor.

"I have a surprise for you," the Ambassador said, stopping in the foyer.

"Another one?"

He chuckled.

"Thank you for the graduation gift." Nefi wished she had brought the new digital camera but had not yet read the instruction booklet. Seven years ago, he gave her a tiny camera along with the Brazilian passport she needed to travel to the United States. "The old camera still works."

Nefi suspected the surprise was that the Ambassador's family was in residence. She had not seen them since her visit to Brazil in 2008.

He guided her toward the stairs, so Nefi headed to the second floor. He led her into a lovely room with pale yellow walls. It had two areas where sofas and chairs sat around low tables. As Nefi turned to see the rest of the room, she spotted an oval dining table for six, where two women and a tall man stood smiling at her. Nefi's heart raced, and she sharply inhaled when she recognized them.

Uncle Hamilton and Aunt Louise took turns hugging her.

The Ambassador's wife stepped from behind Aunt Louise. Mrs. Morales laughed as she held Nefi. "Oh, to see your face!" She released Nefi and held her shoulders at arms' length. "How beautiful you are!"

Nefi was glad she had worn makeup. Though her best friend Martina had introduced her to makeup, Mrs. Morales had refined its use to high art. "Thank you, thank you!" Nefi's heart overflowed. She wiped her eyes with her hand. For good measure, she hugged Ambassador Morales again. What a thoughtful surprise this was!

They took their seats with Nefi in between her aunt and uncle and the Ambassador and his wife facing them. A young gentleman entered to fill Nefi's water glass and asked if she wanted coffee, tea, fruit juice, or a soft drink.

Nefi answered automatically in Portuguese, "*Chá gelado, obrigada.*"

"*Sim, senhorita.*" He nodded and left the room.

"Now, tell me why on earth you want to relinquish

your Brazilian citizenship." The Ambassador placed his napkin in his lap.

Nefi pulled the thick cloth napkin from her plate and set it on her lap. "Even though I treasure dual citizenship, the FBI does not allow their employees to have it. I suppose they consider it a potential conflict of interest."

The Ambassador nodded. "Have you been offered a position?"

"I begin an internship at Quantico in June. I can't apply for their full training program until I'm twenty-three."

"Why not wait until then to surrender your citizenship?"

Nefi felt a bit ambushed. Turning in paperwork to a stranger in a bureaucratic process was one thing. It was far more uncomfortable to tell the Ambassador himself why she no longer wanted to keep her citizenship in his beloved country. He had ordered swift service for her the day she arrived hungry, scared, and wearing tribal face paint at the consulate in Manaus. Paperwork which usually took weeks had been completed within hours. Orphaned and in the company of strangers, she showed up in need of a passport and immigration papers to allow her to travel to the United States, to grandparents she did not remember meeting and an aunt and uncle she didn't know existed.

Years later, she learned that when Ambassador Morales heard Nefi's parents were murdered, he dispatched notices all over the country to be on the lookout for Nefi. Her parents had named him as her godfather, the person in charge of her religious upbringing, and over the years, he'd mailed Bibles and children's books to her village.

She wanted to explain her decision without offending this kind man. "Nine thousand people applied for these internship positions. Four hundred were chosen. I want to demonstrate my seriousness."

The server delivered a glass of iced tea near Nefi's plate and left the room. Nefi's village never had ice. Throughout her childhood, the only times she saw ice was in Manaus once a year when her parents took her to the pediatrician. Her reward for not biting the doctor or the nurse was a big meal at a restaurant, a soft drink with ice, and ice cream for dessert. Almost everyone Nefi knew in the United States took ice for granted.

When the Ambassador did not respond, an awkward silence fell over the room. She studied his face as he and Mrs. Morales exchanged a look. Nefi longed to discuss a pleasant topic.

Nefi asked, "How is Antonio?"

Mrs. Morales set down her water glass. "He's studying in Switzerland."

"Your son has come a long way from driving your limousine, Al," Uncle Hamilton said.

The Ambassador nodded with a grin.

Uncle Hamilton had taken time from the vital work of the Senate to be here. Aunt Louise had traveled from their rental home in McLean, Virginia. Ambassador Morales had arranged it all. Such a thoughtful man! Did he understand? Was he sad or insulted about surrendering citizenship? Nefi sighed. This had been a difficult decision, and she stood by it, though she deeply regretted hurting her godfather's feelings.

The server returned with a cart laden with covered plates, a bread basket, a fruit basket, and a decanter of white wine. He placed the covered plates and the rest on the table. With a flourish, he lifted the covers from Nefi and Aunt Louise's plates. He performed the same service to Mrs. Morales, and then he revealed Uncle Hamilton's plate and, lastly, the Ambassador's.

Sea bass, plantain, rice, and broccolini filled their plates and scented the air. He remembered her favorite dish. Ambassador and Mrs. Morales had treated her to this for dinner when she visited them. At the time, she suspected they wanted to match her up with Antonio. During that visit, Mrs. Morales groomed Nefi to dress, behave, and think like a lady. The week had been a crash course in etiquette, makeup, hair styling, and posture as well. Though Mrs. Morales might have intended the makeover to benefit her son, Nefi longed to apply everything she learned to impress Vincent. Nefi had wanted Vincent to see her as a twenty-one-year-old woman and forget about the feral teenager who had attacked him in the jungle.

"Nothing," Nefi said, "will change my love for you and Brazil."

Mrs. Morales reached across the table to place her hand over Nefi's. "You are always welcome in our home."

Nefi's eyes stung. "Thank you." Her invitation felt like forgiveness.

After the Ambassador said the blessing for the food, they feasted. Intermittent conversations about graduate school, Hamilton's re-election campaign, and Antonio's studies in Switzerland were followed by the Ambassador's announcement that he planned to retire at the end of the year.

Mrs. Morales gazed lovingly at her husband. No one asked why he wanted to retire. He appeared to be in excellent health and similar in age to Uncle Hamilton in his mid-fifties. Perhaps the political winds were changing against the Worker's Party. Nefi had met the President, His Excellency Luiz Inácio Lula da Silva, at the Sambadrome during Mardi Gras. He had been charming and smelled of smoke and aftershave.

"How is President Squid?" Nefi asked.

Ambassador Morales laughed and clapped his hands together. Once he regained composure, he turned to Uncle Hamilton and Aunt Louise and said, "I must tell you about when I introduced Nefi to His Excellency. He had invited us up to his viewing box to watch the Mardi Gras parade. Nefi asked why I called him a squid. His nickname, Lula, in Portuguese, also means squid."

Mrs. Morales gasped.

"She did not say this in front of him," the Ambassador said, holding his wife's hand. Ambassador Morales's countenance grew somber. "I think this will be His Excellency's last term in office. His cough is getting worse. He is a heavy smoker, I'm afraid."

So, there it was. The Ambassadorship was appointed, so someone else would likely replace him under a new administration.

Aunt Louise and Mrs. Morales discussed plans for their Viking River Cruise next spring and the men joked about being dragged to museums in every country along the route.

The server silently removed empty dishes and served dessert and coffee while the conversations continued. As the leisurely lunch wound down, Ambassador Morales accepted Nefi's passport and forms and excused himself to process them.

Mrs. Morales and Aunt Louise said goodbye to Nefi with hugs on their way out to shop.

Alone with her uncle in the lovely room, they moved from the table to a sofa.

"Did you know about my parents' trust fund?"

He nodded.

"Grandmother Wright started sending me two-thousand dollars a month when I went to college. She told me I didn't have to report it when I applied for student grants and loans."

"That sounds like her." He cleared his throat. "Sorry. I shouldn't have said that."

Nefi shrugged. "I wondered if her middle name was Always."

"Jane Always Wright." He chuckled and draped an arm around her shoulders. "She can be irritating, it's true, but she sent two thousand dollars a month for your school. It helped. Be kind to her. I suspect she would have been happier as a lawyer than a mother."

"Why didn't she go to law school?"

"Oh, she did. She even passed the bar in Virginia."

"What? Did she practice law?"

"Marta told us that Jane worked for two years, and then she got pregnant."

At the sound of her mother's name, Nefi sighed. Whatever maternal instincts her mother had did not come from Jane Always Wright, Esquire. Nefi leaned her head on her uncle's shoulder.

"Louise and I will pay for your wedding, so don't put it off."

Nefi sat up so she could read his face. Her first thought was about their generosity. The second was about the urgency in his tone. "Thank you. We haven't set a date.

Martina and Oscar haven't set a date for their wedding either. We don't want to have dates that conflict."

He nodded and bit his lower lip. "I'm happy you're getting married. So many young people these days get pregnant before they get married or don't get married at all. It breaks my heart."

Nefi threaded her hand between her uncle's arm and ribcage. "Even if Vincent lived in Boston instead of three-hundred kilometers away, I couldn't get pregnant. We haven't had sex."

Uncle Hamilton patted Nefi's hand and grinned. "I didn't ask but thank you for telling me."

When Nefi was brought to her aunt and uncle's home to live, she often shocked them with her directness. Aunt Louise said she was honored by Nefi's honesty. Uncle Hamilton tended to excuse himself from the room when Nefi asked Aunt Louise questions about sex and personal hygiene. Nefi had confided in Aunt Louise about her promise to her mother to remain a virgin until married. Aunt Louise had vigorously supported that promise and told Nefi it took great strength of character to stand by beliefs when the whole world tended to mock them. Nefi believed her values made her a light in darkness rather than an oddity. She was, nonetheless, comfortable being treated like an oddity.

The Ambassador returned with a stamped, signed, official paper that declared Nefi was no longer entitled to use her Brazilian passport, vote in Brazil, or enjoy any rights of citizenship as of today.

Nefi hugged him and tucked the paper into her satchel. It was her choice to let go of her past, but Brazil would remain in her heart and memories. She felt a loss in letting go of her citizenship and childhood.

"When are you going back to Boston?" Uncle Hamilton asked.

"My flight is at nine."

"Wonderful. Then let me show you off at work."

The Ambassador chuckled. "Nothing like being seen with a beautiful young woman to make the press pay attention."

"Let them talk," Hamilton said.

Soon after saying goodbye to her godfather, Nefi and her uncle rode in the back of a town car toward the Senate building. Nefi's cell phone chimed with a call from the 804 area code, which included Richmond, Virginia.

"Hello?"

"Hello, Nefi." Grandmother Wright's sounded friendlier than usual.

Her uncle elbowed her and whispered, "Speak of the devil, and she appears."

Nefi had read that in the Middle Ages, people believed a superstition that the devil was summoned by the sound of his name. Nefi grinned. "Hello, Grandmother."

"Oh, grandmother makes me sound so old. How about if you call me Mimi?"

The perfect nickname for a narcissist. Rather than point out her grandmother's age, Nefi gave in to her request. "Hello, Mimi."

"Much better. Now, I believe we need to sit down together to talk about the trust fund. I know you have questions, so how about if we meet for lunch tomorrow? Find a nice restaurant near campus, say around eleven-thirty?"

Grandmother Wright had not visited Nefi in the four

years she'd been at Harvard. Had grandmother avoided Harvard because it reminded her of Marta? Had she avoided Boston because that was where Marta had married Herman Jenkins?

"You're coming to graduation, aren't you?"

"Of course. Although, I doubt we'd have any privacy to discuss personal financial matters with friends and family there."

"Yes, ma'am. I'll get a reservation for noon at Modelo's Market Cafe."

"Excellent. See you then, dear."

Why did every encounter with her grandmother feel like a business transaction? She marked the date and time of lunch with "Mimi" on her cell phone calendar. Nefi tucked her phone into her satchel.

Uncle Hamilton bit his lower lip. This was his way of showing he overheard the conversation and hesitated to speak.

"Say whatever is on your mind."

"Have you ever wondered why your mother moved thousands of miles away from home?"

"I used to." Nefi sighed. *Grandfather was kind, but grandmother? Her personality would not change.* "Grandmother is family. My challenge is to understand her, accept her, be forgiving of her, and, most of all, avoid becoming like her."

He leaned close and kissed Nefi's head just above her ear.

Nefi spent the afternoon meeting Senators, a state governor, Uncle Hamilton's secretary, and an intern. The building bustled with urgent and vital activities of the second session of the 111th Congress though no bill was being voted on that day. Uncle Hamilton brought her into the Senate chamber's visitor's gallery and pointed down at his seat on the right side. In whispers, he noted where the President, the Majority Leader, and the Minority Leader of the Senate sat. Fewer than a dozen people were in the chamber. One man appeared to be grandstanding for the cable channel broadcast.

Her uncle took her to dinner at the Capital Grille. Afterward, he sent her to the airport by limousine in time for her night flight back to Boston. By the time Nefi collapsed, happy and full, in her seat on the plane, she marveled at the amazing day. Seeing family and friends was a sweet surprise. She could visit the Smithsonian another time.

She pulled the strap of her satchel over her head and tucked the whole thing under the seat. As she bent forward, her cell phone chimed. She dug it out of the satchel and was about to answer it when the flight attendant strode by.

Nefi answered the call. "This is Nefi."

"Hello, Nefi. This is Helen Cho. I'll be in Boston on Wednesday. Can we meet in the morning, say around nine-ish?"

Wednesday, Wednesday. She remembered she was supposed to be at her apartment on Wednesday. "I don't have a car. Could you come to my apartment?" She buckled her seatbelt.

"Sure."

"Thank you!"

"See you then."

The flight attendant helped an elderly woman stuff a carry-on suitcase into the overhead compartment.

Nefi entered the time and date in her calendar to meet with Helen Cho and then quickly turned off the cell phone.

She tucked the phone into the satchel and put it under the seat in front of her.

Nefi settled into sleep to the roar of the engines. Tuesday lunch with Grandmother. Wednesday meeting with Helen Cho to learn about the trust fund. She had a list of questions to ask Miss Cho on Wednesday. Why did she need to be home in the middle of the week? Nefi searched her memory. Trash day? Appliance repair?

Wednesday was the nineteenth of May. Nefi's eyes popped open. Vincent was arriving on the nineteenth.

·7·

Tuesday, May 18, 2010

THE FLIGHT FROM Richmond, Virginia, had arrived on time at Boston's Logan Airport. Jane had easily found the rental car booth and her rental. She used the rental car company map to locate Modelo's Market Café and Bakery on Medford Street in Somerville, Massachusetts, a suburb two and a half miles northwest of Harvard Square.

Jane wore a gray cashmere coat for warmth and style. Carrying a red Prada leather tote bag with the handles tucked in the crook of her left arm, she strode from her rental car. She gazed up at the building's purple sign and the pink awnings. Is this the place? It looked like a Bohemian grocery store. How many businesses named Modelo's Café could there be?

The door swung open, revealing Nefi in khaki pants and a pale blue sweater. Her hair, as usual, hung loose past her shoulders, and she was wearing a bit of makeup in that girl-next-door natural look that seemed so popular these days.

"Mr. De Souza has reserved a table for us."

"Why would a place like this need reservations?"

Nefi scowled and held the door open.

Jane entered and removed her gloves. The place smelled of melted cheese and freshly baked bread. She followed Nefi past a long glass display case of pastries, bread, cakes, cookies, and pies, through the grocery section to the back, which was set up with tables and chairs. Before they could sit, a man in a white apron bounded toward them with his arms open wide. He spoke in what sounded like gibberish.

He hugged Nefi and turned toward Jane.

She braced herself for an unwanted hug, but the man extended his hand instead.

"May I introduce Mr. Joe De Souza, the owner." Nefi then turned toward the man and said something to him, followed by "Jane Wright."

His meaty hands gently enclosed Jane's right hand. "It is an honor to meet you, Mrs. Wright. My family and I welcome you."

"Thank you."

He pulled out her chair and then Nefi's before he returned to the kitchen. The menus were already on the table. It was a table for four. Nefi and Jane sat facing each other.

A young woman approached them. "What would you like to drink?"

Nefi ordered iced tea and a large Asiago cheese bread. Jane ordered coffee, and the server left them alone again.

Let the game begin. Jane tucked her gloves in her purse and set the purse on the empty chair to her left, where she could keep an eye on it. "What do you want to know about the trust fund?"

"I received the first monthly deposit." Nefi fidgeted for a bit before folding her hands on the table. "I understand you sent two-thousand dollars a month to Uncle Hamilton for school while I lived in McLean. You sent the same amount to me in college."

Jane nodded.

"The records show each monthly payout from the trust fund was eight-thousand dollars. Where did the other six thousand a month go?"

Though Jane had not pegged the girl as greedy, this challenge to account for the balance of the payouts made her sound ungrateful.

The server delivered their drinks along with a large flatbread covered in melted cheese then she stood at attention with her pen poised over her order pad.

Leaving Nefi's question hanging, Jane lifted the menu. "I need a minute."

The young lady excused herself.

Meat-filled turnovers, fried and stuffed sourdough, a pancake stuffed with marinated chicken, Acai bowls with granola and nuts, omelets, sandwiches, wraps, and fried bacon pork belly with yucca fritters were not on her diet. Pasta, rice, and beans with meat, salads, and soups were listed on the last page. When she looked up from the menu, Nefi waved the server back.

Jane selected grilled chicken, spinach, and broccoli.

Nefi said to the server, "*Eu gostaria do meu pedido usual com carne e banana frita.*" To Jane, she said, "I always get the same dish. It's a Brazilian specialty."

That explained Nefi's choice of restaurant. Here, the girl

could speak her childhood language. Now it was time to speak about money, a foreign language to Nefi. "Let's discuss the trust. After Marta and Herman passed, I became the trustee. I invested in real estate." She sipped her coffee and found it surprisingly flavorful for a small cafe.

Nefi bowed her head for a few moments, and then she tore off a handful of the cheesy bread. "You paid for the real estate with six-thousand dollars a month?"

"No, child. Follow along. I used the life insurance proceeds to buy real estate. Richmond, Virginia, is considered one of the top twenty-five cities to live in, and real estate tends to grow in value no matter what the stock market does. Someone has to maintain this particular property, so I paid five thousand a month for a man to tend to it."

Nefi swallowed the bread and washed it down with the tea.

Oh, to be young again with a high metabolism. Jane sighed. If she smelled a doughnut, fat formed on her hips. Discipline kept her body from going large and slack. Upkeep took effort, but it was worth it. "Which reminds me, I haven't paid the property manager this month. Since the payment goes to you now, you'll need to reserve five thousand each month to cover his salary. It might seem like a great amount of money, but I assure you that without someone watching over the property, it would deteriorate and lose its value."

The server seated a family of three at a table by the window.

"I don't have it."

Jane leaned forward and whispered, "Didn't you receive eight-thousand dollars on the fifteenth?"

Nefi tore off another handful of bread. She seemed

fixated on the bread instead of paying attention to the conversation. "I mean, I don't have it *anymore*."

Jane pushed her coffee and saucer to the side while she gathered her thoughts. Her heart raced. How would she cover the man's salary this month? *That stupid pin-striped fool at Attucks, Bird, and Copley should have notified her before he signed the trust over to Nefi.* Her hands trembled, so she pressed them on her lap. She whispered intently, "You spent eight-thousand dollars in three days?"

Redness flushed Nefi's neck and ears. Her voice came out a whisper, "I can set aside the money next month."

Jane sighed heavily, relieved that she'd convinced Nefi to pay the property manager. She took a drink of coffee to calm herself. "It's all right. Not everyone is cut out to manage money. I might have spent the money at your age." She smiled at Nefi to let her know she was forgiven. Though she would not ask where the money went, she suspected Nefi had blown it on tattoos or clothes. Easy come; easy go. While she could understand the desire to dress well, she couldn't comprehend why young people crowded into tattoo parlors while claiming tattoos demonstrated their individuality. "I suppose I can draw the money from my savings. You know, Ted and I aren't getting any younger. We must prepare for retirement."

"Grandfather's retiring?"

"Eventually." Jane moved her coffee and saucer to the right of her place setting. Her untouched bread plate sat to the left where it belonged.

"Momma taught me how to remember which cup and bread plate are mine." Nefi formed her left hand into a lowercase 'b' and her right hand into a lowercase 'd' and said, "bread plate on the left and drink on the right."

Nefi sounded like Marta, fresh from her fourth-grade etiquette lessons. The program called White Gloves and Party Manners lasted one evening a week for two months over a summer a lifetime ago. Jane used to set Marta's hair in curlers and dress her up in crinoline and puffy-sleeved dresses for the class. She was the most beautiful child in the class with the posture of a ballerina. It was peculiar to see that lesson echoed decades later from a girl who grew up barefoot in the jungle.

A group of businessmen arrived and stood by while servers slid tables and chairs together to accommodate eight. Mostly in their twenties and thirties, one business-man appeared to be their leader. He had dark black hair salted with gray. He smiled and nodded at Jane.

Jane nodded back at him. The restaurant section was filling up and a long line formed at the bakery counter as if a tour bus had emptied at the door.

Mr. De Souza himself served them and rubbed his hands together. While Nefi complimented the owner, Jane smiled up at him until he returned to the kitchen. They ate. The fresh broccoli, spinach, and chicken burst with flavors.

"That leaves one thousand each month." Nefi con-sumed great forkfuls of what looked like cooked bananas.

"What did you say?"

Nefi swallowed. "You sent two to me and five to the property manager. That leaves one."

A twinge of panic seized Jane. She should have told Nefi to send her six thousand dollars a month. She forked a chunk of chicken and reminded herself to breathe. "That's for property tax."

Nefi stared for a while before she said, "Please send me the property manager's mailing address."

Breathe, breathe. "Of course, dear."

"I'm sorry you have to draw from your savings." Nefi appeared contrite.

"You are far more responsible than your mother was at this age. We sent Marta to the finest schools so she would have great opportunities in life. I didn't recognize her rebellious streak until it was too late." Jane speared broccoli to a chunk of chicken with a sharp, fast stab of her fork.

"What do you mean?" Nefi stared wide-eyed across the table.

"Well, now Marta didn't need a Harvard education to run off to the jungle with that Jenkins boy, did she?" Jane bit the food off her fork.

Nefi set her fork on her plate and lowered her hands to her lap.

Jane let the reminder of Marta's failures sink in deep. If the girl imagined pouting would draw an apology, she would be mistaken. If Nefi couldn't accept the truth about her mother's irresponsibility, then so be it. The truth is the truth. Often the most profound truths hurt. Three years after Marta graduated from Harvard, she lived in poverty in a mud hut in the Amazon rainforest with savages. *Who would take a baby there? Honestly, such insanity.* Marta's life in the jungle turned out as dreadful as Jane had expected.

Conversations among the families and the business people surrounded Jane and Nefi while Jane let Nefi stew in her thoughts. Nefi had not suffered and sacrificed and lost a daughter and a fortune because of other people's reckless choices. Jane believed she, not Nefi, should control the ten-million-dollar trust fund.

After estimating she'd consumed six hundred calories, Jane set down her fork.

The server boxed up the remainder of Nefi's lunch while Jane paid the bill.

Nefi didn't speak again until they left the restaurant to go their separate ways. "I'll see you at graduation."

"See you then." Jane plucked her gloves from her purse and put them on.

Marta had squandered her life just as Nefi had squandered eight thousand dollars in three days. What if she decided to cash in the trust? If her friends knew of the money, they would con her out of it with sob stories and absurd investment scams. Who knew how long it would take to lose it all? A psychology degree did not prepare a college student to oversee a ten-million-dollar trust fund. Nefi was too trusting, too naïve for her own good.

Jane vowed to review the trust agreement again. There had to be a loophole or spendthrift clause to preserve the trust.

·8·

Wednesday, May 19, 2010

Early Wednesday, after her morning run and shower, Nefi sat with Cassie at the dining table under the chandelier to set up the gift Ruis sent. The gift had been charging up overnight.

Cassie recited the specifications of Nefi's new Apple iPhone 3GS, "Cellular network C-D-M-A and G-S-M, nice."

Nefi leaned toward Cassie's shoulder. "Is that good?"

"This sweet device will work anywhere in the world. Well, maybe not in remote areas of China or at the North or South poles. Let me get this straight. Your best friend's older brother gave you this phone, and he paid the bill for twelve months?"

Nefi nodded.

"He sure likes you."

Nefi snorted. "Like another baby sister."

Cassie rolled her eyes. She was dressed for running but wasn't sweaty, so she hadn't gone yet. "If you say so."

"Stop that. He was one of the three men who found me in the rainforest and brought me to my aunt and uncle. I went to his wedding."

"And he knows you're engaged?"

"And he knows Vincent."

Cassie handed the new cell phone to Nefi. "The good news is that this is a seriously fabulous cell phone. The bad news is you have to enter your contacts manually."

Nefi opened the contact list on her old cell phone and set it on the table. "Okay."

Cassie laughed. "Okay? You have to physically type in their names, phone numbers, addresses, emails, everything."

"I understand." Nefi typed Vincent's name into the new phone. "It won't take long. I have most of them memorized." She entered Vincent's phone number and email address.

Cassie picked up Nefi's old cell phone and scrolled through the contacts list. "That's the saddest thing I've seen all week. You have only twenty-three friends?"

"And family."

Cassie set down the phone and hugged Nefi, then she left the table and entered the kitchen. "Where's Mutt?" She stepped back into the common room with the clean blender in her hand. "He hasn't made his green breakfast slime."

Nefi checked the wall hook by the front door, where he left his keychain. She picked it up for Cassie to see and then hung it back in place. Cassie, Nefi, and Mutt kept their keychains on their hooks to show who was home and away.

Nefi shrugged. Mutt left his bedroom door open except when sleeping or changing clothes. Because of his PTSD, he preferred to have open spaces and open doors. Nefi followed Cassie through the kitchen toward Mutt's room. The door was open, so they both peered inside. Mutt's bed was made.

Cassie stepped into Mutt's room and soon came back out. "His bathroom door's open." She set the blender on the counter by the refrigerator.

"Why don't you run by yourself?"

"First of all, I'm not as fast as you," Cassie lowered her head. "And second, I like to keep an eye on Mutt. It's not just sounds that can set him off. Sometimes, it's a chemical smell or smoke."

Nefi nodded. Last night Nefi told Cassie and Mutt she'd be home all morning. Mutt wouldn't need his keys for a run. Nefi was expecting Helen Cho at nine and Vincent later. It was a four-hour drive from New York City with no traffic accidents or delays, so Vincent's arrival time depended mainly on how early he left the city.

Nefi returned to the dining table to enter more contacts into the new phone.

"You won't have to worry about making friends once people find out how rich you are." Cassie's voice carried from the kitchen. The clink and clang of dishes sounded like Cassie emptying the dishwasher. She never balked at handling clean dishes.

"I hope you aren't telling people."

"Relax. I'm just teasing."

The doorbell rang. Nefi checked her watch. Nine

exactly. She stepped through the kitchen and opened the door to the apartment.

A petite Asian woman carrying a black briefcase lowered her sunglasses and looked up. Her pale gray suit offset a bright red silk top that matched her lipstick. Her shoulder-length straight black hair reflected light like smooth plastic.

"Miss Cho?"

"The one and only Nefi Jenkins?" Helen Cho parked her sunglasses behind her hairline and extended her right hand.

Nefi gripped her soft, manicured hand and gently tugged her through the doorway. "Thank you for coming!" She closed the door behind Helen. "Cassie James, meet Helen Cho."

Cassie smiled warmly and shook Helen's hand. "You're the forensic investigator? Wow. I expected someone more—"

"Geeky looking?" Helen said.

Cassie and Nefi nodded.

"Glad to disappoint you." Helen entered the common room and slowly pivoted in the middle, stopping when she faced the dining table. "Let's sit here."

Nefi swept the phone's package, user manual, and old cell phone to the table's far side, clearing half the table for the expert.

Helen seated herself at the head of the table with her back to the kitchen. While she removed papers and a small laptop from her briefcase, Nefi took a seat with her back to the curtains.

She was tempted to open them but decided outside light might cause a glare on the laptop screen. Remembering her manners, she immediately stood. "Would you like coffee, tea, or a soft drink?"

"Nothing, thank you." Helen powered up her laptop.

"I'd like Cassie to join us." Nefi watched Helen's face for a reaction.

"That's fine with me."

Cassie pulled a chair close to Nefi and sat with her hands clasped on the table.

Helen handed Nefi a black 3-ring binder that held a three-quarter-inch thick stack of paper. "This is the detailed report for you to review. I'll summarize it and then answer your questions." She pressed the enter key, which brought up an income chart with the value of the trust fund measured on the vertical axis and each year named on the horizontal axis from the inception of the trust fund. "The original trust began when your mother inherited four million from her grandfather in December 1988. Your maternal great-grandfather divided his estate between his daughter Jane Wright and his only grand-child, Marta Wright Jenkins."

Nefi was two months old when her great grandfather died.

Helen's manicured finger ran along the bottom of the chart. "Between 1988 and 2002, the trust was invested in bonds, stocks, and municipals and grew to six million. When your parents were married, they established a family trust and named the trust as the beneficiary of their life insurance policies." Helen slid her fingertip on the chart to 2002. "The policies paid into the trust, and your maternal grandmother, Jane Wright, became the trustee." She glanced at Nefi.

Nefi nodded at the four-million-dollar jump in value from the life insurance policies.

"And here," Helen's fingernail pointed to a four-million-dollar drop followed by a four-million-dollar increase in value, "a withdrawal was made to purchase real estate, which was titled to the trust. This real estate increased in value, along with the value of the stocks, bonds, and municipals to today's value."

The ten-million-dollar figure impressed Nefi once again. So many zeros.

"Any questions?"

Nefi and Cassie shook their heads.

Helen pressed the enter key, calling up a chart labeled Expenses and Withdrawals. It, too, listed the values on the vertical axis and each year on the horizontal axis. "Attucks, Bird, and Copley charged fees to manage the investment portion of the trust and to incorporate the real estate holding as well. Their fees were well within the norm for this size trust."

A small black line labeled ABC INVST ran the length of the chart. It looked like the management fees ran at one percent of the total per year.

Helen's fingertip landed on a green line of withdrawals labeled PAYOUTS. "Since 2002, the trust has paid ninety-six-thousand dollars a year to the Trustee. Last month, the trustee changed from Jane Wright to you. You were entitled to become the trustee on your twenty-first birthday, but you told me it took a while for the investment advisor to locate you."

Nefi nodded. Helen's full report and this briefing had taken some time to prepare, but was it worth four-thousand dollars to hire an expert? Everything Helen said,

Nefi already knew. What did the third blue expense line represent?

The sliding glass door to the balcony slid open, startling the women, who turned toward it. Cassie and Nefi were on their feet facing the balcony when the curtains parted and Mutt, wearing only pajama bottoms, stepped into the room.

"Sorry. I overslept." He tugged a blanket through and closed the balcony's sliding glass door.

Nefi exhaled and said, "Helen Cho, meet my other roommate, Michael Trace the third."

Helen stood slowly. Her expression of shock changed as she raked her eyes over Mutt. Even Mutt read her last expression as Helen reached out to shake his hand.

"Did they kick you out, or do you usually sleep on the balcony?"

Nefi and Cassie exchanged a knowing look. Mutt's bouts of claustrophobia and panic often struck at night, and when they did, he occasionally calmed himself by going outside. Never mind that last night's temperatures fell to the forties. Being in the open air brought him peace. Perhaps all soldiers carried terrors with them in varying degrees for the rest of their lives. Ruis and Vincent avoided crowds whether they admitted it or not. Terri had confided in Nefi that a sudden noise at night would launch Blake to his feet. He couldn't relax until he had found the source of the noise and, in Terri's words, "neutralized it."

Mutt cradled the guest's hand in his giant hands. "I am pleased to meet you, Helen Cho."

Perhaps Mutt didn't notice that Helen had asked a question. It hung unanswered in the air like a child's balloon. Standing side by side, Nefi and Cassie elbowed each other as they studied Helen and Mutt.

Without turning away from Mutt, Helen spoke again. "Nefi, does Vincent know Michael lives here?"

"Yes, Miss Cho," Nefi said.

Mutt's expression remained calm. His pupils widened, and his breathing quickened. He released Helen's hand. "Excuse me. I'm going to get dressed." He left the room.

Helen sighed and looked at Cassie. "Is he your—"

"Friend. We served together in the Marines." Cassie returned to her seat at the table.

The moment Helen turned away, Nefi glanced at Cassie, who flashed a grin. Nefi sat and tried to focus on the chart again.

"Where was I?" Helen stared at the laptop screen.

"I believe you were going to explain the blue line on the expense chart," Nefi said. She schooled her face into a neutral, relaxed expression. The interaction between Mutt and Helen reminded Nefi of mating behavior she had witnessed in the jungle.

"Yes. Yes. So, the blue line shows other expenses to the fund, such as annual tax preparation fees, maintenance of the property such as improvements, renovations, and property taxes."

"I believe the property taxes are paid out of the monthly payout," Nefi said.

Helen blinked twice and opened the binder. Without turning it around to read the pages upright, she flipped to a page and said, "According to the records provided by Attucks, Bird, and Copley, the property taxes are paid quarterly from the fund." She pointed to a detailed list of expenses by year.

There, in black ink, listed under each year, sat a figure labeled property taxes. Nefi leaned back in her chair. Her grandmother had looked away when she talked about the property taxes. *Was grandmother mistaken?*

"Property taxes are that high?" Nefi pointed to the figure on the expense page.

"The property is near downtown Richmond, Virginia, across the James River. Prime real estate." Helen paused and pursed her lips. "Which brings me to a delicate matter. I didn't find any income from the real estate deposited into the trust. Equity, of course, would not be calculated until the property is sold, but it seems odd that the property isn't earning income. When I talked to the investment account representative, he confirmed that the trust had not received income from the property."

"Grandmother told me she paid a property manager five-thousand dollars a month from the monthly payout. Could the property be an empty shopping center?"

Helen's hands worked the laptop keyboard. "I searched online for the property and found this." She pressed the ENTER key.

An image of a furnished apartment appeared framed with information about the industrial-chic Stockton Lofts with multiple units near the James River, Forest Hill Park, and the historic area of Shockoe Bottom.

Nefi's heart skipped a beat at the realization her grandmother had lied to her. Twice.

Helen's eyebrows creased her perfect face, and the corners of her mouth flinched downward. She flipped to the back of the binder. "This is a copy of the property appraisal from the month it was purchased. And this is a copy of last year's property tax bill that shows its current assessed value. I could investigate the real estate for you, but hiring a private detective would cost less. That's my recommendation. Hire someone to go to the property, take photos of it, count the number of units, and find out the rent for each. The website didn't give that information."

Mutt emerged from his room, fully dressed in khaki pants, a turquoise polo shirt, and brown deck shoes. A faint scent of soap followed him into the common room. He sat at the table across from Nefi and Cassie. "So, what's the news?"

Cassie eyed him. "Miss Cho discovered a huge discrepancy in Nefi's trust fund."

Mutt turned his face to Nefi. "What kind of discrepancy?"

Nefi bowed her head. The next trust payout would arrive after graduation during her internship in Washington, D.C. "I'll hire a private investigator."

Helen closed her laptop and set it inside her briefcase. When she closed the briefcase, it locked with a click. "Nefi, I need to speak with you in private."

Mutt bounded from his chair, opened the curtains, and slid open the glass door to the balcony. "This is where I find refuge from the estrogen storm."

Helen smirked on her way out to the balcony. Nefi swatted Mutt's stomach as she passed by him. Mutt grunted and closed the door.

"I'm so sorry to bring you bad news," Helen spoke softly. "Do you want me to recommend a private investigator?"

"I know one. Let me get my checkbook."

"Make it out for two grand."

Nefi raised her eyebrows.

"This research didn't take me as long as I thought it would. You'll need money for the private investigator."

"Thank you, that's generous." Nefi hugged her new friend.

"You also need a lawyer. I'll send you the contact information of one I recommend."

Nefi opened the door and picked up her new phone from the table on the way to her room. Once in her room, she dug the checkbook from her satchel. As she wrote the check, she realized Blake was right about Helen Cho. This was money well spent, even though the news shocked her to the core. She wanted to crawl into bed to cry. She also wanted a rational explanation that didn't involve her grandmother stealing from her trust fund.

She drew in a deep breath and closed her eyes.

Lord, please, reveal the path I should take. Strengthen me to do the right things, to think clearly, and to act out of reason and not emotion.

Rather than dash back to Helen with the check, Nefi decided to call Arlo in private. She could remain the victim of a crime or fight back. She despised being a victim. She found his business card in her desk drawer. After entering his name, nickname, and phone number into her contacts, she called him.

"Barlow Investigations, how can I help you?"

"Hey, stalker. I have a job for you."

"Nefi Jenkins?"

"Wait. Is your name Arlo Barlow?"

"Are you sure you want to make fun of my name? Because I know your real first name."

Nefi gasped. "How?"

"I am a private investigator."

"I'm impressed, and I apologize."

"Apology accepted."

Nefi took a deep breath. She wasn't accustomed to spending great sums of money, but knowledge is power, and she needed to know the truth. "I want to hire you to investigate a property I own in Richmond, Virginia."

"You want to know about a property you own? What am I missing here?"

"It's owned by my trust fund. I need to know what it is and why it isn't earning money. And can you photograph the property and the neighborhood?"

"Where is this property?"

"Richmond, Virginia. I got a new phone, so I can text you the address. There's also a property manager who makes five thousand a month taking care of the property."

"And you can't ask the property manager because...?"

"Income from the property has not been paid into the trust fund." Nefi signed Helen's check.

"Oh. Got it."

"I'm not sure I can trust anyone involved," Nefi's voice cracked. She took a deep breath. "Do you need payment in advance?"

"Not from you. Give me a few days."

"Thank you, Arlo."

"Thank you, Miss Jenkins."

Nefi tore the check for Helen from the checkbook. Next, she texted the address of the Richmond property to Arlo's cell phone. Holding back tears and judgment, Nefi told herself to stay calm and wait for more information. She reasoned that she wasn't in denial but needed more facts.

Clutching the check, she returned to the common room to find Helen and Mutt deep in conversation. Heat emanated from them in waves. Cassie watched the interaction as if it were the NCAA basketball finals. Mutt's posture improved as Helen gazed up at him. They stood close enough to foul or fumble. Helen disarmed Mutt with a smile, then she turned her head, but not her body toward Nefi.

Nefi handed Helen the check. "I really appreciate your advice, and I'll read the report." To prompt Mutt, she added, "Where are you parked?"

Before Helen could answer, Mutt asked, "May I walk you to your car?"

"Absolutely."

Mutt even carried her briefcase. "Where do you live?"

"Maryville, Tennessee."

"What a small world. I grew up in Alcoa. My parents are still there." He followed Helen to the apartment door and opened it for her. As she stepped through the doorway, Mutt glanced back at Nefi and grinned.

Nefi and Cassie followed them to watch. Mutt waved them away, so Cassie and Nefi paused to grant him space and the illusion of privacy.

When Mutt and Helen moved out of range of hearing, Cassie snorted. "There goes a fine example of lust at first sight."

Blatant mating behavior. "It reminds me of life in the jungle." Movement near the street caught Nefi's attention.

A tall man dressed in dark casual clothes and wearing a backpack turned from the sidewalk to the walkway toward the apartment. He froze as Mutt and Helen approached. Vincent! Nefi fast-walked toward them.

Helen stopped and balled up her fist. A moment later, the petite woman punched Vincent in the shoulder.

He saw the punch coming. Why didn't he move out of the way?

Mutt scooped Helen off her feet. "Whoa! Let's not pick a fight here." He carried her away.

"You know it's a felony to strike an FBI agent," Vincent said to Helen.

Helen laughed. "You didn't identify yourself as an FBI agent."

Cassie caught up with Nefi and whispered, "Ex-girlfriend?"

"I'll tell you later," Nefi whispered.

✵

Vincent rubbed his shoulder. As he continued up the walkway, he glanced at the bulked-up young man who carried Cho in his arms.

He spotted Nefi, looking amazing, standing beside a tall woman who had a military bearing. Her roommate? He hadn't met Nefi's roommates because he hadn't been to Boston in years. He usually spent Christmas with her at her aunt and uncle's new house.

In five long strides, he reached Nefi and lifted her in a hug.

Nefi wrapped her arms around his neck and sighed.

Her embrace renewed him. Holding her felt like home, happiness, and all things wonderful. He set her feet back on the ground and kissed her. "I missed you."

"I missed you more." Nefi released him and patted his chest. The habit was a holdover from her childhood in the Amazon. Her aunt had explained that the villagers greeted a returning villager this way as if to confirm the person was truly present and not imagined. Nefi turned and placed her hand on her roommate's shoulder. "Cassie James, meet Vincent Gunnerson."

Cassie shook his hand. "I've heard a lot about you for years. I was beginning to wonder if you were real."

Cassie's bright eyes and warm, firm handshake welcomed him. She was taller than he expected. He chuckled and stuck his left thumb under the backpack strap. "I'm impressed to meet an engineering grad student. Nefi brags about your grades and your baking skill."

Cassie shrugged. "I do all right. It looks like you travel as light as Nefi."

"This contains graduation gifts."

"Nice." Cassie headed back to the apartment.

Vincent placed an arm around Nefi's shoulders. "How do you know Helen Cho?"

"I needed advice on my trust fund. Blake recommended her." Nefi kept pace with him. A lavender scent wafted from her, reminding him of every hug and kiss. "Speaking of gifts, Ruis gave me a cell phone."

Vincent smiled.

"You knew?" Her golden eyes widened.

"Of course. We didn't want to all get you the same gift."

By *we*, he meant himself, Blake, Ruis, and Senator and Mrs. Jenkins. They had formed a protective pact to watch over her. Blake and Ruis behaved like big brothers, except for the time when Blake didn't recognize her and flirted with her at a wedding. After Nefi reached age twenty-one, Vincent's protectiveness developed into love. Nefi once said that in the remote Amazon village where she grew up, age differences meant little. He had grown up in New York City, where culture, law, and his Catholic faith labeled her as a child until age twenty-one. Their seven-year age difference felt vast to him.

During their pre-marital counseling, Vincent discovered that Nefi treated God as a benevolent father, watching and protecting her with a still small voice of wisdom here and grace there. In her personal faith, the empty cross symbolized Christ's ascension into heaven after serving as a sacrifice for all humanity's sins. She had once asked Vincent if the Catholic faith was a guilt-based sensibility because they kept Christ perpetually hanging on the cross. He hadn't questioned the symbolism of it until then, so he couldn't answer her. It was refreshing to talk about their mutual faith. He thanked God daily for bringing Nefi into his life. He also prayed Nefi would not talk about Martina. It pained him to keep a secret from his fiancée, but it was part of his job to keep cases secret. He wanted Nefi to trust him, but he had also promised to keep Martina's secret. Honoring both women put him in an awkward position.

After they entered the apartment, Vincent set his backpack on the dining table.

Nefi held up her new cell phone. "I can look up things on the internet." She pressed the internet icon and started typing.

Vincent laughed. This was her very first smartphone.

"What?" Nefi paused.

"You don't have to type. Just press this microphone symbol and talk."

Nefi squinted at him as if deciding whether he was teasing her. She pressed the tiny symbol. The phone chimed, and Nefi asked, "What is the capital of Brazil?"

A female voice answered, "The capital of Brazil is Brasilia."

Startled, Nefi dropped the phone on the table. "That's amazing!"

Cassie's laughter followed her from the kitchen to the dining table.

"Did you know about this?" Nefi picked up her phone and pointed it at Cassie.

Cassie sank into a chair at the dining table. "Girl, everyone knows about it. Your dumb phone belongs in a museum."

"It's not dumb. It's just old."

Cassie smirked at Vincent and slowly shook her head. "I'm not insulting your phone. That's what a non-smart-phone is called."

"Oh."

Smiling, Vincent removed a crudely wrapped box from the backpack and set it gently on the table. "This is from Blake and Terri."

Cassie returned to the kitchen. "I have lemonade. Do you want some?"

"Sure, thanks." Vincent stood waiting.

Nefi tore off the red wrapping paper and bow to reveal a heavy, dark gray plastic case. She unlatched it. Inside, nestled in gray foam, sat a black M&P 9mm Shield mounted with a Crimson Trace laser and three empty magazines. She ran her fingers over the textured grip and ridged slide.

Vincent remembered Ruis saying he had taken Martina and Nefi to the shooting range a few times. Of course, Ruis had drilled them on the safety rules. Always assume the gun is loaded. Never point the gun at anything you don't want to kill. Never put your finger on the trigger until you are ready to fire. Be aware of what is behind and around your target. Keep weapons locked away when not in use, especially if children are around.

Cassie handed Vincent a sweating glass of lemonade. Her head pivoted toward the handgun. "Will you look at that? You have great friends."

"Quality beats quantity." Nefi grinned.

Cassie raised her hands. "When you're right, you're right. Vincent, how many contacts do you have on your phone?"

Nefi gave Cassie the side-eye.

It felt like he'd stepped into a debate. He checked his phone and scrolled through the list. "I suppose it's somewhere around three hundred. Why?"

"Nefi, show him." Cassie waved her hand.

Nefi bit her lower lip and handed her phone to him. Though he didn't know why it mattered, he scrolled through Nefi's contacts. He recognized most of the names. The list ended so abruptly his mouth fell open. He handed the phone back.

"I ask you," Cassie said, looking at Vincent, "is that normal?"

Feeling cornered, he was about to say that Nefi was selective when the apartment door opened, and the bulky young man who had carted off Cho strode into the room.

He headed straight for Vincent. "Vincent Gunnerson, I presume?"

Vincent shook his hand. He was a few inches taller and a few years older than the roommate with the high-and-tight haircut. "Good to meet you."

"Good to meet you, too. Call me Mutt."

"Seriously? I've heard Nefi call you that, but—"

"It's my initials. I am Michael Ulysses Trace the Third."

He turned toward the table. "Ooooh. Is this a gradua-tion gift?"

Nefi nodded. "From my friends Blake and Terri Clayton."

"Is Blake a Marine?" Mutt sat at the table.

Vincent answered with "Semper Fi."

Cassie smiled.

Vincent took two wrapped boxes from his backpack and gave one to Cassie and the other to Mutt. Nefi often described her roommates as adventurous people who loved sports, so Vincent hoped they would like their gifts. Anyone important in Nefi's life was important in his.

Mutt grinned, and his eyebrows shot up. "Hey, thanks, man."

"Well, thank you, Vincent." Cassie tore off the wrap-ping paper.

Mutt opened his gift as well.

Inside each box was an envelope which they opened and silently read. Cassie reacted first by hopping from her chair to hug Vincent.

Mutt stood and shook hands with Vincent. "That's a perfect gift. Thank you. Thank you so much." He showed Nefi the paper. It was a certificate for the NASCAR Rich-ard Petty Driving Experience.

Cassie shouted, "Road trip!" and she gave Mutt a high-five.

"And this is from me." Vincent handed Nefi a thick envelope.

"Thank you." Nefi kissed him.

"Open it," Cassie said.

Inside the envelope was a receipt for a conceal-carry class, a year of access to the Boston Firearms Training Center, and registration for the multi-state firearm licensing course paid in full. Nefi squealed with joy and flung her arms around his neck. After the hug, she handed the receipt to Cassie and Mutt to see.

Vincent felt relieved. Oscar had recommended jewelry, luggage, or a weekend at a spa, but those were things Martina would enjoy. Nefi was different in so many ways.

Cassie lowered her drink to the table. "You two are such a perfect match." She wiped her eye. "It's so romantic."

"Pull yourself together, soldier," Mutt muttered to Cassie.

"Says the man who walked a geek to her car." Cassie batted her eyelashes.

"I carried her most of the way." Mutt headed to his room and stopped. "I need to run," he said to Vincent, "but tonight, I want to know how you ticked off the lovely Miss Cho."

Vincent cringed. "Yeah, okay."

Cassie rose from the table and shouted toward Mutt's room. "I'll run with you." She turned to Nefi. "I'll take my keys. Have fun."

Vincent pulled two small boxes of 9mm rounds from his backpack and set them on the table by the handgun. Next, he withdrew two sets of sound-suppressing ear protection, his own and a new one.

"Are you sure you don't want to tour Boston?" Nefi looked ready to abandon whatever she had planned.

"I've been here before."

Nefi let out a squeal, danced in place, and then bolted from the common room.

He reminded himself to tell Blake and Terri about Nefi's excitement over the gifts. Of the women he dated, Nefi was the only one who understood the value of learning how to use weapons. Her eagerness to shoot warmed his heart. He hoped she would practice, especially because she wanted to join the FBI. Half the agents he knew practiced only the minimum required. Sure, most agents never needed to fire their weapons, but it was far better to master such skills and never need them than to be unprepared when you do.

Nefi returned with her satchel strapped across her body. He recalled the day he first met her. She wore a leather satchel with loose clothes. She was barefoot, and her face was covered in black and red tribal paint. Today, she wore a hint of makeup, just lipstick and mascara. Years ago, when she was a fierce, starving, heartbroken teenager, he had admired her. After they found her in the jungle, she stopped to pray before eating her first meal in a week or more. This small act of faith had filled him with awe. She continued to surprise him over the years. Occasionally he wondered why she loved him. If she loved him out of gratitude for helping her reach her family in the U.S., then why hadn't she fallen in love with Blake? Women flocked to him for his good looks and easy-going humor. Or Ruis?

Who can reason out love and attraction? Whatever her reasons were for choosing to love him, he was grateful. He surrendered to her.

She helped him put what they needed back in his backpack. He handed her the receipt, which she tucked into a pocket of her satchel.

Vincent shouldered his backpack and followed Nefi, who grabbed her apartment keys on the way out the door.

As he followed her, his heart swelled. This astounding woman loved him. He longed to spend the rest of his life loving her.

·9·

ON JANE'S DRIVE to pay the property manager, she seethed. She had not expected to waste two hours of her life to borrow five-thousand dollars from her own life insurance policy. The agent finally relented and then lectured her against borrowing more. After that, she had to cash the check at the bank because she always paid the property manager in cash.

Jane was confident Ted would never notice the withdrawal because it wouldn't be reported to the IRS. Ted paid attention to their tax forms, combing through them, line by line, as if he would catch something the expert had missed.

None of this inconvenience would have happened if she were still in charge of the trust. After managing the trust for seven years and increasing its value, Jane considered it galling to endure Nefi's questions about how she'd spent the monthly payouts. And then to find out Nefi had already squandered her first monthly payment, well, it was simply infuriating. Nefi proved to be as irresponsible with money as Marta.

Neither Marta nor Nefi had ever held a job. Nefi had a work-study job at Harvard, but she was just a research assistant in some behavioral sciences program. They didn't appreciate the value of their inheritance because they hadn't earned a penny of it. In Marta's high school years, Ted had insisted Marta spend her time studying and socializing, enjoying her childhood. He said she'd have the rest of her life to work. Marta hadn't worked during college either because she needed time to study. *Ha! In the end, she majored in boys and graduated with an M-R-S.*

Jane motored through downtown Richmond, Virginia, over the James River on the I-95 bridge, and exited into Old Town Manchester. Passing quaint restaurants and coffee shops, she gripped the steering wheel at the deep injustice of losing control of the trust fund. How long would she have to pay for her father's stupidity?

As an only child, Jane had expected to be the sole beneficiary of her parents' estate, including the mansion in Richmond, the cottage in Cape Cod, the stocks, bonds, and all their earthly possessions. That's how normal parents set up their last will and testament. But no. Mother died and left Daddy in charge of things. Why would any father take away half of his estate from his only child to give it to a grandchild? And in Daddy's last few months, he always talked about the great-grandbaby. Nefi was a beautiful, quiet baby with gorgeous eyes. Nefi. Nefi. Nefi. Maybe holding his great-grandchild made him feel immortal, and he wanted to pay Marta back for that feeling.

Marta would have inherited everything eventually. Jane clenched her teeth.

Marta returned from Boston with that Jenkins boy to attend the funeral. She stayed just long enough for the reading of the will and to flaunt her baby girl, Nefi. Ted had dismissed the division of the inheritance as a 'great-grandparent thing' and said he understood it. Jane did not understand it then, and she still felt cheated. She had used her part of the inheritance to buy a mansion and renovate it.

And what did Marta do? She sold the Cape Cod cottage and parked that money with all the stocks, bonds, and other liquid assets into a trust fund. After Daddy's funeral, Marta and Herman announced they were running off to the Amazon rainforest to teach Portuguese to indigenous Indians. *Portuguese!*

Marta was so irresponsible. Even Ted argued against bringing a baby into the jungle. Marta and Herman set up significant life insurance policies as if that made them more responsible parents. They named the trust as the beneficiary. Creating the trust fund was the one intelligent thing they did before they left.

For now, Jane resigned herself to being the responsible adult and handling things the way they should be handled. Burdened with cleaning up the blunders of her father, her daughter, and now her granddaughter, Jane sighed heavily. If Nefi followed through to pay the property manager, then Jane could adjust to the changes forced upon her. If not, she would have to explore other options.

Because the parking lot was empty, Jane parked close to the property manager's apartment. Taking a moment to calm herself, she refreshed her lipstick and checked her hair in the visor mirror. She turned off the engine, unbuckled her seatbelt, and looped her purse handles over her arm on her way out of the car into the sun.

Her heels clicked on the pavement of the parking

lot and the concrete walkway to the four-story red brick warehouse that had been renovated into one of those high-ceiling, open-concept apartments known as lofts. She used a card key to enter the lobby and then knocked on his door like a boss.

The door swung open, and Jimmy Jones broke into a smile. "Right on time. Come on in." He was an unhealthy fifty-year-old with his brown hair pulled into a short pony-tail. In his coffee-stained sweatshirt and dark blue jeans, he looked older than he was. Jimmy's face was rough and thick like leather boots.

Jane eased by sideways to avoid brushing against Jones' beer belly. "We need to talk."

"I hate it when a woman says that." He shut the door.

Jane led the way down the corridor to the living room.

The outside walls were brick adorned with wide win-dows that arched on top. Wood plank floors and ceilings warmed the industrial feel of the spacious room that con-tained the kitchen, living room, and dining room. The stark white interior walls, slate-gray granite countertops, stainless-steel oven, and refrigerator had a cold, clean style. More than apartments, these high-ceiling units were lofts.

Jane pulled the envelope containing a pack of fifty one-hundred dollar bills from her purse and held it out for him.

He pinched the envelope in the middle and tugged at it. "What's the matter?"

Jane released the money and leveled her gaze at him. "This might be the last one."

"What?"

"I no longer manage the trust that owns this property.

Of course, I advised the new owner to keep you on as the manager."

Jimmy slouched into a large, overstuffed recliner that faced a 72-inch flat-screen television. He held the envelope of cash to his chest. "Does he want to hire somebody else?"

"She. The new owner is barely in her twenties. I doubt she has the time or the interest to replace you, but it's out of my hands."

"Then what's the problem?"

"She could decide to sell."

Jimmy frowned and worked his jaw. His IQ number fell on the downhill side of the bell curve, close to room temperature. His work history of short-term jobs in heavy labor suggested problems with authority and a complete lack of initiative. He would never be able to afford both this apartment and earn this salary on his own.

Jane let him stew about an uncertain future.

"If she sells, I could work for the next owner." He looked up at her.

Jane sighed. She'd have to walk him through the reality of his situation using small words and simple concepts. "Have you spoken to the property managers of the other renovated buildings in the neighborhood?"

He shook his head.

"Perhaps you should. Ask them how much they get paid and whether they get a furnished apartment rent-free."

Jimmy squinted at her and leaned back in his chair. "All right, I will."

Jane sat on the black leather sofa, facing Jimmy at an angle. "You see, I wanted you to be here on-site to make it easier for you to handle problems and repairs. Some property owners either pay a salary or let their managers live in an apartment for free. I've done both." She knew he had a part-time job cleaning a law office nearby because he had left his paystub on the counter last month when she delivered his payment. She stood and sighed. Jones needed to understand a new owner wouldn't pay him in cash. "Ask the other managers how much gets taken out of their checks for taxes."

Jimmy's eyes widened. The word taxes struck home.

"I wanted to prepare you in case the new owner doesn't take my advice."

Rising to his feet, Jimmy faced her.

Jane intended to awaken Jimmy's fear to motivate him to trust her as an ally. Like children, people of lower IQ tended to react emotionally without considering the consequences.

Had she said too much? Did he think she was threatening him?

Fear could quickly become anger and cause Jimmy to strike out. She stood. As the nearest target, Jane became fearful. Stepping back out of his reach, she regretted leaving her pepper spray in the car. Her heart pounded, and she heard herself breathing. She suspected the other occupants of the building were at work.

With his eyelids half-closed, Jimmy stepped toward her. "I appreciate what you done. My sister makes out my taxes for me. She says it's a good thing to get paid in cash. You can tell the new owner to visit and ask around. Most of the residents appreciate me."

Jane exhaled. "I'll do everything I can to keep things the way they are now." She quick-stepped toward the hallway. When she glanced back, Jimmy was counting his cash.

·10·

MUTT AND VINCENT grilled steaks on the porch while Cassie stood by, draining her glass. Nefi watched them through the sliding glass door. From the few words that carried to the common room, it sounded like Vincent was explaining how he accidentally broke Helen Cho's arm during a training exercise at Quantico.

Nefi set the table and placed the salad, the aluminum foil-wrapped baked potatoes, and Boston baked beans in the center where everyone could reach them.

Cassie slid open the glass door, entered, and closed it behind her. After placing her drink at her usual seat at the table, she spoke. "What did Vincent say about the missing money?"

"I haven't told him yet."

"Why not?"

"He might feel obligated to do something like interrogate my grandmother."

"And why is that a problem?'

While straightening the silverware at the place settings,

Nefi worked her way around the table. "I hired a private investigator to gather facts about the property. Maybe my grandmother mishandled the money. Maybe she stole it, but I need proof before I confront her."

Cassie slowly shook her head. "Why would you confront her? If she lied and stole money from you, do you think she's going to apologize and give the money back?"

Nefi understood Cassie's advice on an intellectual level but not an emotional one. Grandmother Wright lied, but that didn't prove she was stealing. Grandfather owned a newspaper, and they lived in a giant historic mansion. *Why would grandmother steal?* Nefi glanced through the window at Mutt and Vincent, who loaded the steaks onto a platter. "Maybe the property manager embezzled the money. I'm not going to do anything until I have irrefutable evidence."

Cassie scowled. "Once you get irrefutable evidence, then what?"

Nefi wrung her hands. "It's not about the money. A month ago, I didn't know the trust existed. I thought having money would make my life easier. Mr. Lancaster warned me that the money could change my life."

Cassie hugged Nefi. "Don't change. And promise me you won't do anything until you brief Vincent." Cassie released Nefi. "He adores you. Doesn't your fiancé deserve to know what's going on?"

Nefi nodded.

"Remember, he loved you when you were poor."

True. Would her life be defined by the day she inherited money? Once people knew, would they treat her differently?

The men entered with a cloud of smoke and a platter of two-inch thick, sizzling ribeye steaks. Mutt sat beside Cassie, and Vincent sat beside Nefi, facing the sliding glass door. Mutt's black t-shirt announced in large white letters, "I enjoy long romantic walks" and in smaller print, "to the gun store." Cassie said a simple prayer of thanks over the meal, then they all ate.

Vincent nudged Nefi with his right shoulder. "Are you okay?"

"The trust is a bigger responsibility than I imagined," Nefi said softly.

Vincent rubbed his left shoulder where Helen had punched him. "Cho knows her stuff. I'm sure she'll give you sound advice."

Nefi and Cassie nodded.

Mutt chuckled. "And she can pack a punch."

Cassie glared at Mutt.

"How long before you get your carry permit?" Mutt asked Nefi.

"The man at the range said it could take up to ninety days to get the card. I can't wear the gun until I get the card." Nefi looked at Vincent for confirmation.

Vincent nodded. "You have time to figure out where you want to carry it. You have the usual holster options, of course. I've heard an undercover agent talk about wearing a thigh holster for her backup weapon under a dress."

Mutt smirked.

Cassie swallowed and took a sip of her drink. "I'll help her find one."

"Spoilsport," Mutt whispered.

Nefi snorted at Mutt. It was time to change the subject. "I saved today's targets." She dashed to her room and unrolled them from her satchel. Returning to the table, she held up the first one.

The twenty-three-inch by thirty-five-inch silhouette

target had holes scattered all over it from her 9mm M&P Shield. The target was labeled 50-yard Police Target. Only one of the twenty-five holes was inside the dark head and torso area marked on the target.

"You shot at fifty yards?" Mutt said.

"Fifteen." Nefi realized Mutt and Cassie could probably shoot more accurately one-handed at twenty-five yards than this. "Even with the headset on, the gun was loud, and I flinched. Then Vincent told me to hold the gun tighter like my life depended on it and gently squeeze the trigger."

Vincent waved his empty fork toward Nefi. "Show them the second target."

Nefi set the first one on the table and held up the second target. Five holes created by her first five shots on the new target formed a line from the bottom left outside the torso toward the center of the torso. Twenty of the twenty-five holes dotted the torso at the center of mass.

Mutt and Cassie applauded.

Mutt added, "I read that most civilian shootings happen within fifteen feet, so you're good."

Nefi returned to her seat at the table. "As long as the target stands still."

Mutt pointed his steak knife at Nefi. "You're more accurate with a knife."

Vincent looked up from his plate. "What do you mean?"

Nefi groaned.

Cassie leaned forward. "You didn't tell him?"

"We should eat before our food gets cold." Nefi cut a piece of steak and popped it in her mouth. Nothing like a perfectly seasoned, medium-rare ribeye steak to celebrate with friends.

"I'm almost afraid to ask," Vincent said.

Though Nefi refused to look at Vincent, her scalp tingled with the sensation of being watched.

"We can wait until after dinner, right?" Mutt asked Cassie.

"Absolutely." Cassie spooned a large dollop of sour cream onto her baked potato. She turned toward Vincent. "Are you a sports fan?"

"Don't know much about soccer except that the players have to be amazingly fit to run the whole game. I like football, baseball, basketball, and hockey." Vincent ate a heaping spoonful of baked beans.

"Did you play?" Mutt asked.

Vincent swallowed. "I played basketball in high school. My dad loved the game. What about you?"

"Football. I played tackle. We won the state championship my senior year. I was recruited to a big ten college team, but it's a rough game at that level. Way too many injuries."

Nefi laughed. When the others turned to stare at her, she said, "You were concerned about injuries?"

Mutt's brows bunched up, then relaxed. He grinned and nodded. "Yeah, that's fair."

Nefi placed her hand on Vincent's forearm to ground herself. After a few more moments, she regained her composure. "Do you know what Mutt's job was in the Marines?" Nefi had to focus on Vincent's face to avoid seeing Cassie, who would make her laugh.

"No, what?" Vincent was smiling, no doubt amused by the others.

"Explosive Ordnance Disposal Specialist," Nefi could barely pronounce it while holding back laughter.

Vincent's eyes widened, and his eyebrows rose. "You defused bombs?"

Cassie dabbed her eyes with her napkin.

Mutt shrugged. "One of my high school pals said he joined the Marines because he was tired of being told what to do."

Smiling, Vincent and Cassie shook their heads.

After they finished eating and cleared the table, Mutt strolled to his room and returned with a black canvas gym bag. He called out, "Follow me, Vincent. I'll show you a sport Nefi taught us."

Cassie grabbed her keys off the hallway table and held the door open for Vincent and Nefi. Nefi picked up her own keys and hooked the carabiner keychain to the waistband of her pants. After they left, Cassie locked up. The four of them marched across the lawn to a three-story parking garage. Vincent slowed his gait to hold Nefi's hand. In the cool of the evening, they passed through the shadowy garage to the farthest corner of the ground floor to a parking spot blocked off by three orange rubber construction cones.

Mutt flipped on a wall switch, and two floodlights illuminated the parking spot. The back wall was covered with four-inch cubes of pinewood. At a glance, the wall looked like the ends of stacked wood. Three circle targets were painted on the wood. Red painted lines on the floor marked distances from the target at 2, 3, 4, 5, 6, and 7 meters.

"Since Nefi didn't have a car, we used her parking space," Cassie said.

While Vincent stared at the converted parking space, Mutt opened the gym bag, and Cassie moved the cones. Mutt handed three black carbon steel throwing knives to Cassie. He gave three heavier knives to Nefi and held up three for Vincent.

"I'll watch," Vincent said, stepping aside.

Cassie took the first turn by standing at the five-meter line and throwing overhand. Her knives were the equally weighted blade and handle style, designed to spin end over end. Her first knife spun twice and stuck low at the six o'clock position on the left target. Her second knife landed above the first by a few inches, with the handle angled slightly upward. Her last and most forceful throw stabbed the right edge of the bullseye with a satisfying *thunk*. "The range is cold," she announced before she retrieved her blades. Once back at the five-meter line, she said, "The range is hot."

Mutt stood at the five-meter line to throw. His three throws resulted in three knives surrounding the bullseye of the center target. He and Cassie fist-bumped while he declared the range cold. He pried his knives from the target and moved behind the seven-meter line.

Cassie stepped behind Nefi and pulled Vincent with her.

Mutt said, "The range is hot."

With her eyes on the right-side target, Nefi toed the seven-meter line. She gripped the knife handle and flung the blade-heavy knife hard into the bullseye. Her knife shot straight and stuck straight in the wood. She held the second knife behind her neck, where she often wore one sheathed, and aimed her other arm at the target. After a breath, she swung her free arm back while she extended her knife-throwing arm at the target. When she released the knife, it stuck snugly against the first one. The third also landed in the bullseye.

Mutt's voice rumbled across the empty space. "That's why she throws last."

Vincent said, "You continue to amaze me."

Nefi melted against him. "I'm not sure my aunt and uncle would approve of this hobby."

Vincent huffed. "Probably not."

Mutt declared the range cold and retrieved Nefi's knives.

Cassie held out Nefi's knives to Vincent. "You know you want to."

Vincent picked up one of Nefi's knives and one of Mutt's and weighed them in his hands. He selected Mutt's balanced knives. "The range is hot." He stood at the seven-meter line and threw the knives one after the other. They landed within the second circle, one a borderline bullseye.

Cassie let out a low whistle.

Mutt called the range cold and pried the knives from the wall. He stored all the knives in his gym bag.

On their walk back, Vincent said he had a long drive back to New York. Mutt and Cassie shook his hand and told him that they'd see him at graduation. They continued toward the apartment.

"Why didn't you fly here?"

"I couldn't find a bulkhead seat on a flight, and first-class was full." Vincent draped an arm over Nefi's shoulders as they strolled on the sidewalk.

Nefi imagined his legs folded up against the seat in front of him and his head touching the overhead compartment and smiled.

The glow of streetlights filtered through ancient oak trees and elms, casting patches of light and shadow. In the shadow of a high-limbed oak, Vincent gently pulled Nefi against his chest and kissed her.

Her whole body tingled and heated up as she wrapped her arms around his ribcage. His warm, soft lips pressed gently on her mouth. Her imagination carried her to the future, to thoughts of their honeymoon, and she was glad they were in a public place, so she wouldn't be tempted to act on this passion. After the kiss, she opened her eyes.

Vincent's pupils were dilated.

Treasuring the moment, Nefi closed her eyes and rested her face on his warm chest. A rhythmic thumping accompanied the bellows of his lungs, filling and emptying. His steady heartbeat accelerated. What was he thinking?

"Have you talked to Martina?" he asked.

The question disoriented Nefi so much that it took a moment for his words to register. "Not since before her exams. Have you?" Nefi lifted her head and broke the embrace. Martina's text said she wanted to talk about something in person. What was her news? Did she and Oscar decide on a wedding date? "Have you talked with her?"

Vincent looked away over Nefi's shoulder. "Not lately."

Avoiding eye contact felt like deception, a minor one perhaps, but it created a sense of unease that unconsciously triggered Nefi to pat her palms repeatedly on Vincent's chest.

Vincent gently pressed his hands over Nefi's. "I'm here."

As if waking, Nefi realized she had been patting Vincent. She blushed. "Martina used to call every other day."

"She's okay. I spoke with Ruis."

Nefi sighed and nodded, knowing Martina would talk when she was ready to talk. Whatever Martina's news, joyful or sorrowful, Nefi would support her. Had Oscar said something to Vincent about Martina? Pressing Vincent to talk might push him to violate his brother's trust, especially if the news turned out to be sensitive or awkward. *Like an unexpected pregnancy?*

No. Nefi wrestled her imagination under control. A scripture from Philippians whispered in her consciousness. "Whatever is true, whatever is noble, whatever is right, whatever is pure, whatever is lovely, whatever is admirable—if anything is excellent or praiseworthy—think about such things."

Vincent lifted Nefi's left hand to his lips and kissed her fingers. "I'll be back for graduation."

"Thank you for the training and the range subscription. It shows how well you know me."

Vincent hugged her firmly, planted a kiss on the top of her head, and turned her toward the apartment. "Go on before I make a fool of myself."

"Goodnight," Nefi said as she glanced over her shoulder. She bolted up the sloping lawn, knowing he would wait until she was inside the apartment before he left. At the apartment door, she turned back.

He waved and headed to his car.

Inside, Nefi dropped her keys on the table and continued walking straight to her room, where she brushed her teeth. The day brought gifts and revelations. Nefi put her shoes in her closet, shed her clothes into the hamper, and pulled a loose cotton nightgown over her head. Grandmother Wright had lied. Martina refused to talk on the phone. Helen Cho told painful truths Nefi didn't want to hear. Nefi sighed and fell into bed.

Vincent was holding back something about Martina. She couldn't blame Vincent for keeping a secret from her while she kept one from him. She vowed to tell him everything about the trust fund discrepancies after graduation.

Surrendering to sleep, she dreaded graduation day.

·11·

ON THE FRIDAY before graduation, rain, temperatures in the low fifties, and wind gusts up to twenty-three knots kept Nefi, Cassie, and Mutt indoors. The washer and dryer hummed with Cassie's laundry. Nefi dragged her dirty clothes basket to the hallway and planted it by the washer to claim the next use of the machines. With forty minutes left on the dryer cycle, Nefi wandered over to the sofa and sat beside Mutt, who was channel surfing. Today's t-shirt was decorated with the message: "There's no such thing as too much ammo unless your house is on fire."

He shouted to Cassie, who was in her room. "What time is the game?"

"Seven." Cassie emerged from her room in a lime green sweatshirt and sweatpants and slumped into the sofa on the other side of Mutt.

Nefi reread the text from Arlo about meeting tonight. In her reply, she invited him to the apartment so Mutt and

Cassie could also sit in on the meeting. Nefi wondered how upset they might be to have their game interrupted. "Which game are you watching?"

Cassie leaned forward. "The Washington Capitals play the Montreal Canadiens in Montreal."

Nefi bit her lower lip. She hesitated to admit that this new information didn't answer her question. The football and softball teams her roommates followed were all in the United States. That left soccer and hockey as possibilities since a Canadian team faced a United States team. "Hockey?"

Mutt and Cassie shook their heads.

"Soccer?"

Cassie said, "It's hockey. We're shaking our heads because we can't believe you don't recognize the team names by now. This is the Stanley Cup quarterfinals."

Nefi leaned forward to see beyond Mutt to Cassie. "The private investigator is on his way here. I was hoping you could sit in to hear what he has to say. I appreciate your judgment."

"What time?" Mutt asked.

The doorbell chimed. Mutt turned off the television.

Nefi jumped to her feet. "Thank you. Thank you. I really appreciate this." She dashed to the door and led Arlo through the kitchen to the common room. "This is Mr. Barlow, a private investigator I hired." She turned toward Arlo. "Mr. Barlow, meet my roommates, Michael and Cassie. They're helping me understand the trust."

He shifted the shoulder strap of his duffle bag to shake hands with them. Though the shortest person in the room, Arlo's posture and presence made him seem in command of the room. "Did you serve?"

Cassie squinted at him. "Marines. And you?"

"Navy. I flew a Sikorski Seahawk."

"Search and rescue?" Mutt asked.

"Among other things." Arlo released Cassie's hand.

"Let me get you a beer." Mutt headed to the kitchen.

Cassie led Arlo to the dining table. Her load in the dryer finished with a buzz and fell silent. Cassie, Nefi, and Arlo sat at the table. Mutt handed Arlo a bottle of Budweiser, and then he too sat at the table. Nefi sat beside Arlo. She hoped he would clear things up about the property in the trust.

Arlo twisted the top off the bottle and took a swig. After rummaging through his duffle bag, he pulled out a small laptop, opened it, and activated it. "You asked me to survey the property, so I photographed it outside and inside. The property takes up a city block in what used to be an industrial area where the factories and warehouses have been renovated. It's on the south side of the James River. This is the exterior." He poked the keyboard, ran his fingers on the mousepad for a few moments, and then turned the laptop toward Nefi.

Detailed photos of a four-story red brick building with arched windows filled the screen. Then the images switched from still photos to video from street level to a higher and higher perspective until it showed a central courtyard through a glass dome. The camera lens zoomed in on the courtyard, revealing a row of ten treadmills, three stationary bicycles, and weight benches.

Mutt sat up straight. "What kind of drone did you use?"

"It's a Parrot AR designed by Henri Seydoux. When I'm not investigating for clients, I photograph property for a prominent real estate company. They love aerial motion video."

Cassie said, "Your geek is showing."

Arlo said, "The drone gets great images."

Nefi and Mutt leaned in to see the screen.

More drone video showed a parking lot filled with Jeeps, SUVs, and cars along the sunlit side of the building. A walkway from the parking lot led to a recessed entrance-way. On the other three sides of the building, the brick walls extended to the sidewalks. Interior photos revealed the entrance, corridors, the inside of one of the lofts, the gym, and a large club-style meeting room.

"The building houses three-bedroom apartments," Arlo said. "Twenty of them."

Chills ran through Nefi as she braced for more terrible truths. This was income-producing property owned by the trust. None of the rental income, according to Helen Cho and the financial records, reached the trust. If the property manager embezzled the rent money, then why didn't Grandmother notice the missing funds? Was she grossly negligent or working with the property manager?

"I went inside and told the manager I was looking for a place to rent. He gave me this brochure." Arlo's voice would have been soothing in another context. He handed the glossy brochure to Nefi.

Photos of a gym, clubhouse room, and industrial-chic apartments graced the brochure. Granite countertops, high ceilings, wood plank floors, stainless steel appliances, and boxy furniture created a welcoming appearance. The brochure called each unit a loft. Nefi's hands started shaking, so she set the brochure on the table. Her fingers curled involuntarily into fists.

Cassie asked, "How much is the rent?"

Arlo took another draw on his beer. "Thirty thousand a year. Each."

Nefi closed her eyes as sums filled her mind. Six-hundred thousand a year in rent on twenty lofts. At least six years of rent, at full capacity, was $3,600,000. "And Grandmother Wright kept one thousand per month of the monthly payouts, adding another $84,000 unaccounted for." Why would grandmother steal from the trust? When Nefi opened her eyes, tears escaped. She cleared her throat. "How do we find out where the rent money went?"

Arlo handed Nefi a slim 3-ring binder. "You have options. Since the trustee is a family member, you could take these photos, my report, and your trust agreement to a trust litigation attorney to get the money back. That's the civil court way. The other option is to pursue criminal charges against the trustee."

"What if the property manager is the one keeping the rent money?" Wiping her eyes, Nefi searched Mutt and Cassie's faces.

Arlo said, "The police would track whoever handled the money and where it went."

Cassie sighed. "How could the manager keep all the rent money without your grandmother noticing it?"

Since grandmother lied about one-thousand dollars a month, certainly she'd lie about larger amounts. Her grandmother bought the property to make money so she'd know where the rent money went. Nefi was stunned by the audacity of the embezzlement. Of course, stealing a thousand dollars a month measured up to grand theft every year, but stealing millions meant she did not fear getting caught.

Nefi sighed. "She probably assumed I was too naïve or stupid to notice millions missing from the trust fund."

Jane had played on Nefi's love and need for her family. It pained Nefi to admit her neediness had clouded her judgment, but it was time to accept the soul-crushing truth and cross the threshold between innocence and knowledge.

I wouldn't have noticed the missing millions. Jane would have succeeded if not for one casual lie.

Mutt's mouth turned down. He looked up at Nefi. "I suspect that even though she robbed you, you want to give her a chance to come clean."

Cassie pursed her lips as if to hold back from speaking. She sighed. "You have a good heart, Nefi. I've seen you give money to homeless people even when you have almost nothing. You're a giver. She's a taker. I've learned that givers have to set boundaries because takers never do. You need to get back what your parents left for you."

"Helen deals with financial stuff all the time," Mutt said. "She might know a good attorney. Do you want me to call her?"

Nefi acknowledged Mutt's eagerness to call Helen Cho with a quick grin. "She gave me a name. I promise to call the attorney after graduation."

"When is graduation?" Arlo asked.

Cassie said, "Next Thursday, the twenty-seventh."

Arlo stood and pulled his duffle bag onto the table. "The most likely people to steal the rent money are the people who handle the money. This puts you in the danger zone between a thief and a fortune." He pulled an object from the bag and set it on the table.

Everyone stood and stared at it.

Nefi's shoulders sagged. "Are you serious?"

·12·

APARTMENT MANAGER JIMMY Jones called Jane to tell her that some guy stopped by asking to rent a loft, even though none were available. Jones hadn't run an ad in months. He said he also saw the guy taking photographs inside the building.

She had been expecting the call and was prepared for it. "I'm on my way. We need to talk." Jane grabbed her coat, her purse, an envelope of cash, and an invitation before leaving the house. This discussion had to be done face to face.

By the time she rang the doorbell of the property manager's apartment, she was convinced her plan would finally undo the terrible injustice of her parents' last will and testament. Her plan would right a wrong.

She was insufferably pleased about finding just what she needed in the trust fund agreement. The singular ironclad clause which would return control of the trust agreement to her was legal. Convincing Jimmy Jones to do his part required finesse.

When she reached Jimmy Jones' loft, she followed him into his living room. "You said the man who came to look at an apartment was taking photos?" Her voice echoed in the narrow hallway.

"Yeah. I saw him walking around outside the building before he came in to ask if one was available."

Jane crossed her arms. "Have you ever seen a potential renter take photos before?"

Jimmy shook his head. "I gave him one of the brochures."

After a dramatic sigh, Jane said, "Maybe the new owner hired a realtor to sell the property. Did the guy leave his name?"

Wide-eyed, Jimmy shook his head again. "No, and he didn't even ask how much the rent was or if we had a waiting list."

That was beyond suspicious behavior.

"I did what you told me to. You know, asking other property managers about what they made." Jones planted his hands on his hips. "That big condo complex down the road don't," he blinked as if resetting his brain, "doesn't give the manager a condo. And he told me a ballpark figure on his salary. So, I asked my sister what my taxes would be if my employer took them out of my paycheck, and she told me the federal government would take fifteen thousand dollars and the state would take another three thousand!" He punctuated his statement with a closed fist.

Jane appreciated his outrage. She silently thanked Jimmy's sister for lighting a fire under him. Apathy was useless to her, but anger, well, that was something she could guide to her benefit. "Jimmy, sit down. I need to tell you something in confidence." After he sank into his easy chair and she eased onto the sofa cushion, she continued,

"The trust fund that owns this property was supposed to be mine, an inheritance from my parents. My mother died, leaving decisions up to my father. In his grief and illness, he changed the trust and cut me out of half of it. Can you imagine having your father give away half of your inheritance to someone else?"

Jimmy shook his head.

Jane set her purse on the floor. "I don't know why he turned against me. Maybe he was angry I quit my law practice after I got pregnant." She paused to control her anger. If she hadn't borne a child, everything would have been hers.

"My daddy didn't like me." Jimmy scowled. "Called me stupid all the time. Said I'd end up dying in the street like a dog."

Though she had never asked about his personal life, she needed to assess his motivation. "Did your father ever manage a luxury apartment building? Or earn the kind of money you do?"

Jimmy straightened his back. "Never. He was a lazy, mean drunk. We lived in a trailer and never had nothing."

The air conditioning system's air handler hummed while Jane and Jimmy replayed dark memories, each blaming their fathers for old soul-deep wounds. Anger thrummed through their bodies like subsonic tones harmonizing a familiar sad song.

"There is a way to fix this problem once and for all. It would mean I'd be in control of the trust fund again, and you would stay here as long as you want. Are you strong enough to fight for this?" Jane opened her arms to the whole loft.

Jimmy stood and paced the room. "I'm too old. I'll

never find another job like this." He combed his fingers through his scruffy hair. With his hair sticking up near his ear, he had revealed a thick, uneven scar that ran from his temple into his hairline. His fingers traced the faded red line. "See this? My father did that."

Jane stood to stoke Jimmy's anger. She needed to direct his emotion into action. "It's up to you. Are you going to live in a luxury loft or die on the street like a dog?"

"I'll do whatever it takes to stay here."

Jane picked up her purse and walked to the kitchen counter. Jimmy followed. There, she laid out the graduation invitation with Nefi's photo on it. Inside the invitation was a separate card about a private dinner to be held at Modelo's Market Café. After presenting these papers, Jane pulled an envelope of cash from her purse and opened it, dumping five-thousand dollars in small bills onto the counter. The life insurance agent had lectured her again that the policy was not a checking account before he finally wrote the check.

She gave Jimmy specific instructions and ended them with, "Get whatever you need. Can I count on you?"

"That's what I do," he said in the lower register of his voice. "I fix things."

·13·

NEFI HELD VINCENT's hand as she led the way through Modelo's Market Café, past the showcases of baked goods and shelves of groceries to the café in the back. "Mr. De Souza opened the café just for us tonight."

Vincent seemed a tad underwhelmed. He probably expected a fancy restaurant because he wore a fine suit and tie and highly polished dress shoes. He looked amazing.

Nefi stopped and faced him. "My aunt and uncle had the same reaction when I brought them here the first time. It isn't the Capital Grille, but I bet you're going to have a meal you'll remember."

He leaned into a kiss Nefi felt to her toes.

"I look forward to the meal and seeing you so happy."

Catching her breath, she led him into the café where her uncle and aunt were talking to Mr. De Souza. The three of them turned and greeted Nefi and Vincent. After hugging her aunt and uncle, Nefi introduced Mr. De Souza to Vincent.

"This is your fiancé?" Mr. De Souza shook Vincent's hand vigorously. "I am honored to meet you."

"It's good to meet you, too." Vincent nodded. "Nefi says this is her favorite restaurant."

Mr. De Souza beamed. "Just so you know," he said, taking on a serious expression, "I don't have a liquor license, but I can give champagne." He waved at one of the servers, who quickly brought a tray with flutes of bubbling champagne.

Vincent and Nefi each took one.

Across the room, Cassie was locked in a friendly debate on handguns with Mutt's father. Mutt had an arm draped around his older sister while Mutt's five-year-old nephew held the hem of his mother's skirt and billowed it. Mutt's family, Cassie's parents, and grandmother were all here. Nefi counted and came up two heads short.

Mr. De Souza tapped Nefi's shoulder. "Who is missing?"

"*Meus avós*," Nefi whispered. Her grandparents had a habit of arriving, as Aunt Louise called it, fashionably late. The Wrights liked to make an entrance. Since they had attended the graduation, they shouldn't be too far away. "*Eu sinto muito.*"

"*Não é um problema.*" De Souza headed to the kitchen.

Cassie beckoned Vincent. "Come here and help me convince Mutt's dad why he needs a 1911."

Vincent turned to Nefi.

Knowing how Marines love their guns, Nefi said, "Go ahead." She set her champagne flute at her place setting and pulled out her cell phone to text her grandmother. She would have preferred texting her grandfather, but he always drove. She didn't want to tempt him to read while driving.

Conversations and echoes filled the already packed room. The five-year-old boy tugged on Nefi's graduation gown. Nefi paused, writing her text.

"Uncle Mutt said you speak Brazilian."

Nefi smiled at him. "I do. What is your name?"

"I'm Chad. I'm five years old," he said, holding his hand out like a proper gentleman.

Nefi shook his hand. "It is a pleasure to meet you, Chad."

"Say something in Brazilian, please."

Crouching, she carefully enunciated a Portuguese phrase she thought he'd like, "*Eu amo minha família*. It means 'I love my family.'" She repeated it and coached him to repeat it until he could speak it confidently.

"Thanks!" He dashed back to his mother.

In her peripheral vision, Nefi sensed movement by the entrance. Still holding her cell phone, she rose to her full height to see over Cassie's parents. Ted and Jane Wright stood in the doorway between the grocery and the restaurant until all eyes turned toward them.

Aunt Louise rushed over to welcome them and introduce them to everyone nearby.

Uncle Hamilton nudged Nefi with his shoulder. "Fashionably late again."

Nefi reached around her uncle's waist with her free hand. "Thanks for being here."

He planted a kiss on the top of her head like her father used to do. A wave of loss rolled over Nefi, threatening to draw tears. A deep breath grounded her once again in the happy here and now. She dropped her arm from her uncle's waist and headed off to greet her grandparents.

Grandfather hugged her and whispered in her ear. "You're as lovely as your mother."

"Thank you." Nefi faced her grandmother and got a pat on the shoulder.

"Where do you want us to sit?" Jane asked.

When Nefi turned away to compose herself, she spotted Mutt.

Mutt mouthed the words, "Is everyone here?"

Nefi nodded.

"Ladies, gentlemen, and graduates," Mutt said, "please be seated." He then scooped up Chad and parked him in the seat next to his own.

Nefi led her grandparents to their place at the table, directing her grandfather to the head as the senior family member according to Mr. De Souza's instructions. Mutt's father sat at the other end of the table as Mutt's family patriarch. For Mutt and Cassie, the graduation ceremony was a landmark in their ongoing studies. They were already mixing graduate-level classes with their senior courses. Their parents had insisted they participate in graduation.

Uncle Hamilton strode to his place setting and pulled out Aunt Louise's chair. The loving gaze from Aunt Louise rewarded him.

Nefi muted her cell phone and set it on the table. When she reached for the back of her chair, a hand was on it.

Vincent pulled out her chair.

Sweeping her graduation gown under her thighs, she eased into her seat. "You're going to spoil me."

"Every chance I get," he whispered in her ear as he sat.

Tingling from the sexy timbre of his voice, she grinned. Surrounded by family and friends, Nefi felt a rare joy. She felt honored that her whole family and Vincent had taken the time to share this milestone in her life.

Mr. De Souza returned from the kitchen as the last of the

crowd settled into chairs. He turned and nodded to some-one in the kitchen. Moments later, servers bearing carafes of juice and platters of food emerged from the kitchen and delivered food and drink to the tables, family-style. After the server's third trip from the kitchen, the center of each table overflowed with steaming meats, vegetables, rice, and bread.

Mutt's father stood and gave a brief blessing. He thanked God for the graduates, this time together, and Mr. De Souza and his staff for working after hours. A unison 'amen' fol-lowed, and everyone served themselves from the platters of food.

Mr. De Souza moved from table to table to answer questions about the dishes. Chad eyed the fried plan-tains suspiciously.

Mutt placed a sampling of it on the boy's plate. "I bet you'll like it."

Chad forked a plantain chunk into his mouth and chewed. He nodded and took another.

Brief conversations popped up during the meal and faded into the sounds of forks and knives on plates and drinks being poured. Mutt nodded to Cassie, who nodded at Nefi, to confirm this restaurant had been a great choice.

Vincent nudged Nefi with his shoulder and whispered, "Why are you still wearing your graduation gown?"

She whispered back, "Are you asking what I have on under this?"

"Never mind."

They had the place to themselves, and the family-style dining put everyone at ease. Mr. De Souza's friendliness topped off the evening. He disappeared into the kitchen to oversee the desserts that Nefi, Mutt, and Cassie had chosen for the party. They had agreed that a large cake would go to waste, so they selected a variety of wonderful sweets from the bakery cases instead.

Nefi leaned back in her chair to relax before dessert. Mutt and Cassie were talking about sports. The men were still eating at Nefi's table while Aunt Louise spoke about her upcoming river cruise in Europe.

Jane Wright signaled to Nefi, so Nefi got out of her chair and walked around the table to her.

"I'm so embarrassed," Jane whispered. "Ted and I rushed out of the car. I left your present in the back seat. We're parked on the side road. Norwood Avenue." She pressed her key fob into Nefi's hand below the table.

The sun had set, and her grandmother was in heels, so Nefi nodded. She headed through the grocery section of the building, and a male server followed her. Nefi turned to him. Carlos had worked there as long as Nefi had been in Harvard.

"I'll unlock the door for you. You're coming back, right?" His voice finally evened out to a smooth baritone from the sudden pitch changes of adolescence. He was almost as tall as Nefi.

"Yes. Just getting something from the car."

Another server called for Carlos from the dining area, so Carlos said, "If you wait, I'll walk you to the car."

"I'll be fine, Carlos. Thank you."

Carlos unlocked the door, Nefi walked through, and he locked it behind her. He made a knocking gesture, and he mouthed that he'd be right back before he disappeared behind the grocery shelves.

Holding the key fob in her left hand, Nefi strode south on Medford Street toward Norwood Avenue and followed the sidewalk around the corner to a line of cars parked on the street. She examined the key fob with a tag on it like a miniature license plate. Oh, a rental car. She pressed the fob to make the lights of the car flash. It was the ninth car along the curb under trees that blocked the streetlights. She passed the corner jewelry store and its empty parking lot.

If her grandparents had arrived earlier, they could have parked closer. Nefi gritted her teeth and walked by the walled employee parking area of the jewelry store into the shadows toward the car. The moment she stepped under the trees, she heard footfalls behind her. The silhouette of a thin man was reflected in the car's windshield.

Where did he come from?

In the reflection of the car's windshield, he pulled something from his pocket bigger than a set of keys.

What was in his hand? Tingling on the back of her neck urged her to act. Nefi took a slow deep breath and expelled it quickly. She pressed the fob again, flashing headlights at the man while she darted behind the rental car to the street.

She touched the driver's door handle and watched the man pass by the other side of the car. If he kept walking, then he wasn't following her.

He looked over the hood of the car at her, but then, at the rear bumper, he turned and stepped behind the car.

Nefi's right hand flew to the nape of her neck for the handle of her throwing knife. She backed away from him in long, quick strides.

The man stepped into the street. At waist level, he gripped a handgun with both hands.

Her heart raced. Anger energized her when the man took a shooter's stance at the back bumper. Nefi pressed the button on the key fob again so the rear lights would give her a look at the man. The lights flashed twice, revealing a face she'd seen before. He looked like the property manager from Arlo's report.

"Don't do this, Mr. Jones." Nefi hoped to shock him by using his name. She held her left arm and the key fob toward him. She planted her feet apart in her throwing stance and pulled her knife from the sheath. Her pulse pounded in her ears.

Half a block from traffic, they stood on the road alone under the trees.

"You don't give me no choice." He raised the barrel of the gun.

Nefi flung her knife with all the accuracy and anger she could summon.

An ear-splitting boom blasted through the quiet and echoed.

A bullet punched Nefi's chest at the sternum. A second shot struck her in the side, knocking her backward. In blinding pain, she staggered a step and fell, unable to draw breath. Deafened, flat on her back on the road, she prayed for Jimmy Jones to run away. If he had bullets left, he could finish her off. She couldn't call for help. She couldn't breathe. Her chest and stomach muscles spasmed. Remembering the key fob, she lifted it to her face and pressed the buttons until she heard a faint honking.

Oh, God, don't let me die.

Soon, Cassie's face was hovering over her. Her lips moved, but Nefi couldn't hear Cassie over the ringing in her ears.

Nefi pulled her right hand to her throat and made the universal gesture of choking.

Mutt ran by. Nefi gasped for air and hoped Mutt wasn't chasing the shooter unless he also had a gun.

Cassie looked away, her mouth moving. Cassie looked

blurry, and flashes of light obscured her. She plucked the key fob out of Nefi's hand.

Darkness flooded Nefi's field of vision, leaving a pinhead speck of light.

Suddenly someone pinched her nose and pulled her chin down. A mouth pressed over hers and blew breath into her lungs. Her rib cage expanded with renewed pain. Light returned. Vincent!

A second breath from Vincent paused the pain binding Nefi's ribcage like iron bands. Nefi inhaled and watched a pantomime between Cassie and Vincent. Vincent's expression was alarm bordering on panic. Though it stung, Nefi breathed on her own. Nefi laid a hand on Vincent's forearm and squeezed it to thank him. He had his cell phone by his ear.

Cassie unzipped Nefi's graduation robe and pointed to Nefi's chest.

Vincent's panic turned to confusion, then relief. Nefi reached up to feel the points of impact on the metal-plated body armor vest Arlo had given her. Each bullet was a hot lump in a small crater.

Cassie zipped up the graduation gown and leaned over Nefi to speak to Vincent.

Soon, the street lit up with flashing red and white lights. Two police officers ran in the same direction as Mutt.

Vincent bent over and kissed Nefi tenderly, and then he moved out of the way of the two paramedics who checked Nefi's pulse and placed an oxygen mask over her nose and mouth. They lifted her onto a gurney and rushed her into the back of an ambulance. Cassie climbed into the ambulance. She spoke to the EMTs. Whatever she said changed their demeanor, and they closed the doors.

Cassie pointed to Nefi's chest and unzipped the robe to

show them the vest. They helped Nefi out of her robe and vest. With gloved hands, they unbuttoned Nefi's top and examined her sternum and stomach with soft touches where deep bruises were forming.

Cassie suddenly blanketed Nefi with the graduation robe and motioned for her to be still. Nefi did what Cassie wanted. The doors opened, and a female police officer stepped in. Cassie closed the doors behind the officer. A more muted conversation ensued, making Nefi wish she could read lips better. The conversation around her sounded like a language of vowels spoken underwater. She read the police officer's expressions like a series of billboards. When Cassie held up the bullet-embedded vest, the officer's skepticism turned to surprise.

The officer spoke facing Nefi, so Nefi pointed to her ears and shook her head. She didn't want to take off the oxygen mask because it pushed air into her lungs. The less she had to move her ribs, the less pain she had. It felt like breathing through a straw, drawing air, but not enough.

Nefi forced her lungs to expand and contract even though her ribs ached, and the air seemed as thin as if she'd just run a race. She tried to calm herself by reminding herself she was alive. For the time being, she was also safe.

She longed to be unconscious because deeper pains crept in that no medicine could reach. As soon as the property manager knew his attempt to kill her failed, he would try again. Had Mutt caught him?

·14·

WHEN THE DOORS to the ambulance closed, Vincent stared at it.

Cassie's words rang in his head. "The shooter worked for Jane Wright. Someone's been embezzling from Nefi's trust fund for years. I can't tell you more right now but keep an eye on the Wrights."

Vincent turned his attention to Jane and Ted Wright, who, like the rest of the graduation dinner guests, had wandered out of Modelo's to see why two police cars and an ambulance were outside. How did a financial crime escalate to attempted murder? Why didn't Nefi say something about this? He tamped down his emotions so he could gather information with a clear head.

Jane fast-walked ahead of her husband to Vincent. "What happened? Where's Nefi?"

Vincent looked down at the thin older woman. Carefully choosing his words, he said, "She's been shot."

Jane's head pivoted toward the ambulance. "Why aren't they moving?"

Vincent longed to record Jane's reaction with his cell phone, but it was illegal in Massachusetts to record someone without permission. He withheld information to watch how she interpreted his non-answer. When Jane turned back to face him, Vincent clenched his jaw and inhaled through his nose.

Jane gasped and clutched her pearl necklace.

Her shock didn't seem genuine, but Cassie's warning colored his judgment. He decided to test Grandmother Wright with another tidbit of information. "That man shot her." He pointed toward the legs sticking out behind the officer who crouched over the body on the road.

A concerned grandparent would ask who the shooter was to piece together a reason for such a tragedy. A concerned relative might cry, pace, or show surprise at having a loved one shot.

"Is he dead?"

Vincent blinked. "Yes." And then, if he hadn't been trained to look for it, he would have missed Jane's fleeting smile. It chilled him to his bones.

"Who was he?" Jane sounded as calm as someone discussing the weather.

Vincent shrugged again. "If he had any ID on him, the police would have it."

Ted stood on the curb with his phone to his ear.

Who on earth was Nefi's grandfather calling? Police and paramedics were here. Was he reporting the news to his newspaper or calling a lawyer? Not much sympathy from this pair. Vincent struggled to keep his emotions and expressions neutral.

Who were these people? They didn't behave like he expected grandparents to act. His loving grandparents were always excited to see him and his brother, Oscar. Grandpa, or *Jah-goo*, told the best jokes. Grandma, whom they called Baba, insisted her *Rosol*, the Polish version of chicken noodle soup, cured everything but stupidity. At the end of every visit, Baba and Jah-goo staged a mock battle to send his parents away and keep Oscar and Vincent for them to raise. Only Polish was spoken in their house. Out of respect, Oscar and Vincent learned to speak the language, but they couldn't write it or read it. Vincent knew deep in his soul that if he'd been shot, Baba and Jah-goo would be in the ambulance telling the paramedics what to do.

Unlike the Wrights, Senator and Mrs. Jenkins were in each other's arms. They had lost a son to drugs, and last summer, they believed they'd lost Nefi in the firebombing. Gently leading them away from the crime scene, Vincent brought them back to the main road, out of sight of the Wrights, where Mr. De Souza was wiping his eyes with a handkerchief. This! This is how people react when a loved one is injured or presumed dead. Vincent drew them into a huddle and spoke softly. "I need you to keep this to yourselves for now, but Nefi is alive."

Senator Jenkins took in a deep breath. "Thank God. I heard gunshots."

De Souza clapped his hands together and held them in front of his face. "She is a fighter, our Nefi."

"Yes, sir," Vincent said, liking this restaurant owner even more. "She is. Please stay until the police question you."

"Yes, of course. Let's wait inside where it's warm." Mr. De Souza guided the senator and his wife toward Modelo's Cafe. "I'll make you strong Brazilian coffee."

Vincent marched back to the crime scene. He had wondered why Nefi, Cassie, and Mutt wore their graduation gowns to dinner. The gown covered body armor. Were Mutt and Cassie also wearing vests?

Cassie and an officer stepped out of the back of the ambulance. Cassie held out a key fob to the officer, who pulled a small clear evidence bag from her pocket and held it open. After Cassie dropped the fob into the bag, she approached Vincent.

The officer crossed the street to Ted and Jane Wright.

Vincent longed to enter the ambulance to see Nefi, but he also wanted answers to the questions swimming in his head.

Cassie hugged him hard and whispered, "Don't go in there while the Wrights are here. Let them think she's dying or dead."

Vincent nodded and released her. Cassie had a good reason to keep Nefi's status from the Wrights. He remembered last summer when Nefi was missing and presumed dead. There wasn't enough alcohol in New York City to dull his pain. It was the only time he ever passed out from drinking.

He and Cassie eavesdropped on Nefi's grandparents and the officer.

"I'm sorry," the officer spoke to the Wrights, "but your car can't be moved because it's part of the crime scene." She held the evidence bag with the key fob at her side.

"It's a rental," Ted said, emphasizing it with a shrug.

"How about if I give you a ride to the station for your statement?" The officer held her arm out toward her cruiser.

Ted scowled. "That's better than standing out here." He draped his arm over Jane.

"It's the least we can do," Jane said. She wiped her eye as if she'd been crying. "We can't help with anything here."

The Wrights followed the officer to her car, which was parked at the corner. Vincent watched the police car drive away. He reached for the handle of the ambulance's back door.

"Hey, Vincent." Mutt shouted, "Come here." Mutt and a police officer stood near the shooter's body.

Vincent sighed and let his hand drop to his side. Couldn't whatever Mutt wanted to talk about wait until later?

"She's in good hands," Cassie said, turning toward Mutt. "They don't need you crowding their workspace."

Vincent nodded. Turning his attention to Mutt, he sighed. He wasn't skittish about seeing a corpse, nor was he eager. He and Cassie hiked the half block to Mutt, who introduced him to a male police officer in his forties.

"And this is Vincent Gunnerson, fiancé of Nefi Jenkins, and he's an FBI agent." Mutt pressed his hand on Vincent's chest. "Watch your step."

Vincent looked down at pooled and sprayed blood which reflected streetlight like mercury. The arterial spray shot blood over the street to the far curb. Nefi's knife must have cut the carotid artery. After walking around to a clean area of the roadway, Vincent shook hands with one of Boston's finest.

The officer quizzed Vincent on where he was and what he saw. It took Vincent three minutes to give his statement. He had been in the restaurant when the shots were fired, and he didn't know the shooter.

A car pulled up and parked in the middle of the street,

then a man with a commanding presence stepped out. As the streetlight illuminated him, he looked a bit familiar.

Mutt greeted him. "Thank you, Mr. Barlow."

"Call me Arlo."

Arlo "Repo" Barlow had been at Ruis Ramos's wedding. He was a helicopter pilot who told hilarious jokes. Arlo's solemn expression suggested he had been called to the crime scene. *Was he with the police?*

"Hey, Vincent, Cassie." Arlo glanced at the body, nodded, and asked no one in particular, "How's Nefi?"

Mutt smiled. "The vest worked."

Arlo let out a breath.

"That was your idea?" Vincent asked Arlo.

"It was." Arlo then held out his hand to the police officer. "I'm a P.I. Nefi Jenkins hired me to investigate her trust fund management. I brought my findings and a copy of her trust agreement. This man," he said, indicating the body, "worked for the previous trustee, Mrs. Jane Wright of Richmond, Virginia, who is also Nefi's grandmother."

The officer raised his eyebrows.

A chill crept up Vincent's spine. He did not believe in coincidences.

Mutt spoke across the huddle to Cassie. "Did you brief the other officer?"

"I did. She invited the Wrights to give a statement at the station. They accepted." She nodded at Arlo.

The older officer, with his pen poised over a notepad, addressed his question to Arlo. "A vest? Trust fund? What are you saying?"

Arlo placed his right hand over his heart. "I'm saying it's time law enforcement investigated the systematic theft Mrs. Jane Wright committed while she was the trustee. In the trust agreement, Jane Wright inherits ten million dollars if Nefi Jenkins dies. These are the facts I can prove." He handed the officer a business card.

Vincent flinched. Ten million? Nefi had mentioned a trust fund. In this context, the trust fund was the motive, and it connected the shooter to Jane Wright. Taking deep breaths, he calmed himself. Nefi was safely in the hands of paramedics. He wished she had confided in him. Why had she told her roommates and Arlo instead?

The officer phoned his partner. "Hold the Wrights." His second call requested a crime scene team. After that, he said, "Mr. Barlow, can you go to the station? Detective Kelly in homicide will need to get your statement and those documents. Here's my card and precinct."

"Yes, sir." Arlo took the card, pivoted on one heel, and marched to his car. Once inside, he executed a three-point turn and drove away.

The officer dismissed Mutt and asked Cassie to answer a few questions. Mutt moved onto the sidewalk and motioned for Vincent to come with him.

It felt like the right time to talk privately with Mutt, Marine to Marine. "I want to thank you and Cassie for watching out for Nefi." Vincent wished he had been able to protect her. He lived and worked two hundred miles away, so she relied on her roommates and friends instead. His footfalls felt heavy on the sidewalk.

Mutt nodded. "Poor kid. She trusted her grandmother."

Vincent sighed. His heart sank. Nefi left him out of the information loop. She knew he was trustworthy and would protect her, didn't she?

"She made us promise not to tell you," Mutt said.

"About what? The trust fund or that her life was in danger?"

Mutt blinked and pressed the back of his open hand on Vincent's arm, forcing him to stop as well. "She promised us she was going to hire a lawyer to handle the embezzlement through civil court."

"Civil court? Oh, man, let me guess. She wanted to save dear old grandma from embarrassment."

Mutt nodded. "She loves her family."

Stung that she trusted her grandmother more than she trusted him, Vincent lowered his head.

"It was tough for her to accept a relative would steal from her. We couldn't tell you what was going on because she knew you'd do something. She didn't want to spoil graduation."

After dozens of comments raced through his mind, Vincent shook his head and laughed. His eyes welled.

"Yeah." Mutt sighed. "I'm so sorry."

The ambulance pulled away from the curb, lit up its lights, and sounded the siren.

Vincent and Mutt inhaled sharply.

Mutt said, "Maybe she has a cracked rib."

Vincent used his cell phone to look up the phone number of the ambulance company. After he learned where they were taking Nefi, he told Mutt.

A crime-scene van pulled into the spot Arlo had vacated. Vincent admired Nefi's friends for their loyalty and foresight. With the situation under control by others, he decided to wait with the Senator and Mrs. Jenkins.

"I'm going back to the restaurant." Vincent left Mutt on the sidewalk.

After Nefi's aunt and uncle gave their statements to the

police, he would tell them about Nefi's body armor. Just the facts. He knew Senator Hamilton and Louise Jenkins loved Nefi. She could tell them the rest of the story since it was hers to tell.

Could Jane Wright steal from her own granddaughter? Did the shooter act on his own, or was Jane Wright involved? If Jane was involved, how would Nefi handle such a betrayal?

·15·

WHY IS THIS happening?

Nefi closed her eyes. She wanted to scream. Every breath expanded her rib cage, causing stabbing pain. She groaned. The vest had stopped the bullets, and she'd felt the warm lead lumps on the vest. So why did breathing hurt so much?

Sucking air didn't help. Nefi fought pain and panic. Her ribcage ached. Her ears rang. She knew her heart was racing because she heard it throbbing in her ears. She opened her eyes. Was the air on to this mask? She tried to follow the oxygen tube from her face to a tank, but the paramedics blocked her view.

The ambulance rocked gently. The paramedics moved inside the cramped space around the gurney. One of the paramedics flashed a penlight in her eyes, left then right, then pressed the cool stethoscope to her chest and her side. An alarmed expression triggered frantic activity from both paramedics. One paramedic secured the gurney and strapped Nefi down at the hips.

The stabbing pain grew stronger. A moment later, the vehicle lurched and sped up. A siren sounded in the distance. It didn't matter where they were going. The pain rode along.

The air felt thick, and Nefi coughed. Believing the air had stopped flowing in her oxygen mask, she pulled it off and gasped.

A hand pressed the mask back down over Nefi's nose and mouth.

Her heart pounded louder than the ambulance siren and the voices of the medics.

Is this what dying feels like? Lord, I don't want to die. Not like this.

She stared at the ceiling of the ambulance. Oxygen must be getting through, but it wasn't enough, no matter how deeply she sucked it in. Could the impact of a bullet on the vest trigger a heart attack?

How awful it would be to be killed over money like mom and dad. What good was it to survive getting shot but die of a heart attack?

She tried to laugh, but it turned into coughing.

One of the medics lifted her mask and aimed a flashlight at the back of her throat before securing the mask back in place.

It felt surreal. Jimmy Jones had shot her. *Twice.* Wanted her dead. If not for the heavy vest, she would be dead.

The oxygen mask tightened and relaxed with each breath. She was alive because Arlo, Cassie, and Mutt bullied her into wearing the sweaty, heavy body armor vest. They were so painfully right.

This wasn't a random crime. Jones came from Richmond to kill me.

Nefi found it hard to breathe under the weight of sorrow and betrayal.

The ambulance turned a corner, causing Nefi to roll within her restraints. The motion put painful pressure on her ribs, but she focused on the cause of it.

A stranger had looked directly at her and fired twice. His expression was not one of hate, anger, or rage. It was decisive and purposeful. Someone she had never met before meant to kill her.

Why?

As soon as his finger had moved to the trigger, she had thrown her knife as hard and as fast as she could. The knife was her only weapon. Then the deafening flash and a bullet slammed into her, then another. As if reliving the shots, sudden pains stabbed Nefi in the chest and side.

I am not a victim! I am a survivor!

She hated being helpless. She sucked air in gulps against the pain in her chest, ribs, and heart. She allowed her anger to rise toward the man who shot her. She refused to succumb to death. He could not win. Evil could not prevail.

Please, Lord, let me live. I believe you have a purpose for my life.

She vowed to find Jones and wring answers from him about why he'd shot her and what he meant when he said, "You don't give me no choice."

The only connection between Jones and Nefi was the trust fund. And grandmother Wright. Jones worked for Grandmother Wright. Was the answer that simple?

She suspected more than she could prove. She suspected her lying grandmother played a role in the shooting to cover up her theft.

Could anyone be that hateful?

Throughout her childhood in the Amazon, Nefi longed to meet her grandparents. Their mystery elevated them to mythic hero status. She ached to meet them and thank them for the clothes and gifts they sent on her birthday and Christmas year after year. In storybooks, grandmothers baked cookies and protected their grandchildren from witches and wolves. Fairytale grandmothers set a high standard. She did not want to believe her grandmother had stolen from her.

She drew in a shuddering breath.

The love of money is the root of all evil. Accept people for who they are.

Jane Wright lied. Someone stole from the trust fund. Jones and Jane Wright had access to the missing money. Whoever was stealing would want to stop an audit or investigation. Her grandmother had witnesses who would say she was inside the restaurant when the shots were fired. Her alibi would be backed up by a senator, an FBI agent, and people who didn't even know about the trust fund.

Jane wouldn't have to worry about getting caught stealing if Nefi was dead. After seven years of visiting on holidays, Jane would never again have to pretend to care.

Nefi wanted to grab her grandmother by the shoulders and shake her until she explained how money meant more than family.

Muted voices called out.

Nefi opened her eyes. The pain in her side intensified, and she gasped for air. When she tried to sit up, strong hands pressed her down.

Lord, please forgive my sins and bless those who loved me.

Lights and doorways rolled by, and the muted voices

grew louder and sharper. A woman in green pajamas with a paper mask over her mouth and nose leaned overhead.

"Hold still!" the masked face shouted.

Lord, forgive me for arguing with my parents.

Something pinched the crook of her arm, and Nefi surrendered, rising lighter than air into darkness.

·16·

NEFI AWOKE IN a stark white room on a bed that wasn't hers. An IV tube taped to her arm ran up to a liquid-filled bag hanging on a metal stand beside her. Her tongue stuck to the roof of her mouth. She assessed her situation.

I am still alive by the grace of God and the wisdom of friends.

Soft hands landed on her forearm, making her flinch and turn to see who was in the room.

Aunt Louise patted Nefi's arm. "You're safe, dear." Her mascara was smudged.

Nefi drew in a deep breath, relieved to see a friendly face. When she tried to speak, it sounded like a croak.

"Allow me." Aunt Louise held a quart-sized plastic mug with a straw sticking out of it to Nefi's mouth.

Nefi took a long draw of water and swallowed it like a cotton ball. "*Tia* Louise." Her voice rasped like sandpaper on wood.

"Vincent was here all night. I took over a few hours ago. You were talking in your sleep."

The dream roared back vividly. In her sleep, Nefi relived a memory of the day her parents died. Guilt and shame clung to the memory. She felt the need to confess. "The morning my parents were killed, we had a terrible argument. My last words to them," she gulped air before continuing, "were so mean."

Aunt Louise set the water bottle on the bedside table and rolled the table out of the way. Her soft hand caressed Nefi's forehead. "Tell me about it."

Nefi sighed and said, "I begged to go to the U.S. I asked why they bothered to teach me science, math, world history, and Spanish if I'm going to spend my whole life in the village. I said it wasn't enough to see the world only through books. Then I ran to the tallest tree and climbed it to look north. I was praying for God to send me to the U.S. when—"

"You blame yourself?" Aunt Louise's expression softened.

"God answered my prayer." Shame crept out from the long-suppressed memory of that day.

Aunt Louise arched an eyebrow. "Did you make a deal with the devil to take your parents away so you could go to the U.S.?"

"Of course not."

"Does God answer your every prayer immediately the way you want, like a magic genie?"

"No, ma'am."

Aunt Louise sat on the edge of her chair. "Then how about if you separate your spat with your parents from their deaths? There isn't a cause and effect going on there."

"I needed to hear that." Nefi felt lighter with this new perspective. "You could have been a great psychiatrist."

Louise waved away the compliment. "Never underestimate the power of common sense."

Nefi and her aunt shared a moment of quiet, each lost in their thoughts.

"You're going to be all right, Nefi."

Nefi nodded.

"Hamilton had to go back to the office. I'll stay until you get discharged."

Nefi reached out and held her aunt's warm, soft hand. "I love you. I can't ask you to stay." When she tried to sit up, pain stopped her. "Go home and tell Uncle Hamilton I'm going to be back on my feet soon."

A door opened, and a man in green scrubs stepped in. He had a high forehead, close-cropped black and gray hair, and stunning, straight teeth. "Ah, you're awake. Can you hear me?" His calm demeanor and soothing voice put Nefi at ease. "Good to see you again, Mrs. Jenkins." He turned toward Nefi. "And it's good to see you awake, Miss Jenkins. I'm Doctor Korley. You have bruised ribs," he pointed to her side where the second bullet hit the vest, "and your sternum is bruised. Last night, the muscles around your ribcage spasmed, and it probably felt like a heart attack. The impact of being shot at close range caused pneumothorax, the collapse of your lung. You were fortunate your ribs didn't fracture."

She wanted to tell him she didn't believe in luck. She believed in the grace of God. Grateful her ribs were not broken, she still ached, but not as much as last night. "I feel better."

"Thank the painkillers. I'm giving you a prescription for more and a mild muscle relaxer," he held up a handful of papers clipped together. "We used a small tube to let the air out of your chest so your lung could expand. You have stitches in your side that need to come out in a few days. I'm sending you home today. You are young and in excellent health. You need rest, and you won't get it here. Until I see you for your follow-up appointment, no flying in airplanes, no scuba diving, and don't lift anything heavier than a quart of milk. If you feel short of breath or cough up blood, return to the emergency room immediately."

Nefi nodded. "Did they catch him?"

Dr. Korley blinked, glanced at Aunt Louise, and then took a deep breath. "I don't know. There's a detective waiting to see you."

Nefi eyed the door. "May I get dressed first?"

"Of course. I'll send in a nurse to help you. And your sister Cassie is here." The doctor's slight grin to Aunt Louise showed his willingness to play along with Cassie's lie. "Do you want me to send her in?"

Aunt Louise smiled.

"Yes, please." Nefi peered over the side of the bed for her clothes. Nothing there.

"A follow-up appointment is listed in the discharge papers. If that date doesn't work, call to reschedule."

"Thank you, Doctor Korley."

After the doctor left the room, Aunt Louise gathered her purse and leaned over Nefi. "Now I can leave. I'm going to leave you in the capable hands of your sister." She kissed Nefi's forehead.

"Thank you." Nefi squeezed her aunt's hand. "Are my clothes over by you?"

Aunt Louise checked around her chair, under the bed, and in a build-in closet between the door and the bathroom. "I don't see any."

A white-haired nurse arrived and handed Nefi a pen to sign a series of forms.

"Excuse me," Aunt Louise said, "where are Nefi's clothes?"

The nurse turned a page and pointed to another place for Nefi to sign. "The detective took them."

Cassie stepped into the room. In jeans and a sweatshirt, with her close-cut hair and brown skin, Cassie would only pass for Nefi's sister if they were adopted. "Hey, sis. You can't leave here in that open-back gown." She deposited an outfit, shoes, and underwear on the bed.

Aunt Louise hugged Cassie. "I'm heading home. Call if you need something."

"Yes, ma'am." Cassie opened the door.

After Louise left, Nefi signed two more papers.

Cassie shut the door.

The nurse, who looked to be in her mid-fifties, eyed Cassie and said, "If you have any questions about your discharge care or follow-up appointment, it's in this packet." She pointed to a business card clipped to the top of the papers. The nurse then recited instructions about changing the dressing on the stitches and avoiding lifting and other heavy activities until the doctor said otherwise. "Do you have any questions?"

Cassie shook her head.

The nurse removed the IV needle from Nefi's arm and pressed a folded white dressing on the spot. She then taped a bandage in place.

Between the nurse and Cassie, they eased Nefi out of the surgical gown into a sports bra, underwear, sweatshirt, sweatpants, socks, and sneakers. The bra pressed on a large bruise at her sternum. A second larger bruise colored her side above the waistband of her sweatpants. The bruises looked more painful than they felt. Once dressed, Nefi was exhausted.

"Stay here. You must ride in a wheelchair until you are released. It's hospital policy." To Cassie, she said, "I'm going to notify transportation about wheeling her out, but for now, I need to let the officer in. He's been here for hours. Give me your phone number, and I'll call you when she's ready to leave."

The nurse backed a wheelchair beside the bed and guided Nefi from the bed to the chair.

Cassie gave the nurse her cell phone number. Next, Cassie handed a roll of breath mints to Nefi. "Sorry, I forgot to bring your toothbrush. I'll be downstairs having coffee."

"Why don't you take the prescriptions and the paper-work?" The nurse handed them to Cassie. "She's going to want them filled today."

Nefi popped a mint in her mouth. Her stomach growled.

Cassie took the papers and followed the nurse out of the room.

Nefi chewed the mint and swallowed it. She tucked her hospital gown under the sheet, and the reaching motion caused a jolt of pain in her ribs. Lifting her sweatshirt, she gently pressed the bandage and felt stitches.

Rap. Rap. Rap.

She pulled the sweatshirt down. "Come in."

A broad-shouldered man in a navy-blue suit entered with his cell phone to his ear. "Hey, I'll call you back." He reached out his hand. "Nefi Jenkins?"

"Yes." Nefi squeezed his hand but did not shake it.

"I'm Detective Kelly with the Boston Police Department."

In his late thirties, fit and business-like, he sat in a cushioned chair facing the bed. "I collected everything you were wearing last night as evidence."

"Do you have my cell phone?"

"No."

"Did you have it with you when you left the restaurant?"

"I don't remember."

She was more upset about surrendering the body armor. It had saved her life. What if Jimmy Jones tried to kill her again?

"I'd like to record your statement about what happened last night. Do I have your consent to record?"

"Yes."

He tapped the screen of his cell phone and placed the phone on the rolling overbed table, which he then rolled in front of Nefi. He also took notes using a small pad and a ballpoint pen. "Please say and spell your name and state your age."

"I'm Nefi Jenkins. N-E-F-I J-E-N-K-I-N-S. I'm twenty-one."

"Thank you. Describe what happened last night. Start with why you left the restaurant."

Sticking to the facts, Nefi told him everything that happened, from taking her grandmother's key fob to riding away in the ambulance. In the ten minutes it took to unburden herself, she felt wrung out.

Detective Kelly's face revealed conflicting emotions as if arguing with himself. His final expression was sadness. "It is illegal to carry a double-bladed knife in Massachusetts. Do you want a lawyer?"

"What is the penalty?"

"That depends. Have you ever been convicted of a felony in any state?"

"No, sir."

"The court could send you to jail for up to two and a half years or charge you a fifty-dollar fine."

Nefi closed her eyes. *Father God, I believe working for the FBI is my mission in life.* She opened her eyes. "I accept responsibility for my actions and waive my right to have an attorney at this time."

His eyes softened, and he cleared his throat. "Do you remember if your knife struck the shooter?"

Nefi shook her head.

"Please state your answer."

"No, sir. I heard and felt the first shot while I threw my knife. The second shot knocked me down, and I had trouble breathing." She grasped the plastic cup and straw from the rolling table and sipped water.

"Why were you wearing body armor?"

"A private investigator and my roommates insisted. There's money missing from my trust fund. My friends believed the amount of money involved put me at risk. I was going to hire a lawyer to get the money back."

"Why not call the police?"

"I wanted to give the…thief a chance to return the money." *Sure, go ahead and say how naïve it was.*

The detective's eyebrows flinched, and then his face relaxed. "I see. Did you hire the attorney?"

Nefi closed her eyes for a moment to acknowledge her poor decision. She didn't know if Jane knew her embezzlement was revealed, but somehow, the shooting was connected to the trust fund. Jane's connection to Jones mocked the idea of coincidence. She opened her eyes and said, "I planned to hire an attorney after graduation."

The detective's mouth formed a thin, straight line,

indicating he, too, saw the decision to wait as unwise. He rubbed a hand over his chin.

Judgment comes easy in hindsight.

Detective Kelly's eyes were a warm chocolate brown with flecks of gold. His breath gave off a minty scent. "Do you know the man who shot you?"

"I recognized him from a photo in the private investigator's report. His name is Jimmy Jones. He manages the property owned by the trust fund."

"The trust fund you own?"

Nefi glanced at the officer's phone and answered for the recording. "Yes."

"The man who shot you worked for you?"

"Yes, sir."

"How well did you know him?"

"Last night was the first time I...met him."

Taking notes, he asked, "How did he get the job?"

"My grandmother hired him when she was the trustee."

Detective Kelly looked up from his notes. "Is your grandmother Jane Wright?"

Nefi's eyes stung with shame that her grandmother was stealing from the trust fund. A part of her believed Jones was the bigger thief because he shot her. Did he know she was looking into the missing money? Maybe, just maybe, her grandmother stole only from the monthly payout. A lesser thief was still a thief, just as a lesser evil was still evil. "Yes, sir. And my grandfather is Ted Wright. He's the publisher of *The Sentinel-Times* in Richmond, Virginia. They're my mother's parents."

The detective nodded. "To clarify, you said, 'Don't do this, Mr. Jones.' Then he said, "You don't give me no choice.' Is that right?"

"Yes, sir."

"What did he mean?"

"I wish I knew."

"Have you spoken to him before? On the phone? By text or email?"

"No, sir."

After reading through his notes, he stopped the recording. He tucked his phone, pen, and notepad into his jacket pockets and pulled out a business card. "If you think of anything else, please call me."

"Are you going to arrest me?" She took the card.

"We will continue to investigate and follow where the evidence leads." He stood.

Nefi juggled curiosity and dread over what happened to Jimmy Jones. If he was on the loose, he would try again. She gave in to curiosity. "Did you catch him?"

The detective blinked twice before he spoke. "How long have you been throwing knives?"

Holding the card, Nefi said, "The village chief taught me when I was seven. He taught all the kids."

"Where was this village?"

"I grew up on the Jurua River in the Amazon rainforest."

"That explains a lot." Detective Kelly's smile flashed and disappeared. "Off the record, you are the only person I know who brought a knife to a gunfight and won."

"Won?"

"We have recordings from security cameras from the jewelry store and a house across the street. It looks like you acted in self-defense. Jones is dead." Detective Kelly quietly left the room.

Jones is dead. *I killed him.*

Nefi wanted a career in law enforcement to protect

people, and yet, the nightmare of crime and its consequences cycled again, tearing her family apart. Greed led
to embezzlement, and from that evil, more crime ensued.

Why did Jones say, 'You give me no choice'? When he
raised his gun, he gave Nefi no choice. Jimmy Jones's crime
made Nefi a killer.

If only she had stayed in the restaurant. Nefi's heart
paused a beat. Jones lived in Richmond, Virginia.

How long has he been stalking me? How did I miss that?

A thread of thought floated through her mind like a
falling leaf. It landed with one end touching Jones and the
other touching the reason Nefi left the restaurant. Grandmother asked her to go outside to retrieve a gift from her
car. Jones was out there, armed and waiting. It was too
much of a coincidence to ignore. Nefi grew up sensitive
to dangers like being stalked. This survival skill remained
strong enough to catch Arlo "Repo" Barlow following her.
Was Jones a better stalker than Arlo? If so, then how did she
miss sensing him? If not, then how did he find her?

The potential collusion between her grandmother and
Jones contradicted Nefi's expectations so completely that
she had to tamp down her emotions to think clearly. As she
calmed her mind, memories of her grandmother flashed
like signposts marking instances of weak moral character. In each instance, Nefi had excused her. Grandmother
declared she was an atheist, so Nefi prayed for her to find
faith. Grandmother excused evil behavior in celebrities as if
being rich exempted them from censure and accountability.

Ever since she caught her grandmother in a lie, Nefi
failed to accept her grandmother's criminal nature because
of a personal normalcy bias. Nefi wanted and expected her
grandmother to be like other grandmothers. She loved her

grandparents and yearned for their love in return. Grandfather Wright was easygoing and friendly. Was his love genuine, or could she have misjudged him? Grandmother Wright seemed sad, which led Nefi to try harder to love her, but all the longing in the world could not change her into the person Nefi hoped she was.

Whether or not grandmother knew Jones was outside the restaurant, she was a thief. By denying and delaying acceptance of the truth—that Jane was stealing from the trust fund—Nefi had allowed the crime to escalate. Jane valued money more than family. Her blatant embezzlement proved it.

Nefi surrendered her fantasy of a loving grandmother to reality. Jane Wright did not deserve Nefi's faith in her. Jane was corrupt and unworthy of being a family elder like those from Nefi's village in the Amazon. Jane did not merit the respect of being an American matriarch of the family. She was a liar and a thief who betrayed the trust she was given. If judged by tribal standards, she'd be beaten and forced out of the tribe for life. Here in America, the legal system demanded formal charges, an arrest, and bail, followed by a trial and sentencing. Innocent until proven guilty.

Nefi longed to be a protector, and yet, this crime had made her a victim and a killer. She rejected the victim mentality and awoke her inner warrior for battle. What had begun as greed somehow led to Jimmy Jones' death. Jones believed he had to kill, but why?

Nefi was justified in defending herself, and yet, she had taken a life. She could never undo that. She took responsibility for killing Jimmy Jones.

From this moment forward, she vowed to force Jane

Wright to take responsibility for every penny stolen. Jane had started this battle. Nefi embraced her mission to bring victims of crime all the justice the courts allowed. No longer a victim, no longer clouded by her hoped-for relationship with her grandmother, she vowed to expose and prosecute Jane Wright to the full extent of the law.

She would begin her internship at the FBI in June. In two years, she'd be eligible to apply for a full-time position as an agent or a profiler. She believed serving in law enforcement was her life's mission. Her calling.

One of Mutt's sayings came to mind—whatever doesn't kill you makes you stronger.

The nurse returned with a young man wearing black scrubs. His name badge read "Tom." The nurse pressed the number keys on her cell phone. "Miss Jenkins is coming down to the main entrance."

Cassie's voice blared from the phone. "No, no, no. There are reporters out front. Is there another way out?"

The nurse blinked, and her mouth fell open.

Cassie added, "She was shot last night. Her uncle is Senator Jenkins."

After a breath, the nurse said, "Oh. There's an unmarked side door past the emergency room entrance by the employee garage." She raised her eyebrows at the orderly and said, "Take her there."

He nodded.

"Thank you!" Cassie said.

After the nurse left the room, the orderly handed a cloth surgical mask to Nefi. "Everyone deserves privacy."

Nefi put on the mask. On the ride through the hospital corridors and elevators, Nefi reaffirmed her vow. She didn't have to wait to become an FBI agent to bring criminals to justice.

The journey through the hospital ended at the employee entrance door, where the orderly locked the wheels of the wheelchair and opened the door to Cassie. They helped Nefi stand and steadied her as she eased into Cassie's car.

Nefi thanked the orderly and fastened her seatbelt. Her ribs ached with each movement. Cassie drove from the employee parking garage past the pack of reporters clustered by the hospital's main entrance. Nefi kept her mask in place.

"We're clear." Cassie sighed.

"Thank you." She would tell Vincent, Aunt Louise, and Uncle Hamilton everything. They deserved to know. She peeled off the mask and closed her eyes.

"What's the matter?"

"My graduation gown was one of a kind. Martina gave it to me."

"If you think about it, it's still a one of a kind." Cassie shrugged, and one side of her mouth pulled back into a half-grin.

"Rips and tears are fashionable. Not bullet holes." She'd have to tell Martina eventually.

"Where's Vincent?"

Cassie cringed. "The reporters were following him, so he's back at the apartment."

"Oh."

"You left your new cell phone at the restaurant." Cassie pointed to the cup holder on the console.

"Oh, good. Thank you!" Nefi sent a quick text message to Martina. *So much to talk about. When are you coming back?*

"How are you holding up?" Cassie asked while watching traffic.

"What doesn't kill me makes me stronger."

Cassie pulled up to a red light. "You are an Amazon."

"I grew up there."

"I mean, you are an Amazon like the women warriors Homer wrote about."

Having read *The Iliad* in high school, Nefi remembered how much she wanted to be one of the horseback-riding warriors depicted in the story. Her first horseback ride was at Blake's family ranch, and though it was fun, she realized how challenging it would have been to fight with a spear or bow and arrow while riding. She identified with the spirit of those women warriors as she suspected Cassie did. Some warrior. She felt as if she'd lost a battle.

"By the way, my family loved Modelo's Café." Cassie gave her the side-eye.

Nefi laughed and held her side.

"Too soon?"

"I don't want to pop my stitches."

After a pause, Cassie said, "You know, Arlo asked a smart question last night."

"What's that?"

"Who inherits the trust if you die?"

Nefi recalled the last pages of the trust agreement. "My offspring."

"And since you don't have any, who would it go to?"

Nefi inhaled sharply. "The previous trustee." There it was—the ten-million-dollar motive.

"Yeah. You need to change that."

·17·

NEFI AND CASSIE arrived at the parking lot near her apartment. Vincent and Mutt stepped out of the shadows by the knife target wall.

Their grim expressions warned of bad news.

"What now?" Cassie asked.

"Reporters," Vincent grumbled.

Vincent helped Nefi out of the car and gently cradled her face in his hands. He kissed her and eased his hands to her shoulders.

She wanted to hug him, but her ribs still hurt, so she leaned against him and sighed. Fighting the urge to pat his chest, she planted her right hand on his shirt over his heart. She imagined falling asleep with her face on his chest.

Mutt cleared his throat. "The reporters have staked out both entrances, so we might as well take the shortest route. How about if Nefi sets the pace?"

Nefi gave Vincent's chest a single pat before she turned toward the apartment building.

Together the four of them walked to the edge of the

garage entrance, where they surveyed the crowd along the road and the sidewalk in front of the apartment building. A news van parked on the curb had a satellite dish on top.

Cassie drew a deep breath and exhaled forcefully. "I'll take point." She stepped into the sunlight.

Vincent and Mutt positioned themselves on either side of Nefi. Vincent's hand rested low on Nefi's back as they crossed the street.

Cassie, Mutt, and Vincent escorted her through a mob of reporters who swarmed, elbowing one another and shouting.

"Is it true you were wearing a bullet-proof vest?"

"How did you know you would be attacked?"

"Did you know the man who shot you?"

"Tell us what happened!"

Cassie charged through the mob, clearing a path for Vincent, Nefi, and Mutt. None of them said a word until they were inside the apartment. Safely inside, Cassie dropped onto the sofa. Nefi lowered herself into a straight-backed chair at the dining table, and Vincent sat beside her.

At the end of the dining table, Cassie's laptop sat open, trailing a power cord to the outlet by the sliding glass door to the porch.

Mutt paced as he stared out the glass door. He had his cell phone to his ear. "Hey, man. This is Michael in apartment two hundred. We have a mob of unfriendlies on the lawn. Would you turn on the sprinklers?" He smiled. "Thanks."

Cassie pointed to Mutt. "I don't care what people say. You are brilliant!"

Mutt spoke to Vincent. "The maintenance man is a Marine."

Minutes later, Mutt pulled the curtain back, and Cassie moved to the window to watch the reporters scatter and shield their cameras from the water with their bodies.

Vincent put his arm around Nefi. "You have the best roommates ever."

Nefi nodded. *Better than certain family members.*

Cassie wandered to the kitchen and opened the refrigerator. She grabbed Nefi's favorite soda and set it on the counter. "Does anyone else want to join me with an adult beverage?"

Vincent and Mutt asked for beers, so Cassie carried them to the table and handed them out. Mutt sat at the table as if expecting something. Mutt and Vincent exchanged a glance and a nod.

Nefi eyed them as she opened her soda and took a long swallow. Aunt Louise would have been silently appalled at having alcohol before dinner, but Nefi understood her friends wanted to ease their stress.

Vincent set his giant hand gently over Nefi's free hand on the table. "It's time to hire a lawyer. Your uncle and the three of us have been discussing it. We found one with an excellent track record and reputation."

"Civil lawyer or criminal?"

"Civil." Vincent gently squeezed Nefi's hand before he let go. "Helen's sister, Mingmei Cho."

Nefi nodded. She spoke softly to Vincent, "I should have told you what was happening with the trust fund."

Vincent smiled. "Everyone has perfect hindsight."

"We can do a conference call now. Your uncle offered to participate." Cassie keyed something on her laptop.

"Now?" Nefi sensed an intervention.

Mutt spoke softly, but it carried across the room. "Last week would have been better."

Nefi nodded.

Cassie opened a link that connected them to Mingmei Cho and Senator Jenkins.

A voice sounded from the laptop and a face, almost identical to Helen's, appeared on the screen. A smaller square flickered beside Mingmei with Uncle Hamilton's image.

"Hello, Nefi." Uncle Hamilton was at his office desk with his bookcase behind him. He looked handsome but tired in his dark blue suit, white shirt, and burgundy tie.

"Good morning, Miss Jenkins," Mingmei said. Like Helen Cho, Mingmei had straight, jet-black hair with a slight bluish shine. "I would like to help recover the funds belonging to your trust account."

"Thank you. The first thing I want to do is remove Jane Wright as beneficiary and backup trustee." Nefi glanced at Cassie.

Mingmei said, "Of course. I'll send a courier this afternoon to pick up a copy of the trust agreement. Mr. Barlow has given me a copy of his report. I'll have Helen send a copy of her financial findings as well. After I review those and update your trust agreement, I'll call you to set up a meeting. What does your schedule look like for the next few weeks?"

"I'm free until June seventh, when I start a six-week internship at Quantico." Nefi focused on Mingmei's image on the laptop. "Detective Kelly said I could be charged for carrying my knife. What happens if he arrests me?"

"When did you speak with him?"

"At the hospital. He took my clothes and the vest as

evidence. Detective Kelly is investigating the shooting. The man who shot me is Jimmy Jones, the property manager of the apartment building owned by the trust."

"I'll talk with Detective Kelly. Let's meet next Tuesday morning at ten. I'll send you a notice with the address. I'm just across the river in downtown Boston. My driver can pick you up."

"Thank you. I appreciate your help. Do you need a deposit?"

"No. My fee will come from the settlement. I'll send a contract by courier so you can review it. Don't sign it until our meeting so we can notarize it. Call me if you have questions." Mingmei nodded and looked down as if writing herself a note, and then she looked back at the screen. "Senator Jenkins, do you have any questions?"

Uncle Hamilton's face appeared in a small box on the right side of the laptop screen. "No, I just wanted to be sure Nefi has the help she needs."

Mingmei nodded. "Excellent. Listen, from this moment on, no one should speak to Ted and Jane Wright directly or by text, email, or smoke signals. Also, you need to say nothing to journalists or social media about the trust fund or the Wrights. If anyone at all asks for an interview or chases you down on the street, tell them to speak to me. I'll see Nefi on Tuesday, and we'll begin the recovery process. Thank you for hiring me. Helen speaks highly of you, Nefi. Not so much you, Vincent."

Vincent, Mutt, Cassie, and Nefi chuckled. Senator Jenkins raised an eyebrow.

"I'll tell you later, Uncle," Nefi said.

The images of her uncle and Mingmei Cho vanished.

Cassie closed her laptop and turned toward Nefi. "There now, that wasn't so hard."

Nefi frowned. "The hard part comes when Mingmei asks Mimi for the money."

Vincent raised his eyebrows. "Who is Mimi?"

"Grandmother wants me to call her Mimi. She said grandmother sounds so old." Nefi rolled her eyes.

Vincent laughed. "That's a perfect nickname for a narcissist."

"It is, right?" Nefi smiled. She and Vincent were thinking alike. It confirmed her belief they would be a formidable couple.

Mutt peeked out between the curtains. "Good, the sprinklers stopped, and the reporters are gone."

Nefi slowly walked to her room to gather the trust fund papers, one of her deposit receipts, and Detective Kelly's card for the courier. She added the detective's contact information to her cell phone. After rummaging through her desk, she found a large mailer and stuffed the trust fund papers, her deposit receipt, and the detective's card inside it and carried it into the common room.

The doorbell rang, and Cassie answered it. Nefi spotted the pizza deliveryman and waved at him. He was the one who knew Latin.

"Oh, man! I thought that was you on the news. Are you okay?"

Cassie paid him and took the pizzas.

Nefi walked closer to the door. "I'm getting there."

"I have a phrase for you. It's not really Latin, but it's worth repeating. *Illegitimi non carborundum.*"

"What does that mean?"

"Don't let the bastards grind you down." He nodded and turned away.

Nefi chuckled and committed the phrase to memory. *Illegitimi non carborundum.*

Cassie closed the door and carried the pizzas to the dining table.

Mutt brought soft drinks and a fist full of napkins to the table. After they took their seats, Mutt said a quick blessing. "Thank you, Father, for your protection. We really appreciate it. Amen."

While they ate, Nefi realized that all that was left for her to do was cooperate. She needed to prepare for the internship so she could help others get justice. She would also take responsibility for her part in this mess.

She thought about spending two and a half years in prison for using her knife to defend herself. Though going to prison would destroy her career in law enforcement, she would accept it as the cost of defending herself. Stranger things have happened. Ruis's stoic sayings reminded Nefi to stop worrying. *Don't suffer imagined troubles. Focus on what you can control.*

"I'm sorry I was so stubborn. Jane Wright is a narcissist. I've known it for years and made excuses for her." Nefi took a big gulp of Dr Pepper.

Mutt raised his can. "Apology accepted."

"Why did you make excuses for her?" Cassie asked.

"My mother was kind and generous. It didn't make sense that my mom could be so different from the woman who raised her."

Vincent kissed Nefi's ear. "She chose to be."

Nefi placed her hand on Vincent's jawline, nodded,

and dropped her hand to the table. "She's not the person I wanted her to be."

Vincent nodded.

Nefi pulled a large slice of pepperoni pizza from the box and bit into it, filling her mouth with cheesy, spicy comfort food. She had not eaten since dinner at Modelo's Café.

Modelo's.

She picked up her phone and found the restaurant's number in her contact list. After swallowing her bite of pizza, she placed the call.

Vincent raised his eyebrows.

Nefi put the call on speaker mode. The call rang twice. "Hello, this is Modelo's. How can I help you?"

Recognizing the voice, Nefi said, "Hey, Carlos."

The next sounds from the phone were a gasp followed by weeping.

"Carlos?"

"I-I sh-sh-should have walked you to your car."

Nefi sucked in a quick breath. "Oh, Carlos, stop. I'm glad you didn't go with me."

"How can you say that?"

"If you had, you could have been killed."

After some sniffling, he said, "I'm so glad you're alive."

"Me, too." Nefi wiped her eyes. "Please tell Mr. De Souza I am well."

"I will. I will."

"Be at peace, Carlos." She ended the call.

It seemed surreal that a teenager she barely knew felt responsible for her while her grandmother felt nothing. She sighed. The people who mattered were the ones who cared. Though there were only thirty contacts on her phone, each name represented a true friend, someone who looked out for her well-being, someone she loved. All but one contact. "Ruis once said, 'Associate only with people who make you better.' I think that's a wise idea." She scrolled through the short contact list to the Ws.

Vincent watched Nefi's phone.

With a few taps on the small screen, Jane and Ted Wright's home and cell phone numbers and address disappeared.

Vincent asked, "How does that feel?"

"Liberating." She took a sip of soda and set the can on the table. Though she rarely talked about her childhood, she felt compelled to share a bit of it with those who loved her. "Back in my tribe, I witnessed a person being sent away. To be kicked out of the tribe meant you could *never* come back. And in the rainforest, being without a tribe usually meant you would die." She examined the faces of her roommates and her fiancé, who were listening intently. "The tribe rejected a man who threw his baby into the river because he said it wasn't his. The adults surrounded him and forced him into the river with their spears. He was waist-deep in the water when something red and black pulled him under. The water churned, and he was gone. The Chief said the Pirarucu avenged the baby."

Mutt and Cassie sat in slack-jawed silence.

Vincent shuddered and spoke to Mutt. "That's a fish the size of a dolphin. It's so aggressive it eats piranha."

Mutt took a deep breath. "Tough neighborhood."

Vincent nodded.

"You are my witnesses," Nefi said. "I am officially evicting my grandparents from my tribe. I will no longer speak to them."

Mutt opened a hand toward Nefi. "You aren't going to toss them in the river, are you?"

"It hurts to be treated like you don't exist. Especially for a narcissist." Nefi stared at her phone. The people who betrayed her and stole from the trust fund her mother and father set up were less than strangers now. They were shadows. Vapor.

The doorbell chimed.

Mutt rose from his chair. "I got this." He disappeared into the kitchen and unlatched the door. "Hey, hold up there!"

"I'm here to see Nefi. Let. Me. Go!"

The familiar voice brought Nefi and Vincent to their feet. Vincent nearly collided with Mutt in the kitchen, where Mutt held a dark-haired woman by her wrist at arm's length.

"Martina!" Nefi wrapped her arms around her best friend in the world.

Mutt released her wrist. "Ooops. Sorry."

Nefi and Martina talked at once in high-pitched tones and held each other. Though her ribs ached, the joy of hugging her friend outweighed the pain.

Vincent said, "Mutt, Cassie, meet Martina Ramos, Nefi's best friend and my future sister-in-law."

Nefi released Martina and stepped back to examine her. She looked thinner than usual. The Louis Vuitton purse Nefi had sent as a graduation gift hung from a strap over her shoulder. She wore a stylish beret that covered her choppy haircut. In one hand, she held a rolled-up newspaper.

Martina shook hands with Mutt and Cassie and gave Vincent a quick hug. They exchanged an awkward acknowledgment, which raised Nefi's curiosity. Vincent and Blake had told Nefi about Martina showing up at the New York FBI office to tell off Vincent after Ruis's wedding. Blake thought it was hilarious. Did Martina accept Vincent now? Did Vincent know something, like maybe the thing that Martina insisted on talking about face-to-face?

"My flight was canceled, or I would have been here in time for your graduation dinner. Surprise!" Martina raised a newspaper to eye level and dropped it on the kitchen counter. "According to the *Boston Globe*, I missed all the excitement. Dinner and a shooting? Really?"

Nefi crossed her arms. "I texted you this morning. You haven't answered my phone calls in twelve days. Why is that?"

As if on cue, Mutt and Cassie backed away.

Martina opened her mouth, closed it, and nodded. "Fair enough." She took a deep breath and sighed before she walked to the table and grabbed a slice of pepperoni pizza. To Vincent, she said, "my suitcase is outside." To Nefi, she said, "Got anything to drink?"

Cassie strolled to the refrigerator. While the others reacted to Martina's false bravado, Nefi wasn't fooled. Martina's face revealed sorrow and an alarming deep-seated fear.

Vincent whispered to Nefi, "Remember Luke 8:17."

In that verse, it said hidden and concealed things would be revealed. *Like secrets?* Was Vincent implying that Jane's secrets would be brought to light? Or Martina's? "My room is this way." She opened her hand toward her room and braced herself for Martina's news.

Cassie carried a soda from the refrigerator to Martina. Martina said, "Thanks, Cassie."

How bad could Martina's news be? Nefi and Martina

pledged to stay virgins until marriage, partly to avoid motherhood before they were ready for it but also because they rebelled against the herd mentality of popular culture. They knew many students who regretted having sex because the consequences lasted far beyond the temporary approval of the herd or the thrill of the moment. If Martina and Oscar had succumbed to passion during their engagement, Nefi could understand it. Her own thoughts toward Vincent heated her with temptation. His embrace and kiss made her tingle and long for more. Nefi would comfort and support Martina through anything, even pregnancy. The Admiral and Mrs. Ramos would be horrified, but they were loving and forgiving people. And they loved grandchildren. Did Martina fully appreciate the blessing of having a loving family?

Whatever Martina's news, they would face it together.

Martina led the way.

·18·

MEANWHILE, IN RICHMOND, Virginia, Jane Wright finished unpacking her suitcase. Ted had slept on the flight from Boston to Richmond, so they hadn't talked about the shooting or their long evening at the police station where an officer and then a detective had asked question after question. What had Ted said to the detective? She and Ted were both inside the restaurant during the shooting. They both heard and saw the same things in the aftermath.

"Jane!" Ted's voice carried up the staircase.

Why did he always expect her to come to him when he called? He could just as easily come to her to speak to her. Jane sighed heavily. He probably wanted to tell her they were out of cream for his coffee because he couldn't find it in the refrigerator. If they were out of it, he fully expected her to dash out immediately to buy it at the nearest store. She trod down the stairs to the kitchen. He wasn't there. "Ted! Where are you?"

"I'm in the study."

If he asked her to help him find his glasses again,

she would get a lanyard to hang them around his neck. Did he really need his glasses if he kept taking them off? She strode down the hallway to the study and stood in the doorway.

Ted inhaled. "We need to talk." Sitting in a Queen Anne chair in front of his wall of bookshelves, he opened his hand toward the other high-back cushioned chair.

Jane walked to the empty chair, sat down, and folded her hands in her lap. Their chairs faced the desk and the wall of framed photos of them with famous writers, sports figures, and politicians, along with framed certificates of merit, awards, and diplomas.

"Tell me about Jimmy Jones."

Unsure what he wanted to know, she stuck with the most recent news. "He shot Nefi."

Ted stared at her as if waiting for more.

What had the police told him? What had they asked? To prevent Ted from speculating or paying too much attention to Jones, she decided to tell him what she'd told the police. "He's the man I hired to manage a property in the trust fund."

Ted slowly nodded.

This alarmed Jane because if Ted already knew this, then either the police told him or someone else did. "Why do you ask?"

"Detective Kelly asked me quite a few questions about him. He also seemed terribly interested in Nefi's trust fund for some reason. What kind of business did Jones manage? Was it a shady business?"

"I don't like your insinuation. Are you accusing me of buying into a shady business?"

"I'm asking what kind of business it was."

"It was an old warehouse I had renovated into rental units. I certainly had no idea the man was dangerous. Trust me, before I hired him, I did a background check. He'd worked as a handyman at a hotel for years."

Ted exhaled through his nose. "All right. I'd like you to go with me to the office. The editor wants to talk to us about the shooting."

Jane was about to argue that she didn't want to, but then she realized this was a golden opportunity to shape the narrative. "When?"

Ted blinked twice before he said, "I'll be ready in two minutes."

Jane stood and marched upstairs for her purse. By the time she reached the bedroom, her hands were shaking. She thought she had planned for everything, but she had not planned for Jones to fail. If he had succeeded and escaped, he would have been written off as a random criminal. No witnesses. That kind of thing happens all the time in big cities.

How could he shoot and miss every major organ of a five-foot-ten-inch-tall woman?

But now, because Jones failed, the police identified him and connected him to the trust. They would search for a motive. She could keep attention on Jones because dead men don't talk. What could she do to encourage the theory that Jones wanted to kill Nefi? What would a plausible motive be?

She freshened her lipstick, hung her purse straps over her arm, and headed downstairs.

·19·

In Nefi's room, Martina and Nefi stretched out on a queen-size bed as they had through high school, side by side with their backs on pillows against the headboard.

Martina removed her hat and sighed heavily. "Before I tell you my news, you have to promise not to tell anyone. Ever. My parents don't know, and it would kill them."

Nefi braced herself. She despised keeping secrets from her family. Martina's big happy family was trustworthy. They wouldn't steal from one another, and as far as Nefi knew, only Martina's father, the Admiral, and Martina's big brother Ruis kept secrets because their professions required it. Ruis worked as a U.S. Marshal, and before that, he'd served as a Navy SEAL. Otherwise, secret-keeping from family felt disloyal. Martina's family trusted Nefi and loved her like one of their own.

Nefi's dread intensified when she considered Martina's secret might be more shocking to a Catholic family than the pregnancy of an unmarried daughter. Her heart sank. Abortion? That would be the kind of personal pain to keep secret forever. She took a deep breath and crossed her arms as if to block the news. "Secrets come out eventually. No matter what the problem is, your family loves you. They deserve your trust."

Martina sat up and twisted her body toward Nefi. "This news isn't about my family."

"If you're pregnant—"

"What? No!" Martina swatted Nefi's arm and glared at her. "Oscar and I haven't done that."

"Oh. Good." Nefi was relieved her best friend didn't have to rush into marriage to beat a nine-month deadline. "Did you get a tattoo?"

Martina snorted. "Absolutely not. That would be like slapping a bumper sticker on a Lamborghini." She combed her fingers through her short hair. "Listen, I know you hate secrets. Just hear me out."

"In that case, you have my promise."

Martina leaned back on the headboard and started her story with the day she accepted a temporary job as a body double for a singer. She told about going to movie premieres and club openings in Europe and America with the singer's fiancé and friends.

Nefi gazed up at the ceiling. "What an amazing first job! Why didn't you just tell us?"

"Secrecy was in the contract." Martina cleared her throat. "The person I was doubling for was hiding out in rehab. No one could ever know." Martina's eyes welled and overflowed. "No one can ever know."

Nefi plucked a box of tissues off her desk and set it between them on the bedspread. "Go on."

"It was all fun until I got kidnapped."

Nefi gasped.

While Martina spoke about her kidnapping in Miami, about being held captive, and how the kidnappers videotaped her ransom message, the timbre of her voice changed as her throat tightened. She paused to wipe her eyes, smearing her mascara.

Nefi so rarely witnessed fear in her best friend it felt peculiar and unsettling. Was she still in danger?

"They drugged me." Martina shivered. "And they took my phone."

"Did they...hurt you?" Nefi whispered, afraid of the answer.

Martina sighed heavily. "One of the jerks punched me in the face."

Nefi exhaled, pressing her hand over her mouth. She wanted the jerk to rot in prison.

"They made me record their ransom demands. They sent the recording to the singer's agent in New York City."

New York City? The ransom video crossed state lines. It was proof of a felony kidnapping. Logically, the agent took the recording to the police or the FBI. "Was that on Monday, April nineteenth?"

Martina turned her head toward Nefi and nodded. "I want to know how you knew."

"That was the day I called Vincent to tell him about the trust fund." *No wonder Vincent sounded so uncomfortable on the phone!* Nefi swung her legs off the bed and planted her feet on the floor. "Vincent knew about this, didn't he?"

"He promised not to tell anyone," Martina spoke through clenched teeth as she rolled off the bed to her feet.

Nefi swung open the door and glared at Vincent.

He turned off the television and stood up from the

sofa. "Mutt and Cassie went for a run." He spoke louder than necessary.

Nefi planted her hands on her hips and raised one eyebrow for emphasis.

Vincent set the remote control on the sofa table. "Let me guess. Martina told her news first."

Nefi nodded.

"Shall I bring a chair in there?"

"We'll come out," Martina announced behind Nefi. "You told her?"

"No." Vincent's voice rolled soft and deep across the room. "But it's about time you did."

"Then how did she know you were involved?"

Though Martina asked Vincent the question, Nefi answered. "When I called him that night, he sounded distracted. I couldn't tell if he was sad, weary, or scared, but he sounded odd, like he was parsing his words."

Martina shook her head. "Nef, you're a human lie detector." She carried the tissue box into the common room and spoke to Vincent. "I got as far as the ransom recording going to your office."

"Want me to show her?" Vincent pulled his phone from his shirt pocket. He tapped his cell phone screen.

Martina let out a sudden gurgling cough. "You have my ransom video on your phone?"

"I've been waiting for you to tell her," Vincent said.

Martina pulled on his arm and said, "Don't make me stand on the couch to watch it."

Vincent sat in the middle of the sofa. Martina sat to his left and Nefi to his right. Vincent turned the phone sideways, displaying the recording in landscape mode. He was about to play the recording when he looked down at Martina and said, "You haven't seen it?"

Martina shook her head. She clenched her jaw while she plucked a handful of tissues from the box and handed the tissue box to Nefi. "Go ahead. I have to tell her the rest before her roommates get back."

Vincent played the recording.

·20·

TED AND JANE arrived at *The Sentinel-Times* building in downtown Richmond, Virginia, and passed through security to Ted's office on the third floor. Jane sat on the burgundy leather sofa to wait for the editor. A stylishly dressed young man in his thirties knocked on the open door.

"Mason, come in," Ted said. "Jane, have you met my assistant?"

Jane gazed up at the young man. "What happened to Mrs. Weatherbe?"

Mason held out his hand to Jane. "She retired. I'm Mason Weatherbe, her nephew."

Jane shook his hand. Mrs. Weatherbe was a dour, tweed-suited woman with a pinched face. Jane liked her because she was not the kind of person Ted would have been attracted to, and now her replacement was equally unlikely to become the cliché office affair. She smiled.

"It's nice to meet you." Mason followed Ted to the large desk, where he placed a small stack of papers. "Here are your phone messages, correspondence, the minutes from the board meeting, and the financials. And the editor asked me to ring him as soon as you arrive. Shall I?"

Ted glanced at the papers, then smiled at Mason. "Send him in."

Mason headed to the door, pausing near Jane. "I'm so glad to hear your granddaughter survived."

Jane sighed heavily. "Thank you."

"May I get you coffee?"

"No, thank you."

Mason left the office. His voice carried from his desk in the wood-paneled reception area of the executive offices. He shared a quiet, open space with the assistants of the chief executive officer and the chief financial officer. The second floor held the newsroom, a bustling, busy maze of low-walled cubicles occupied from early morning until the deadline at 9 p.m. The ground floor held the public reception area, the personnel offices, the cafeteria, and the executive parking garage. The noisiest level was in the basement, where electronic and print machinery churned out the day's news from 10 p.m. to 4 a.m. A separate service elevator at the back of the building funneled supplies into the printing room and bundled newspapers out to a loading dock.

Jane had skimmed the front page of the day's paper by the time the editor and the award-winning investigative reporter, whose name Jane couldn't remember, rushed into the office, and past Jane, to Ted's desk.

Breathless, as if he'd run up the stairwell, the editor said, "Ted, I can't believe you're here! How's your granddaughter, Nellie?"

"She's fine, and her name is Nefi. N-E-F-I." Ted unbuttoned his suit jacket.

At the mention of Nefi, Jane bolted from the sofa to stand by Ted. As she passed the editor and the reporter, the editor flinched.

The investigative reporter wrote in her notepad. "My pal at the *Boston Herald* said your granddaughter was wearing a bullet-proof vest of some kind. What kind? And why was she wearing it? Did she expect to be shot?" She looked up from her notes.

Jane thought she had misheard. "Did you say a bullet-proof vest?"

"Hello, Mrs. Wright," the editor said. He ran his hand down his tie, but the effort didn't change its wrinkles. "Yes. It was also in the police report. You didn't know?"

Ted and Jane shook their heads.

The reporter, what's-her-name and the editor raised their eyebrows and exchanged a look.

This news rattled Jane. The vest was the reason Nefi survived. Why would the girl even own a bullet-proof vest? She was wearing her graduation gown hours after the ceremony, but wearing a bullet-proof vest seemed odd, even for Nefi.

The editor addressed Ted, "I'd like to run a piece with your eye-witness accounts."

Ted scowled and sat on the corner of his massive desk. "We haven't done anything on it yet?"

The editor bit his lip and slowly shook his head. "It happened after the deadline, and we just received a copy of the police report this morning." His gaze bounced to Jane and back to Ted.

"It's all right. Jane has been a trooper through this. I can tell you Nefi begins an internship at the FBI in Quantico in June. I believe it's a six-week program."

The reporter wrote in her notepad. Without looking up, she asked, "Is this internship a prerequisite to getting hired?"

"No," Ted said. "She starts her master's program in the fall. She wants to become an FBI field agent or profiler. I understand she can't be hired until she's twenty-three years old."

The reporter nodded while she wrote and muttered something about "a nice angle." When she looked up, she aimed her question at Ted. "So, is it true the shooter, Jimmy Jones, managed a property held in the family trust?"

Ted breathed through his nose, inhaling and exhaling twice before he spoke. "I'm not sure where this is going."

The editor held up a hand with his fingers splayed. "We want to get ahead of the portrayal of this crime. You know the other news outlets will question the relationship between the shooter and your granddaughter as unusual. I mean, technically, he was employed by her, and it says in the police report that Mrs. Wright hired him."

Jane seethed. She longed to chase the editor and that reporter from the room. They were fishing for a way to sensationalize the shooting.

"If my family wasn't involved, would this be news?" Even sitting, Ted was nearly eye-level with the editor.

"Yes," the reporter said. "People want to know about a girl getting shot right after she gains a ten-million-dollar trust fund. Especially because the shooter works for her."

The editor turned toward Ted. "Don't you want us handling the story?"

"No," Ted said, standing.

"Yes," Jane said.

Ted turned toward Jane and stepped in front of her,

effectively blocking her from the others. "Let it go. Our family is not the news."

"Nefi is." Jane walked around the desk to stand beside the editor and face Ted. "Everyone wants to know about her. Perhaps you could do a profile piece on her. Show who she is, not just the victim of a shooting, but how she wants a career in law enforcement because her parents were murdered."

Ted inhaled sharply. His back stiffened whenever people asked about Marta or her death. He frowned at Jane.

Jane glared back, daring him to get emotional in front of his employees. After a moment, she said, "I think your readers would find Nefi fascinating."

Taking a deep breath, he crossed his arms and said, "She is. I have no problem with a profile piece."

Though Jane got her way, she was fuming. First, her father rewrote the will to the benefit of Nefi, and now Ted agreed she was fascinating. It was like they were under a spell. She certainly couldn't let Ted brag about his only grandchild to the reporter. No. No. This profile had to reveal the real Nefi. Since Ted was so proud of being busy and important, he wouldn't have time for this. She would play the dutiful wife to handle it. "I've got all day," Jane said.

Ted glanced at the pile of papers on his desk and nodded.

The editor and the investigative reporter flanked Jane and practically pulled her out of the room, stopping only to allow her to grab her purse.

The editor said, "Come to my office so we can get background information and contact info on people who know her well, that sort of thing."

While the three of them entered the elevator, Jane made

a mental list of events in Nefi's life that portrayed her true nature. They should interview the high school track coach Nefi tackled. They should know about the bombing and how Nefi faked her own death and ended up in New York City at a nightclub to meet a drug dealer she knew from Brazil. They should know about the friends who gave her weapons for her high school graduation. They needed to know that when Nefi received her first monthly trust fund payout of eight thousand dollars, she spent it all in three days.

Jane told them how she had to borrow from her life insurance to cover the property manager's salary. The poor working man. She would let it slip that in a conversation with Jones, she mentioned Nefi was the new owner of the trust fund and, as such, could sell the property. Jane would hint that a simple working man like Jones might be afraid to lose his job.

Yes, they should find Nefi very interesting. Very interesting indeed.

·21·

IN THE HOUR while Mutt and Cassie ran, Nefi witnessed Martina unburden herself from the awful secret she begged to keep from her family. She told Nefi the story of her kidnapping. Vincent filled in what the FBI did, and the roles Ruis, Blake, and even Terri played in the search. By the end of the story, Nefi understood why Martina had to keep the secret from her family and the public.

Nefi then told Martina about receiving ownership of the trust fund, the trustee's embezzlement, and her experience of being shot twice. Throughout her briefing, she refused to mention her grandmother by name.

"Who was the trustee?" Martina asked.

Vincent answered, "Jane Wright."

Martina covered her mouth with her hands, muffling her, "no."

Unburdened by secrets, the three of them sighed in unison. A comfortable silence followed as they processed their strange, frightful stories. Nefi marveled at how the hand of God had intervened to protect them. Martina's stubbornness and fierce independence helped her through a terrifying kidnapping. And it wasn't luck that protected Nefi from two bullets and a stranger's murderous intent. The body armor did its job, but if Jones's aim had been too high or too low, he could have killed her. If Nefi had not grown up where children learned how to wield a machete and throw a knife, she would have been defenseless.

This was a special moment with the two closest people in her life. She loved her aunt and uncle and trusted them completely, but Martina and Vincent knew all her secrets. Nefi no longer wondered if Martina's friendship was fading. In a way, her world felt right again.

Vincent spoke softly, "It was destroying me to keep Martina's kidnapping from you."

Nefi leaned against Vincent. "I'm so sorry I didn't tell you about the trust fund and the missing money. I kept hoping it was a mistake."

Vincent draped an arm around her. "I'm sorry your grandmother isn't the person you want her to be."

"Cutting her out of your life is her loss," Martina said to Nefi. She turned to Vincent. "I listened to Nefi's messages, and you won't believe—"

Nefi's cell phone rang, vibrating the tabletop. Because Vincent and Martina expected her to answer it, Nefi stuck it under a sofa pillow. "Go on."

"Don't you want to know who's calling?" Martina stared at the pillow.

"This phone can record messages." Nefi felt vibrations through the pillow.

Vincent grinned at Nefi. They then watched Martina squirm. In high school, Martina slept with her phone by her pillow. Vincent's arm lifted off Nefi's back.

Nefi groaned and picked up her cell phone. "Nefi speaking."

"This is Detective Kelly."

Nefi put the call on speaker mode so Vincent and Martina could hear.

"The Richmond police just finished the search of Jones's apartment. They said you are free to clear out his belongings and release them to his sister. They found a personal checking account in Jones' name but no business account. The personal checking account never had more than seven thousand in it at any time until this month when two deposits of five thousand dollars showed up. They're tracing those now."

"One was probably from the previous trustee for his monthly salary."

"All right. We should get his phone records later today. They didn't find any business account for the rent money. According to Miss Helen Cho's reports, the business account should be in the name of the trust, but it could just as well be in an alias or a shell company." He cleared his throat. "And they found an invitation to your graduation and dinner in Jones' kitchen."

Nefi inhaled sharply. *That's how Jones knew where to ambush me.* Vincent and Martina had grim expressions.

"Just for the record," Detective Kelly said, "did you address the envelopes by hand?"

"Yes, sir. How did you know?" Nefi stared at her cell phone.

"One of their crime scene technicians found impressions on the back of the invitation that spell out a particular name and address."

Nefi knew whose address it was.

"Be patient. We don't have enough to make an arrest yet, but every bit of evidence builds the case. One more thing, our crime scene technicians opened the gift that was in the rental car. It's the framed bachelor's diploma from Harvard of Marta Jenkins."

Nefi remembered that Jane said, "Marta didn't need a Harvard education to run off to the jungle."

"It seems like an unusual gift."

A wave of anger washed over Nefi. "I believe the diploma meant nothing to the giver, and I doubt she expected the gift to be opened."

"I see," Detective Kelly said. "I'll text you the name of the Richmond Detective who has the keys to Jones' apartment. We still don't know where the rent money was deposited each month, so if you come across anything, let me know immediately."

"Yes, sir." Nefi set her phone on the table as if to distance herself from this confirmation of her grandmother's evil.

Martina patted Nefi's back. "I'm sorry I hugged you earlier. Your ribs must hurt."

Nefi nodded. Her heart ached, too. She turned toward her best friend. "What were you going to say before this interruption?"

"When I finally got my phone back, I had hundreds of messages to go through." Martina pulled out her cell phone and scrolled through recorded messages. "You won't believe this one. I was kidnapped on Saturday, April seventeenth, around midnight. This is the message you left on Friday, the sixteenth." She turned on the speaker mode and played the recorded message.

"Martina, I know you don't believe in this sort of thing, but this dream was so real I had to tell you. I saw you in a sparkly red dress—the short kind your dad wouldn't let you wear in high school—and you were on a boat. You were terrified. The boat was in a dark place. You screamed, and people laughed. You didn't know anyone at the party. Even if you think I'm crazy, promise me you won't accept an invitation to any boat party. Please. Please."

The message ended.

Vincent and Nefi stared at Martina's phone. Chills crept up Nefi's back and neck. Vincent rubbed his arms. Nefi remembered the intensity and the detailed feel of the dream.

"Can anyone explain that to me?" Martina shook her cell phone. "Then Nefi sent a message every day asking how I was and begging me to call back. The Friday after that, I got this message." She poked her phone again.

"I got the invitation to your graduation. I couldn't be there even if you had enough room for your entire family and me. The FBI internship starts on June seventh. I'm so sorry. Call me when you get a chance. Vincent and Oscar want us to pick dates for the weddings. I also apologize for my bizarre message last Friday. No, I'm not on drugs or drinking. I just had the worst vivid nightmare. You can tease me about it for the rest of our lives, but I had to send that message to get back to sleep. There's more news, but I'd rather talk to you. Call me back, okay? Oh, yikes. I forgot about the time zone. Sorry! You will ace your exams. Goodnight, Martina."

Nefi laughed. "Oh, I wish I could share that with Doctor Sloan!"

"Who?" Vincent asked.

"Her shrink during high school," Martina said. "Sloan tested her for extra-sensory perception."

"Uncle Hamilton's mother and grandmother were psychics," Nefi said, "and he was ashamed of it. So, of course, he was horrified that I thought I was psychic."

"This proves you really are psychic," Martina said. "Just not all the time."

"Exactly. I can't depend on visions." Nefi stood. "Doctor Sloan convinced Uncle Hamilton I was simply highly intuitive because I could read facial expressions and body language like a Mossad Agent." She paced from the kitchen to her bedroom door.

Dr. Sloan explained how people's major facial expressions lasted one to three seconds. It took specific training for most people to notice and correctly interpret expressions flashing by in fractions of a second—and it was the faster expressions that revealed hidden emotions.

Vincent stood in her path and gently wrapped his arms around her. "Doctor Sloan? Why does that name sound familiar?"

"Everyone has some level of intuition." Martina smiled up at Nefi. "I say pay attention to yours whenever it happens because these messages prove how real it is."

Nefi sighed. "So much for four years of psychiatric counseling."

Vincent's jaw dropped. He had the expression of someone doused with ice water. "Wait a minute. Does Doctor Sloan consult for Quantico?"

Uh-oh. Nefi bit her lower lip. She often heard that confession was good for the soul. Was it time to test that adage? In 2009, Sloan invited her to show her unique ability to read people at the U.S. Law Conference and Exhibition in Washington D.C. The other two women on stage were genuine psychics who specialized in finding missing people.

When Nefi agreed to participate in the conference, she didn't even consider Vincent might be among the hundreds of DEA Agents, FBI Agents, psychologists, Texas Rangers, and Police Chiefs attending. At that time, Vincent was a new agent at the FBI in New York City.

Vincent snapped his fingers. "I saw a presentation on non-confrontational interrogation techniques led by Dr. Sloan. Three women dressed in black with big black sunglasses. You were the youngest of the women. I knew that was you!"

Martina crossed her arms and leaned away from Nefi. "Wait. You went to a conference with your shrink?"

Nefi maintained eye contact with Vincent. How much of that day did he remember?

"Doctor Sloan was very protective of you. He refused to tell me your name," Vincent said. "I wanted to talk to you, but you ran off."

"I hadn't seen you in six months." Nefi added, "Since Ruis's wedding."

Martina faced Vincent. "When you broke Nefi's heart."

Vincent groaned and slumped into the sofa. He had brought Rose to Ruis's wedding. "Up until Ruis's wedding, I hadn't seen you in seven years. I thought Blake was kidding when he said you were attracted to me. You changed a lot. I didn't recognize you until Blake danced with you."

"Just for the record, Blake didn't recognize me at first either," Nefi said. "The wedding was an eye-opening experience for me. Then, at the conference, I was still trying to get over you, and there you were, talking to me in front of all those people."

Vincent grinned. "You couldn't think straight?"

Nefi confessed, "I ran off stage to the nearest bathroom to cry." She snorted and glanced at Martina. "Unfortunately, it was the men's room."

Vincent and Martina were laughing when Mutt and Cassie returned from their run.

Mutt peered into the common room from the kitchen. "Sounds like it's safe to enter."

Cassie stepped around him. "Good."

Mutt and Cassie disappeared to their separate rooms.

Vincent stood. "I have a flight back to New York this afternoon." He put out his hand and pulled Nefi into a hug.

They embraced.

"Before you go, what kind of wedding do you want?" Nefi asked with her face close to his.

"The groom is mostly a prop at a wedding. Say where and say when and I'll be there in a tuxedo with a marriage license."

"I'd elope, but it would break Aunt Louise's heart. I don't need a big wedding. Is it weird to have less than thirty contacts on your phone?" Nefi asked Vincent.

Martina answered, "Yeah. But you are a freak, so—"

Vincent and Nefi turned in unison to stare at Martina.

"What?" Martina shrugged. "Freakish in a good way."

Nefi grinned and laid her head on Vincent's shoulder. His strong, warm arms grounded her.

He said, "I'll bet any one of your contacts would drop everything to come if you called."

Nefi nodded. He understood. Quality mattered more than quantity.

Martina sighed. "Having lots of contacts is like having followers on social media. Go on back to the city, Vincent.

I'm staying with Nefi until Thursday. I'll keep her out of trouble."

Vincent and Nefi chuckled.

"That's harsh. Okay, I'll be with her," Martina said, emphasizing her correction with an eye roll.

The responsibility of ownership fell hard on Nefi's shoulders. She had so much to do and only nine days before she had to be at Quantico. "Looks like Martina and I are going to Richmond. I'm going to need to draw money from the trust. And hire a new property manager."

"I've been thinking about that." Vincent pulled a paper from his pocket and unfolded it. "Here's a sample job description for the property manager that includes general maintenance, handyman skills, that sort of thing." He handed it to Nefi.

Nefi read it. Maintain grounds, collect rent, basic plumbing, electrical, and carpentry skills a must, apartment provided. The details fit what Nefi considered important in a property manager. It included things she hadn't thought about as well. "This is wonderful, thank you! Should I list the salary?"

Vincent smiled. "I'd give a salary range." His expression turned pensive. "If you blast this out on the internet, all kinds of unqualified people will show up. What do you think about listing this on a veteran's job board?"

Nefi and Martina nodded.

"If I can't find someone in a week, I'll have to turn this over to an agency." Nefi appreciated Vincent's thoughtfulness. The idea of hiring someone intimidated her. Sure, she could spot a lie in an interview, but she didn't know what questions to ask. This job description gave her specific skills to ask about to narrow the applicant pool.

"Want me to list it?" Vincent raised his eyebrows.

Nefi dashed to her room and set up her laptop on the dining room table. "Please. And put the salary range in the forty to fifty-thousand-dollar range." She laid the paper beside the laptop. "Don't mention the live-in loft."

Vincent seated himself in front of the laptop.

Nefi leaned to whisper in his ear. "Thank you." She then sat on the sofa beside Martina.

Martina elbowed Nefi.

Nefi grunted in pain.

"Oops. Sorry. Bad habit. There's another thing I wanted to discuss in person. Oscar and I have an idea. What about having a double wedding?"

The sudden change of topic surprised Nefi. "I was hoping you'd be my maid of honor."

"Aw, thanks. And I want you to be mine, but my sisters have asked if I've chosen a maid of honor. You know how competitive they are." Martina sighed and picked up momentum. "If we had a double wedding, then it would be too odd for us to be both a bride and a maid of honor, juggling bouquets and stuff. And the maid of honor basically helps the bride prepare for the wedding. My sisters really, really want to be involved, and I think they'd be thrilled if they could be our maid and matron of honor. Besides, for the most part, don't we have the same friends? You know, make it one big party?" Martina clutched her cell phone to her chest.

Nefi warmed to the idea. Would it be possible? Martina used to talk about a lavish wedding. Nefi wanted a simple ceremony. "When would we have the wedding?"

"I can get a license on Monday," Vincent announced as he typed.

Nefi grinned.

"Oscar and I were thinking about December," Martina said.

Vincent turned around in his chair. "This December?" His smile and enthusiastic tone warmed Nefi's heart.

"Yes." Martina bit her lower lip.

Eagerly, Nefi pulled up the calendar on her phone. "I plan to start my master's program in January."

Martina looked up from her phone. "How about Saturday the eighteenth?"

Vincent and Nefi answered in unison, "Yes."

Vincent's phone was still in his shirt pocket.

"Are you okay if we hold the wedding at St. Luke's?" Martina's family attended that Catholic church in McLean, Virginia.

Nefi looked to Vincent. His family was Polish and Catholic. Would his priest from New York City come to Virginia?

"Are you and Oscar in a hurry?" The corner of Vincent's mouth flinched a tentative grin.

Martina stood to her full five-feet-two-inch height and planted her hands on her hips. "No more than you two."

Vincent held up his hands and smiled.

Martina sat. "Schedule your tuxedo rental."

"The eighteenth works for me," Nefi said.

Vincent slapped one hand against the other. "Works for me. Oh, and by the way, I own a tuxedo."

Martina rolled her eyes.

Mutt entered the common room casually dressed and smelling of soap. He sat at the head of the dining table and started a conversation with Vincent. Martina gently patted

Nefi's knee, and then she called Oscar. Cassie entered the room, and Vincent told her about the wedding plans.

In the midst of the conversations around her, Nefi's ribs ached. It felt life-affirming to plan the wedding. The trust had become a responsibility and a danger to her. She readily accepted the responsibility because she had brilliant people like Vincent, Martina, Helen, Mingmei Cho, and Arlo Barlow helping.

As for the danger, she had already survived an attack. Was the murder attempt intended to cover up embezzlement? If Jones embezzled the rent money, then the threat was over, but Jane had worked with Jones to plan the shooting. Why else would an invitation to Modelo's Cafe be in the property manager's possession? In her heart, Nefi suspected Jane sought to cover up her embezzlement. It was an elegant solution. If successful, the killing would look like a random act of violence while Jane played the role of the grieving relative with a solid alibi. If Jones had been caught, he would have been treated like the lone gunman, the scapegoat for the plan. With Nefi's death, the embezzlement investigation would end.

Nefi prayed for Detective Kelly, Mingmei, and Helen Cho to find the evidence needed to expose and convict the guilty. Maybe Jones had embezzled the rent income, but Jane still stole a grand a month for years. That was grand theft.

What would Jane do next?

·22·

Saturday, May 29, 2010

Nefi and Martina spent the morning flying to Richmond, Virginia, where they rented a car and drove directly to the police department to meet with the local detective investigating Jimmy Jones. In his late thirties, Richmond Homicide Detective Avery, a bald, muscular man, told Nefi and Martina that the department was done processing the loft. He then explained the rights of Jones' sister, as his next of kin, to take his possessions.

He ended his briefing by saying, "However, she lives out of state, and she said it could be months before she can come to clear out the apartment. As the owner of the property, you can remove his stuff and rent the place. You could ship everything to her or place it in a storage unit." He gave Nefi a set of keys and an electronic key card. "We processed these already. They go to the apartment. I recommend you avoid contact with his family."

Nefi nodded. "We can move his things to a storage unit."

"You can leave the location and key to the storage with us."

When they arrived at the parking lot of the Stockton Lofts, Nefi and Martina climbed out of the rental car and gaped at a four-story red brick warehouse. It filled the whole block.

Martina cleared her throat. "Maybe he has a small loft."

Nefi gazed at the stark beauty of the building. The photos and the drone recordings made it look smaller. After draping the strap of her cross-body satchel over her neck and shoulder, Nefi drew in a deep breath and headed for the entrance.

Inside, they found a directory of residents beside a wall-mounted phone and a set of locked double doors in the lobby. Nefi used a key card to open the doors into a larger open space which had two sofas facing a low round coffee table on one side and elevator doors and a brightly lit corridor on the other side. On the wall by the elevator was a diagram of the four floors with a small red arrow labeled YOU ARE HERE. The trendy flooring looked like wood planks, but it was tile.

The manager's loft was marked in bold letters, like the gym and the club room. All the other spaces were numbered lofts. According to the diagram, the manager's loft was the first door on the right in the corridor. One ceiling light in the hallway appeared to be burned out.

While Nefi dug the key from her pocket, a woman entered the corridor from another loft door.

Martina tugged a playing-card size piece of yellow crime scene tape off the door frame.

The shapely woman, who appeared to be in her early thirties, walked toward them and stopped within arm's reach. "Are you with the police?"

Nefi transferred the loft key to her left hand and held out her right hand. "Hello, I'm Nefi Jenkins, the owner of the building."

The woman shook Nefi's hand. "The police said Mr. Jones shot someone."

"He did." Her aching ribs reminded her of it with every breath.

"Did he go to jail?"

"He went to the morgue." Nefi unlocked the door to the manager's loft.

"Oh." The woman handed Nefi held a check from the Navy Federal Credit Union for $2,500. "That's my rent for next month. I'm going on vacation."

Nefi tucked the check, made out to the Stockton Lofts, into her bag. "Thank you. Did Jones collect the rent in person?" Nefi asked. It seemed odd. She, Mutt, and Cassie paid their rent electronically from the bank to the rental agency.

The woman grunted. "He told women to knock on the door and hand him their checks. He told the guys to slide payment under the door."

Nefi cringed.

"Yeah. He was the kind of guy who talked to your chest," the woman said. To Martina, she added, "You know what I mean?"

Martina nodded.

"I'm so sorry." Nefi pulled her shoulders back slowly into the posture her aunt reminded her to use. "I didn't hire him."

"Good." The woman eyed Nefi.

"When is the rent due?"

The woman raised her eyebrows. "First of the month. How old are you?"

"I'm twenty-one. This building is in a trust I inherited."

The woman's expression softened. "It's nice to meet you. I'm in number three. My husband's in the Navy. I'm going to San Diego to meet him."

Martina smiled. "Homeport of the Pacific Fleet."

Her expression brightened. "Jacob works in the Military Sealift Command, logistical support."

"My dad and brother served," Martina said. "One of the reasons we're here is because we're trying to find the business account. Do you know which bank the manager used?"

The woman blinked a few times and chewed her lower lip. "I think it's on the back of the checks I get with my statement. Do you want one of them?"

Nefi and Martina answered in unison, "Yes!"

"I'll be right back."

Nefi and Martina entered the manager's loft. Nefi left the door open while she and Martina looked around. The loft was essentially a large rectangle with a corridor along one wall, which opened into a high-ceiling kitchen and living room space with a set of windows facing the parking lot. Along the corridor were doors to spacious rooms, one a bedroom, the second to a bathroom, and the third to a sloppy office or study. A broad granite countertop with bar stools separated the kitchen and living room. A flat-screen television on the living room's far wall faced a black leather sofa and an oversized leather easy chair.

Hearing a knocking sound, Nefi peered down the hall-way and saw the renter. "Come on in!"

The woman looked around as she headed toward the kitchen. "Smells like cigarettes. We're not supposed to smoke in the building." She waved a hand in front of her face then she gave Nefi a canceled check.

Nefi picked up a black pen from the granite counter and crossed through the numbers at the bottom of the check. "I'm going to give this to the detective. He doesn't need to know your account number."

The woman smiled. "I appreciate that."

"This is a huge help." Nefi waved the check.

"Are you going to raise the rent?"

"Is the rent low for this area?" Nefi asked.

The woman's direct gaze matched her candor. "I've been here five years, and it hasn't gone up."

"I am not planning to change anything but the manager."

"Sweet." The woman gave a small wave and headed down the hallway to the door.

Martina's voice came from a back room, "San Diego has a great zoo."

On her way out, the woman said, "He's been deployed eight months. I hope we don't leave our room."

Martina's laugh echoed in the loft as she emerged from a bedroom. When she reached Nefi, she said, "I think we can fit all the bedroom stuff into six large moving boxes. How's the kitchen?"

Nefi took a photo of the back of the check with her cell phone. "I haven't looked in the cabinets yet. I need to send this to Mingmei and the detectives." She texted the check photo with a message to both detectives. Next, she sent a copy to Mingmei Cho with a request for advice on hiring a property manager. The rent money belonged to the trust, but somehow it was being redirected elsewhere. How did embezzlers hide money from the Internal Revenue Service?

"Why not just give the check to the local detective with the storage key?"

"I will. It takes time to get a subpoena. The sooner, the better." Nefi set her phone on the check. She and Martina then inventoried the kitchen. Most of the cabinets were empty except for paper plates and a few pots and pans. The kitchen trash can, filled with fast-food wrappers and beer bottles, gave off a sour stench. Nefi considered taking the trash out but didn't know where the dumpster might be. She decided to tour the building and take notes after packing Jones' belongings.

The second bedroom held a pull-out sofa, a one-drawer desk, a wheeled desk chair, and an end table stacked with smutty magazines. A wireless router sat on the corner of the desk. The police probably confiscated Jones' computer. The desk drawer sat open, revealing hanging files, each filled with rent contracts.

Nefi wandered from room to room and met Martina back in the kitchen. It would take hours to pack up the personal belongings of a sad life. Two framed photos sat on his dresser. One showed a smiling teenage boy and girl on a beach, and the other bore the stern faces of a man and woman with gray hair. Other than these two displays of humanity, the loft felt as welcoming as a prison cell. No bookshelves, posters, or artwork adorned the walls. No plants or pillows or throw blankets brightened the living room. Cassie had a more impressively stocked toolbox than Jones' assorted worn tools stuck in a bucket. Jones's hobbies appeared to be watching television, collecting pornography, and drinking beer.

Martina closed the refrigerator. "Packing and cleaning will take one day max. Hiring someone to manage this building will be harder."

"I've been thinking about that. I texted my attorney about how to do background checks on applicants." Nefi picked up her phone and the cleared check, which she placed in her bag. She made a mental list of things to buy, including boxes, packing tape, a large black marker, gloves, cleaning supplies, and an air freshener.

Nefi's phone pinged in her satchel, so she fished it out and checked her text messages. Ronald Lancaster confirmed the transfer of emergency funds from the trust to Nefi's checking account. This money should be plenty to cover airfares, supplies, the rental car, food, and a hotel in Richmond. Her stomach growled.

"I'm hungry, too." Martina stepped up beside Nefi. "I saw a Mexican restaurant by the storage rental company two blocks from here. I bet the storage place sells boxes and tape."

Nefi wondered how many boxes it would take. As far as she knew, Martina grew up in the same house in McLean, Virginia, where they'd met. Her parents still lived there. Nefi had abandoned her few belongings when she fled her village in Brazil to the U.S. Years later, when her uncle's house was firebombed, she lost her car and everything she had acquired during high school. "I've never packed before."

Martina stared for a while with her mouth opening and closing as if trying to speak but not finding the words.

"You have, right?"

Martina nodded. "I packed tons of clothes and shoes when I moved to Oxford." Martina turned around in the kitchen. "We can do this. How hard can it be?"

Nefi shrugged. Everyone suffers hardships. Besides, stuff was stuff, and it was mostly easy to replace. She treasured the framed photo of her parents from Aunt Louise. Some days it reminded her of loss. Most days, it reminded her of love.

Nefi's phone rang. Mingmei Cho's name showed up on the screen. "Nefi here."

"Thanks for the check images. I'll file to put a hold on the account and get the transaction records."

"I sent them to the detectives, too."

"Okay. The police will freeze the account, but eventually, you'll get whatever is in there. I'll know more after I get the account records."

Nefi said, "What do I do with rent payments that are due on the first of the month?"

"You need to set up a new account just for the Stockton Lofts. I'll send you exact instructions on how to name the account and word the account ownership. Does your bank have a branch in Richmond?"

"I'm sure it does. I didn't bring the trust fund papers."

"No rush. Do it when you're back in Boston. When you hire a property manager, he can deposit the rent payments at the local branch into the new account."

"Oh, okay. And then what do I do with it?"

"You should talk to the investment company that manages your trust and your tax preparer about that." Mingmei's voice sounded clear and relaxed. "I have an incoming call. Gotta run."

Nefi stuck her phone back in her satchel. There were

so many moving parts of the investigation and managing the trust fund, which Nefi found challenging to track. She trusted the detectives, her attorney, and others to follow through with integrity and skill. One day she, too, would be someone who helped others find justice after a crime.

"Ready to go?" Martina stood in the corridor.

Nefi nodded and followed, locking the door behind them. "For where your treasure is, there your heart will also be." Her treasures were her friends, Aunt Louise, Uncle Hamilton, and Vincent. Poor grandmother. She valued something which could never satisfy, so there would never be enough. Greed, like hatred, consumed like fire.

She suddenly pitied Jones. He couldn't keep anything he valued. Perhaps he'd even lost his soul.

·23·

Monday, May 31, 2010

MARTINA WAS RIGHT. It took all day Saturday to pack up and move Jones' personal possessions into a storage unit. On Sunday morning, they cleaned. On Sunday afternoon, Nefi composed a letter to residents to notify them Jimmy Jones would not be managing the property and that this month's rent payment should be forwarded to her Attorney, Mingmei Cho. In the letter, Nefi explained a new property manager would be hired. At Martina's suggestion, Nefi asked residents to email her if they had repair requests or issues they wanted to bring to her attention. It had taken hours on Sunday to create a master list of the residents with their contact information. Using the hotel's business office, Nefi printed the letters and mailing labels.

At the hotel restaurant Monday morning, Nefi sorted through emails on her cell phone and found one from Vincent that included a link to the job board. Her job listing had twelve replies with resumes and cover letters. Nefi had only applied for one job in her life, and it was as a research assistant in the psychololgy department. Her own resume was one page long, yet she was supposed to hire someone. Martina had held a job, albeit a part-time one that ended badly, but at least she'd been through the hiring process. She could help sort through resumes and applications.

That left stopping at the post office to buy stamps and mail the letters, then taking the storage unit key to the police station. They had a late-afternoon flight back to Boston. Martina had helped tremendously and hadn't whined about a thing. Sure, she insisted on wearing thick rubber gloves to handle Jones' belongings, but that seemed reasonable. Martina had to protect a lovely manicure.

Martina sat across from Nefi, devouring avocado toast and washing it down with coffee.

Nefi checked her text messages and found one from Martina's brother, Ruis.

Nothing in life is so exhilarating as to be shot at without result. –Winston Churchill

It made Nefi smile.

"Nef," Martina whispered.

Chagrined at her poor manners for engaging with her phone instead of her best friend, Nefi set down her phone.

"The couple over there is staring at you. Do you know them?" Martina shielded her mouth with her hand.

Nefi turned to her left. This early, the only other diners were a man and woman in their forties dressed in business suits at a table by the window. The man looked away from Nefi to his newspaper while sunlight glared through the half-closed blinds, illuminating them from the shoulders down. The woman squinted toward Nefi, then leaned toward the man to whisper.

The man folded his newspaper and whispered back to the woman.

Nefi watched their expressions shift as if in a polite battle of wills. She and Martina had packed and moved twenty boxes of stuff from the loft to the storage unit down the road. They had met a few renters and people at the police station, but Nefi didn't recognize the people at the table.

The man turned back toward Nefi and then lowered his head. He pushed back his chair and picked up the newspaper while the woman gathered her purse and stood. On their way toward the exit, the man paused by Nefi and held out the newspaper.

"We're done reading. You can have it."

"Thank you, sir." Nefi set the newspaper on the table. Once the couple left the restaurant, Martina and Nefi were alone. "Were they staring at you because you were staring at them?"

Martina unfolded the paper. "They stared first." She opened the newspaper to the front page. Her lips moved as she read, then she clenched her jaw.

Nefi finished her tea and popped a piece of bacon in her mouth.

Martina suddenly slapped the paper on the table and pointed to the masthead. "Tell me this isn't this your grandfather's newspaper."

The Sentinel-Times banner appeared across the top of the front page. Below, a bold headline announced, "Heiress Kills Employee."

Nefi gaped at her own college graduation photo under the headline. Her skin tingled. The fight or flight response she'd studied in psychology and anatomy classes hit her hard. Though she told herself she was breathing deeply to stay calm, her heart rate and blood pressure increased, moving oxygen to her major muscles as her body prepared for battle.

Martina paced the restaurant. She returned to the table and leaned close to Nefi. Her pupils were dilated. She was experiencing the same response. "I can't believe their gall."

Nefi gently uncurled Martina's fists. "I'll call Mingmei."

Martina nodded stiffly and dropped into her chair.

While clearing the other table, the server nudged a glass with the side of a plate. Nefi watched the glass tip and fall over the edge of the table. It struck the tile floor with a loud *pop* and shattered.

Martina jumped up.

Nefi flinched as if the sound of the breaking glass plucked her nerves. She picked her cloth napkin off the floor. "We're jumpy. It's a classic fight-or-flight response."

The server apologized and knelt to pick up the glass shards.

"Like PTSD?" Martina clutched her hands together.

"It will take about twenty minutes for the adrenaline to wear off. To feel normal." It stung to have her reputation destroyed in such a public way. Nefi steeled herself to read the article later. She folded up the newspaper, then pulled enough money from her pocket to cover breakfast and a decent tip and set it on the table. "Let's go back to the room."

Martina rubbed her hands over her arms. "It's cold here."

Nefi led her to the elevator. "That's your body moving blood to your core and your major muscles."

Martina's eyes welled. "Maybe you're used to this, but I haven't felt normal since Miami."

"I'll help you. I've learned a few things about overcoming trauma." Between her psychology classes and life experiences, she could help Martina cope with her memories. Martina had a huge loving family and Oscar to support her emotionally. Nefi used to think of Martina as the pampered baby of the Ramos family and often wondered how she'd face the real world. Now she knew. Martina had survived a kidnapping, which was far more dangerous trouble than Nefi ever expected. Martina showed evidence of a stronger faith.

Martina wiped her eyes. "How are you feeling?"

"Words don't hurt me unless I allow them to." She had hoped her grandfather was not part of the embezzlement, but the personal attack in his newspaper revealed his bias. As the publisher, he allowed the article. Nefi interpreted the public attack article as the growl of cornered animals. The battle line was drawn.

They entered the elevator and rode in silence to the room. Once inside, Martina resumed conversation while they packed their suitcases.

"That smear article makes it look like you attacked Jones." Martina gathered handfuls of cosmetics into a zippered bag.

"I no longer value the words of my grandmother or those who work on her behalf." Nefi pulled her cell phone from her pants pocket and called Mingmei. Her hands shook a little, so she pressed the phone to her ear.

"Hello, Nefi."

"Today's Richmond newspaper, *The Sentinel-Times*, has my photo on the front page with the headline, 'Heiress

Kills Employee.'" Nefi sat on the queen bed she'd made up out of habit before they left for breakfast.

Martina flung the bedspread over her own unmade bed and sat on it.

"Oh. I'll get a copy of it. I'll also check social media."

Nefi closed her eyes. She was afraid to think about what was on social media. "What do I do about it?"

"Don't talk to anyone about this," Mingmei said. "Detective Kelly is an exception, but even then, I'd prefer to be with you when you do."

Nefi nodded. "All right." She calmed herself and gathered her thoughts. "I posted a job listing for a new property manager. I'd really like to hire someone before I go to Quantico."

"Fine. Do that. But tell your friends and family to avoid the media. No matter what they say, quotes can get changed to make you look bad. We fight this battle in court, not in social media or on television or other public communications, got it?" Her stern tone reminded Nefi of Martina's mother.

"I'll pass along your advice."

After a moment of quiet, Mingmei said, "Talk to me. Convince me you will keep your friends and family from jumping into this fight."

Nefi imagined life in the future for perspective. "I'm not on social media and won't talk to reporters of any kind."

Mingmei said, "The public is fickle. We need to let them move on to the next horrible thing in the news. Anything you do or say will keep this in the public eye."

Martina slouched on her bed.

"Hang in there while the detectives and I do our jobs.

I'll see you Tuesday at my office. My driver will pick you up."

"Thank you." With the call completed, Nefi copied and sent individual text messages to her contacts, starting with Vincent.

Please do not talk to the media about me. They are twisting truths to attack me. My lawyer will fight for me in court where it matters most. Thank you, Nefi.

Nefi read the front-page news article carefully. Though every quote was truthful, there were seriously absurd omissions of context. Did this article meet the qualifications for slander or libel? Perhaps not, but it was written with an agenda to ruin her reputation. Her high school principal confirmed Nefi had attacked a coach and a student, but out of context, it looked like she was violent by nature and the attacks unprovoked. Yes, she had killed Jones with a knife, but there was no mention of his handgun! This was not journalism. The fourth estate was designed to keep the government in check. This was tabloid trash.

She did not have a social media account, but she suspected the story from the newspaper was spreading at the speed of gossip. People would choose sides, and few would defend her, but taking an unpopular position on anything was tantamount to begging for abuse. From what she read about social media platforms, they were based on popularity, not facts. An electronic rumor mill. The whole social media environment fostered and rewarded the herd mentality and not independent thought or rational debate. Nefi's favorite psych professor called social media the hive mind. It reminded Nefi of the Borg on the science fiction series "Star Trek: The Next Generation." The Borg destroyed the individual to make it part of the collective.

Martina's phone pinged. "You sent me a text? I'm right here!"

"That includes social media."

"I know. I know." Martina shook her head. "You are such a freak."

Text messages pinged from Vincent, Blake, Aunt Louise, Cassie, Mutt, Arlo, and a few friends from high school. Their quick replies encouraged Nefi to stand strong. She had better things to do than read a newspaper. With all of Jones' belongings in the storage locker, she needed to deliver the storage locker key to the Richmond detective. She tucked the storage locker papers and key in her satchel and slipped the strap over her head and shoulder. Wearing a cross-body satchel reminded her of life in the Amazon. *Carry only essentials. Travel light. Keep your hands free.*

Nefi stuffed the folded newspaper in her suitcase. "Are you ready to go?"

"I'll drive." Martina sat up and shouldered her purse. Somehow, she managed to walk in spike-heeled shoes without twisting an ankle.

"Deal." Nefi preferred shoes she could run in during an emergency.

Martina nodded and pulled the rental car key fob from her purse.

They loaded their suitcases in the trunk and were soon on the road to the Richmond Police Headquarters.

At the five-story gray building, Nefi asked for Detective Avery. Instead of bringing her back to his office, the plump, bright-eyed clerk directed her to take a seat.

The wooden framed chairs in the lobby had cracked leather cushions. A small plain wooden end table separated two groups of chairs. Two outdated sports magazines and a copy of *The Sentinel-Times* covered the end table. Nefi and Martina took seats on either side of the table.

A muscular man in a suit entered the reception area and showed his ID badge, and the clerk buzzed him through to the offices.

Nefi elbowed Martina, who was clutching her designer purse to her ribs. "That looked like Detective Kelly."

"I thought he was bald." Martina grabbed the newspaper and folded it.

Nefi sighed. "Detective Avery is bald. Kelly is the one from Boston who's handling my case."

Martina's lips parted, and she blinked twice. "Did you get a really good look at him?"

Nefi shrugged. She hoped Martina would not shred the police station's copy of the newspaper.

"This is outside his jurisdiction, don't you think?"

Nefi nodded.

Two men dressed in suits entered the lobby and handed papers to the clerk at the reception desk.

Martina folded the newspaper once more and set it on her lap. She whispered, "Nice. Armani and Tom Ford."

"You know them?"

Martina sighed and whispered, "Those guys are wearing suits designed by Ford and Armani. They're probably lawyers." She carried *The Sentinel-Times* to a trash bin by the door and stuffed the paper into it. Her high-heeled shoes clicked on the tile floor.

One of the men, a gentleman in his early thirties, eyed Martina and smiled.

As Martina walked back to Nefi, the gentleman watched Martina with a gleam in his eye. Had Martina smiled at him or ignored him? Men paid attention to her either way. She always looked stylish and well-groomed, but her confidence, like a powerful pheromone, attracted men.

Detective Kelly re-entered the lobby from the secured office entrance and walked straight to Nefi. Richmond Detective Avery followed him into the lobby, where he pivoted toward the well-dressed men.

"Miss Jenkins?" Detective Kelly's expressions of shock and suspicion spoke louder than his words. "What brings you here?"

Nefi stood and held out her hand. "I'm dropping off the storage key to Jones' belongings."

Detective Kelly relaxed and shook her hand. "Oh."

"This is my best friend, Martina Ramos. Martina, this is Detective Kelly from Boston."

Kelly smiled warmly at Martina and shook her hand. He tilted his head slightly. "Has anyone told you how much you look like that singer...Ruby?"

Martina blushed. "I'll take that as a compliment."

On the other side of the lobby, the two well-dressed men handed papers to Detective Avery and then left the building. Detective Avery approached Nefi in long strides.

"Good to see you, Miss Jenkins, Miss Ramos." He shook hands. He turned to Nefi with a questioning look.

Of course, he was a busy man with other cases, so Nefi dug in her satchel and pulled out the storage unit rental agreement and the key to the unit, which she held out to Avery. "The storage unit is rented for ninety days. Jones' contract says the loft was furnished, so the furniture stays. We put the television and stereo in with the boxes."

"Thank you. I'll see to it his sister gets this."

"Thank you, gentlemen." Nefi turned on her heel and

headed to the door. Even though she heard Martina's voice, she continued to the sidewalk.

Martina caught up with her. "What's your hurry?"

"I got the feeling they wanted us to leave." Mindful to shorten her stride so her best friend could keep pace, Nefi headed toward the parking garage.

"Yeah, I picked up on that. I asked if there was any news on the investigation."

Nefi clenched her jaw at the mention of news. "Why?"

"To find out, of course." Martina grabbed Nefi's elbow.

Nefi stopped inside the parking garage and faced her friend. Martina had good intentions, but her curiosity sometimes outweighed her judgment. If the detectives read the paper and believed any of it, they would still follow the evidence and not let public opinion or the media influence them, wouldn't they? "What did they say?"

"Detective Kelly said to tell you to be patient." Martina let go of Nefi's arm and put her hand over her mouth as if to cover her giggle. "I was tempted to tell him just how really patient you are."

Martina's laughter made Nefi smile.

"I mean, you waited for what? Seven years for Vincent to ask you out." Martina laughed as she dug in her purse and dropped the keys to the rental car at the entrance to the parking garage. Her voice echoed off the cement walls.

Nefi crouched and plucked the keys off the concrete. She stood and handed the keys to her best friend, nudging her toward the rental car. "That's not funny."

"Yes, it is." Martina paused near the back bumper.

A shadow drifted by Nefi's feet, alerting her that someone was following them, so she spun around with her fists up in a boxing stance.

The younger of the stylishly dressed lawyers froze with his hands up. "I wanted an autograph." He held a pen and paper in one hand.

Martina stepped up beside Nefi. "I'm a graduate student at Oxford. I am not Ruby."

As the man backed away, Nefi lowered her fists to her sides. Martina unlocked the car, and both women climbed in and locked the doors.

"Does that happen often?" Nefi flexed her hands in her lap.

"Ruby played a lot of concerts in the northeast." Martina gripped the steering wheel with unnecessary force. "And she danced like a stripper."

Martina had been a high school cheerleader, a flyer, the one tossed in the air. Her father, Admiral Ramos, had voiced his horror at the midriff-baring uniforms introduced in Martina's senior year. "And having crowds stare at you while you make sexy dance moves is nothing like cheerleading." Nefi smirked.

"That's not funny."

"Yes, it is." Nefi chuckled even though the movement stung her bruised ribs.

Martina rolled her eyes and backed the car from the stall. Nefi buckled her seat belt. It felt wonderful to ride in a car with her best friend. The simple joy of spending time with Martina meant more since they'd faced their mortality. They were survivors!

And even if the rest of the world believed the newspaper profile and judged Miss Nefi Jenkins as an heiress and a killer, her true friends, her aunt, uncle, and Vincent knew the truth. Four days ago, she had been lying on her back in the middle of the road, struggling to breathe. Having survived an attempt to end her life, she would survive the attempt to smear her reputation. The attack on her reputation wounded her more profoundly than the shooting. Public opinion had been wielded against her with wicked intent in a sneak attack. The attack was personal and cowardly and hurt even more because it came from her grandfather's newspaper.

They rode in silence to the post office.

Before they opened their doors, Nefi said, "Character is like a tree and reputation like a shadow. The shadow is what we think of it; the tree is the real thing. Abraham Lincoln."

Martina studied her. "I like that."

·24·

LATER THAT MORNING, in another part of Richmond, Jane gloated over the article on Nefi. The front page, no less! She considered mailing a copy to Nefi. Anonymously, of course. During breakfast, Ted fumed over the article, though he couldn't name a single untrue word in it.

He even called the editor to complain that the article made the paper look petty for its harsh depiction of a crime victim. He worked himself into a red-faced fury by the time he stormed out and slammed the garage door.

Finally alone, Jane sipped coffee in the Florida room, a glass-enclosed space at the back of the house overlooking the garden. A collection of overstuffed outdoor-style furniture and a ceiling fan created a tropical mood. Her argument with Ted replayed in her head.

Ted, the sentimental fool, felt sorry for Nefi. He had no idea who the real victim was. *Boo hoo hoo.* No matter how she tried to explain the trust fund should have all been hers, he always sided with her father and said it was perfectly reasonable for him to leave something for his only granddaughter. Marta didn't appreciate the great gift.

Marta always had Ted around to attend her sports games and help her with homework. Throughout her own childhood, Jane ached for her father's attention and affection, but he was constantly out of town or working late to build his trucking empire. The time he spent with family felt like an afterthought or duty—Christmas and Easter services at church, graduation from high school, college, and law school. He showed up, but his mind was at work. He loved his work and the fortune he built from it.

She sighed. Her half of the inheritance went into this mansion and gardens and the wall surrounding the property. This was her castle, and she was the queen of it. Ted liked to present the house as a symbol of his success, but he knew whose money had bought it. His income merely maintained it.

When in full bloom, the yellow forsythia hedge looked stunning against the red brick wall, and the blue hydrangeas lining the side walls framed the yard beautifully. Her years in the garden club had not been wasted. She knew what she wanted and told the gardener exactly where to plant it. The old willow needed trimming, and the roses were due for fertilizer. One of the misters tended to spray the bottom of the living room window, but otherwise, the gardens were perfect. Brilliant tulips and daffodils lined the flagstone path from the porch to the garden's wrought iron bench.

Though it was late in the growing season, Jane's tulips and daffodils had just begun to fade. She had extended their blooming period with compost made of coffee grounds.

She often dragged Ted out to the Florida room for

dinner. The garden had a magical quality at night, espe-cially when the strings of tea lights were lit. Jane sighed. Ted would probably work until he was in his mid-seven-ties because he did not know how to relax. Yes, he loved his work, but it was time to pass the mantle on to someone else and start seeing the rest of the world. She picked up a brochure on cruises to Australia and New Zealand. If Ted preferred to live at work, she'd let him. She would explore the world without him. It was folly to put off vacations. One never knew the future, and she wasn't getting any younger. She wanted to travel while her health allowed.

The doorbell rang. She wasn't expecting anyone on a Monday morning. The gardener worked on Tuesdays, and the cleaning lady came on Wednesdays. She set down her coffee and strolled through the house to the front door. Two large silhouettes darkened the etched glass window. She pressed the intercom button. "Who's there?"

"This is Detective Avery of the Richmond Police Department." One of the shadowy figures held a wallet badge up to the glass.

Unintimidated, Jane flung open the door.

The detective stepped toward her, forcing her to back out of his way. He handed her a paper while more men, one in a dark suit and the other in a police uniform, walked past her.

"What are you doing?" she demanded while two more uniformed officers strolled through the open front door. "I did not give you permission to enter!"

The bald man who handed her the paper spoke in a flat tone. "Mrs. Jane Wright, we are here to execute a search warrant. This officer will escort you to the backyard." He nodded to a uniformed officer.

"You can't barge in here and—"

The officer stretched out his arm, blocking her from approaching the detective. "Come with me, Mrs. Wright. Is this the way to the backyard?" He pointed to the back of the house.

"I'm going to call my lawyer." She fisted the paper and stomped out of the house to the bench under the willow in the backyard. There, she read the warrant carefully to see what they wanted and why. The broad description of items included in the warrant named tax documents, banking statements, and records, both paper and electronic, including personal finance and business records, payroll records, bonuses, expenses, and income.

Tamping down rising panic, she glared at the officer. "I can save everyone time by telling you where Ted keeps these files."

The officer glanced at the house, and then he faced Jane. "I can relay your message to the detectives."

Plural? She looked at the house and counted five men in the kitchen. "We keep our financial papers in the filing cabinet in the study, the one near the desk."

The officer used the radio on his shoulder to repeat the message. A voice responded with, "Got it."

Jane pulled her cell phone from her sweater pocket and called Ted. The call rang five times, and then a voice told her to leave a message after the beep. She tightened her grip on the phone and crisply enunciated her message. "This is Jane, your wife, and there are detectives and officers executing a search warrant on our home. Please call the attorney if you can spare the time."

Confident the warrant related to a libel lawsuit, Jane settled herself on the bench. *Let Nefi try to disprove the facts.*

The lawsuit would fail, but she gave Nefi credit for putting up a fight.

If the papers about the trust were rounded up with the rest, so be it. They would find the paperwork in order. There was no paper trail between Jones and Jane outside the trust. Jones alone had attacked Nefi.

After a deep, cleansing breath, she pulled out her phone and read snippets of international news. Hurricane Agatha struck El Salvador, Guatemala, and Honduras killing 150 and leaving thousands homeless from flooding and landslides. She mentally crossed those countries off her vacation list and scrolled to the next news item.

·25·

BACK IN BOSTON, Nefi and Martina were rolling their suitcases through the parking garage at Logan airport. They were marching toward the cab line when Nefi's phone rang. Believing the caller might be one of her renters, she answered it.

"Is this Nefi Jenkins?"

"Yes."

The caller introduced himself as the FBI's summer internship program manager. His voice sounded flat and businesslike.

Two adults led three children toward the rental cars. The children's high-pitched voices mingled with an announcement blaring over the public address system. Nefi parked her suitcase against the wall on the side of the corridor and held her free hand over her ear to better hear the caller.

"I'm sorry, but due to a change in your status, we believe it would be best to withdraw your internship position this summer."

"What? How did my status change?" Nefi spoke louder than necessary.

"We understand you are involved in an active investigation involving a shooting."

Nefi's skin tingled, and her pulse throbbed in her ears. Of course, the FBI monitored social media and the news. "Yes. I was shot twice and defended myself."

Martina raised her eyebrows and hissed with her index finger raised by her lips. Adults nearby gawked and pulled their children away.

"I'm sorry to hear that, but we believe it would be in everyone's best interest for you to be available to resolve this ongoing investigation. You are welcome to reapply next year."

No, no, no! "I have not committed a crime."

"I did not imply that. Your letters of recommendation and your background fit our program. As much as you may be ready for the internship, we believe your attention will be divided between the training and the felony investigation."

His words droned on as the meaning of the call hollowed her out. It took a year of well-timed paperwork, including an application, education records, and letters of recommendation, to apply for the elite six-week internship program. Nine thousand people applied for four hundred positions, and she had been one of the chosen. Now, they were taking back their offer. What could she say to change that?

"If the investigation caused you to withdraw partway through the program—"

"Excuse me. Would you please call Detective Kelly? He's with the Boston Police. He can tell you the facts."

Nefi realized she was violating Mingmei's instructions by talking about the case. Emotion compelled her to protest. Reason warned her to listen.

"I'm so sorry, but the administration's decision is final. You understand many others are on the waiting list, and we want every intern to participate in the entire program. You are welcome to reapply next summer."

The voice of reason whispered for Nefi to be still. Nefi sighed heavily under the weight of disappointment. In the stillness, she realized there were worse things in life than having to reapply to a training program. If not for the grace of God and body armor, she would be dead. With a fresh perspective, she inhaled and said, "Would you please send me this message in writing?"

"Yes, of course. We hope to see you next summer, Miss Jenkins."

She ended the call because her throat tightened so much that her voice would have squeaked. She took a deep breath.

"Who was that?" Martina whispered.

"The FBI canceled my spot in the internship program." It hurt to speak the words.

Martina covered her mouth with her hand.

JANE PACED THE garden until Ted and the lawyer arrived. Both were escorted directly to the backyard and told to wait there. Jane handed the search warrant to the attorney, who pulled his glasses from his suit jacket and sat on the bench in the shade.

While he read, Jane brought Ted up to speed with a brief description of the morning's events. The police allowed her to go escorted to the nearest bathroom as often as she requested. Anxious and caffeinated, she'd entered the house every hour. Each time she saw more boxes accumulating by the front door where an officer with electronic tablets took photos and spoke as if dictating an inventory while another man in a suit observed. The detective in the suit had a gold badge clipped to his belt.

Among the items stacked by the door were her laptop, a desktop computer Ted used for work, and twelve banker's boxes of files.

"They've been here for three hours," Jane said to end her briefing.

"It looks more like twenty banker's boxes," Ted said softly. He scowled at the house, then at the lawyer. "Well?"

"We were served papers this morning about a defamation lawsuit," the lawyer said.

Ted glared at Jane. "Why am I not surprised?"

"Truth is the best defense, Ted. Everything in that article happened." Jane crossed her arms and stood her ground.

The lawyer turned the last page and handed the warrant to Ted. "I can't see how this search has anything to do with the newspaper. This warrant includes personal financial records and investments. Since I represent the newspaper, you should call another attorney. This is a personal matter." With that declaration, the attorney marched toward the back door, where an officer escorted him through the house.

"Personal? I have to figure this out." Ted swatted the warrant on his open hand and then parked himself on the bench to read. He called his CPA and paced the garden in animated conversation, which ended with him facing the far wall.

He was an educated man, but Jane knew he was out of his depth in understanding legal documents. *He had people for that, well-paid people, like the useless man he'd brought home.* She waited for her husband to ask her what the document meant. She was, after all, a lawyer. At least she had been, once.

In the fifth hour of the search, the bald detective in the rumpled suit came out to the garden. The other man in a business suit followed him. Both men wore latex gloves.

"Are you Ted Wright?" Detective Avery asked, clasping his hands.

Ted rose from the bench and looked down at the detective. "I am. What is all this about?"

Jane sighed. Ted was naïve if he thought the detectives would give him a straight answer.

"I'm Detective Avery of the Richmond Police Department. This gentleman is Detective Kelly from the Boston Police Department." He nodded toward the man who had been reviewing the items seized. Detective Avery braced his feet shoulder-width apart. "Let's get to my questions first."

"I don't have to answer any of your questions without my lawyer present," Ted spoke like he was reprimanding an employee.

Avery ran his hand over his bald scalp and cocked his head slightly. "Wasn't that your lawyer who just left?"

"He's the company attorney. I thought this police harassment stemmed from one of the paper's news articles."

Avery grunted. "Tell you what, how about if I ask two questions? You can answer them or not."

Jane wanted to slap the attitude out of the bald detective.

Ted breathed in and out through his nose. "You can ask."

"Do you have your invitation to Nefi Jenkins' graduation?"

Ted furrowed his eyebrows and turned toward Jane.

Remembering she left it with Jimmy Jones, Jane paused, squinted, and shrugged. "I don't know. At my age, I don't keep every invitation we get. I don't do scrapbooking." Her heart rate accelerated. A wave of nausea struck her.

"I see," Detective Avery said. "And how many grandchildren do you have?"

Ted glowered at him.

Jane stared but did not take the bait. Slapping him would not help her situation. "Is that your second question?"

Detective Avery shook his head. He aimed his next question at Jane. "Why do you have twenty-three boxes of family-size frozen lasagna in your deep freezer?"

Jane felt the ground shift. No. There is no way. Why would they look in the basement freezer?

Ted shook his head. "Is this a joke? Are you taking inventory of our canned goods as well?"

"Are you refusing to answer the question?"

Ted puffed out a mouthful of air. "Look, I don't know what's in the freezer, but you must be mistaken. We don't eat that stuff." He glanced at Jane. "Were you stocking up for a garden club meeting?"

Jane couldn't move. She stared at the detective, wishing with all her might he would evaporate like a vampire staked in the heart.

Detective Avery waved to an officer on the back porch who carried over a banker's box filled with family-size frozen lasagna boxes covered in ice crystals. With his gloved hands, Avery gently opened the top box to reveal folded papers.

"What are those?" Ted was so far behind the investigation he couldn't find his place.

Jane recognized the bank statements to the Cayman Islands account. She took a step backward as if to distance herself from the evidence.

Detective Avery tucked the box flap back in place, and then he pocketed his gloves.

The police officer carried away the evidence.

Avery nodded to Detective Kelly. "Have we confirmed Jane Wright is named on this Cayman account?"

"Yes, we have." Detective Kelly smoothed out the front of his suit and took out a set of handcuffs.

Avery said, "Mrs. Jane Wright, you are under arrest for embezzlement and aggravated murder. You have a right to remain silent."

Jane gasped and breathed through her mouth.

Detective Kelly attached the handcuffs to her left wrist.

Ted took a step toward Detective Avery. "This is outrageous!"

Detective Avery planted himself between Ted and Jane and said, "You have the right to have an attorney present during questioning. Anything you say can and will be used against you in a court of law."

Kelly pulled Jane's right hand behind her back and secured the handcuffs to her right wrist.

Outraged over the revelation about the Cayman Islands statements, she drew blanks when she tried to think. Sounds became muted and distorted. She raised her face as if breaking the surface of the water to breathe.

"Do you understand your rights as I've stated them?"

Suddenly angry she would spend the night in jail, she said something in reply which was vulgar, emphatic, and physically impossible.

Because the detectives had probably heard the same insult during countless arrests, they remained unfazed.

"Jane!" Ted raised his voice as if scolding a teenager.

She was being charged with felonies, and Ted was upset about her language. "Snap out of it, Ted. Find the best criminal lawyer in the state and bail me out."

Detective Avery led Jane to the back door. Detective Kelly backed toward the porch as if he expected Ted to charge at him.

Once inside the house, Jane looked back through the glass door. She expected him to be on the phone searching for an attorney.

Ted stood like a statue. The search warrant fluttered from his hand into the bed of tulips and daffodils.

·27·

MINGMEI'S DRIVER RESEMBLED a Sumo wrestler, square-built, muscular, and unsmiling. Having picked up Nefi at her apartment, he eventually escorted her through the office building's security to the eighth floor.

Nefi had read somewhere that the number eight is considered lucky in Chinese culture for being associated with wealth, wholeness, and completeness. Though Nefi didn't believe in luck, she prayed to prevail against her grandmother for stealing and for that hateful news article. In a knee-length navy blue V-neck dress and low-heeled pumps, she followed the driver from the elevator past offices for insurance brokers, investment advisors, and a psychiatrist to the far end of the corridor. Her leather cross-body satchel nudged her hip. Her pumps had a one-inch square heel with rubber soles, so they didn't click on hard floors. She hoped she had dressed appropriately to meet her attorney.

She realized she was wearing the same dress she had worn to her FBI internship interview. Her breath hitched.

Glass panels slid into the walls, welcoming them into elegant minimalist surroundings. Inside, a woman sat behind a blond bamboo desk that curved toward the back wall, which had three sections. The center section of the wall framed the desk, and it was adorned in a fire red textured wallpaper. Bookending the desk were floor-to-ceiling carved wooden panels. Above the desk in gold Chinese characters and in English was "Mingmei Cho, Attorney at Law." The walls and floor seamlessly continued the bamboo paneling. Other than the reception desk, there were two sturdy wooden chairs against one wall, and against the opposite wall sat a love seat with royal blue cushions.

The driver parked himself in a chair and rested his arms on the armrests. Nefi stepped up to the desk.

A petite, middle-aged woman behind the desk spoke while looking down at her desk. "Miss Jenkins is here."

Subtle Asian twelve-tone instrumental music played, but Nefi didn't see the usual mesh-covered speakers in the ceiling or wall. The music seemed to emanate from the walls.

"Ms. Cho will see you now," the receptionist said, glancing up.

Nefi wondered where to go and was about to ask when the carved panel wall to the left of the desk swung out of sight. Light shone through the doorway, so Nefi walked into the light. Mingmei stood in the center of the room, illuminated by sunlight from windows that ran the length of the room from the dark wood-beamed ceiling to waist-high cabinets and shelves. Mingmei, like her sister Helen, dressed in understated elegance, a style that suited their professions. To her immediate left, Nefi found a wall of recessed cabinets and shelves filled with books and carved jade bookends.

Behind a table-style desk the size of a door, a lush landscape mural covered the wall. Between Mingmei and her desk were two burgundy cushioned armchairs facing each other with an oval wooden coffee table between them. The oval tabletop was protected by a layer of glass where a lovely silver tea set and two clear glass cups and saucers appeared like a display.

"Your office is spectacular," Nefi said. Her mood was lifted by the beauty and serenity of this place.

"Thank you. I spend so much time here I wanted it to feel peaceful." She held her left hand toward a glass wall. "That is the conference room."

A chandelier of clear and colored glass corkscrews hung over the black wooden conference table. Eight royal blue Parsons chairs circled the table. Their dark wood and bright cushions appeared to float on the pale bamboo floor. The far wall had a large, framed painting of a crane standing in a marsh. It was the only artwork in the conference room.

"Would you like tea?" Mingmei opened her hand toward the chair closest to Nefi.

"Yes." Nefi eased into the chair. Inside her teacup sat what looked like a ball of grass with streaks of yellow and green.

Her attorney poured steaming water into Nefi's cup and her own. "This tea is known for its calming effect."

Nefi leaned over the teacup and inhaled a scent that reminded her of the rainforest, slightly sweet and earthy.

"This is yellow lotus flower tea," Mingmei paused before adding, "Blue lotus is illegal to consume in the United States."

While Mingmei spoke, Nefi saw the wad of green magically expand into a pale-yellow flower. It took a few minutes for the flower to fully open, and Nefi watched it in awe. More than a drink, this was a thing of beauty.

Mingmei sipped her tea with her eyes closed.

Nefi lifted her cup to inhale the lovely scent and then taste the tea, which amplified the experience. She set her tea down to let it steep. She lifted the strap of her satchel over her head and set it on her lap. From her satchel, she retrieved a clear sandwich bag and handed it to her attorney. "This is the canceled check from one of the renters."

Mingmei, in turn, gave Nefi a stack of mail with return addresses of the Stockton Lofts. Rent payments!

Nefi told Mingmei about the bank account she had established for the trust. She briefed her on all she and Martina had accomplished over the weekend. When she started talking about the call canceling her internship position, her voice broke.

Mingmei set down her teacup. "Did they tell you why?"

Nefi wiped her eyes with her hand and said, "They said my status changed. That my attention would be divided because of the ongoing investigation. They said I could apply next year." Her eyes burned and leaked no matter how much she willed the tears to stop. How embarrassing it was to cry like a child!

Mingmei pulled a box of tissues from her desk and planted it in front of Nefi. "Can you re-apply next year?"

Nefi nodded, nabbed three tissues, and blew her nose.

Taking two more, she dabbed her eyes. "I told them to send me a letter with what they said."

Brightening, Mingmei said, "Excellent! Did you get the caller's name?"

Nefi shook her head.

"That's all right."

"I don't want to cause trouble with the FBI."

"Of course not. The fact that the internship position was withdrawn because of the crime is further fuel for suing *The Sentinel-Times* for defamation of character. We will demand a front-page retraction since the smear article was on the front page."

A front-page retraction would be worth including in the new application. Nefi's voice came out a raspy whisper. "I applied last summer and missed my interview because of another crime."

Mingmei folded her hands on the table. "I remember seeing it in the news. So how did you get into the summer internship?"

"The Director and the previous Director of the New York City FBI Office wrote strong letters of recommendation, so my interview was rescheduled."

Mingmei's eyes widened. "Then you should apply next year. I know you don't want to hear it, but they're right to remove you this year. My sister Helen was in the summer internship after her senior year of college, and she told me how much work she did. Besides, ongoing investigations need your attention here—the defamation case and the felonies involving Jane Wright."

Nefi slouched in her chair and reluctantly nodded. Remembering the contract in her satchel, she pulled it out.

Mingmei stood and touched a screen on her desk

and said something in Mandarin. Her secretary entered through the wall panel. She had a pen and an odd-shaped silver device in her hand.

Nefi signed the contract to hire Mingmei. Mingmei signed it and handed it to her secretary, who inserted the bottom of the signature page into the device and squeezed the handle. The device left an embossed seal and a square for her to sign and date, then she carried the contract out with her device and pen.

The panel slid shut as Mingmei said, "She will make a copy for you." She lifted two newspapers from her desk and handed them to Nefi. "Perhaps this will encourage you."

Nefi returned to her chair. The top one, a national newspaper, had a colored slip of paper sticking out from the pages of the front news section. She unfolded the pages, opening them to the marked page. The headline caught her attention. "Wife of Newspaper Publisher Charged in Murder-for-Hire Scheme."

Nefi inhaled sharply. Murder for hire! Though she shouldn't gloat over another person's hardship, it felt right to celebrate that her grandmother was being held accountable. Oh, and grandmother's name was ignored. She was reduced to being labeled the "Wife of" in a national newspaper, and that could leave a permanent scar on her cold-hearted soul. That slight would enrage a narcissist more than being arrested. Nefi read quickly through the article about the search of the house and the description of items taken by the police. "Can they prove she hired Jones to kill me?"

"Detective Kelly's reputation suggests he doesn't make frivolous arrests."

One item removed from the house, as described by the reporter, caught her attention. "They confiscated boxes of frozen lasagna?"

Mingmei picked up her tea and smiled. "A feeble attempt to hide bank statements."

Nefi's heart stirred. The police had real evidence. *Praise God.*

She unfolded the Boston newspaper and saw two photos side by side. The headline read: *Harvard Grad Target of Murder-for-Hire* alongside a photo of a body draped with a white cloth. "*According to police reports, Jimmy Jones died last week after he allegedly shot recent Harvard Graduate Nefi Jenkins. Jenkins survived. Police records show she defended herself with a knife.*" The photo on the right was of Jane being led in handcuffs into the police station. She had her face down and turned away from the camera and her shoulders raised. "*Richmond police arrested Jane Wright, wife of The Sentinel-Times Publisher Ted Wright, yesterday on felony charges related to embezzlement and aggravated murder.*"

After reading the entire article in the Boston paper, Nefi had mixed feelings. There was no mention of her grandfather except by association. How did he account for millions of dollars of extra income when his wife didn't work? Unless she hid it from him. Even so, he allowed his paper to attack her publicly. He was the publisher. How could he not know? She took a deep breath. Because of the defamation lawsuit, she couldn't talk to him. One day she would know if he were friend or foe. Until then, she would keep her distance. After folding the Boston paper, she looked up at Mingmei. "Detective Kelly seems very thorough. He warned me about my knife."

"I spoke with the District Attorney. He said he'd look

like a fool prosecuting a young woman for using a knife in a gun fight. However, you need to stay out of trouble and stop carrying a knife."

Nefi relaxed and rested her hands on her lap.

Mingmei sipped her tea. "Keep your eyes open and avoid all contact with the Wrights." She stood and walked to the wall of windows overlooking Boston.

"I deleted their phone numbers."

"That's not what I mean. They are still a danger to you." Mingmei lowered her gaze. "I filed for an emergency restraining order to keep Ted and Jane Wright away from you."

"I appreciate the restraining order, but it's a paper shield. I have already underestimated her capacity for evil." The public humiliation of being arrested harmed Jane Wright's reputation, but it did not restore Nefi's. Jane Wright was dangerous before being publicly outed for her crimes of greed, and now she would likely seek revenge. An animal was most dangerous when wounded. "She might target you for helping me."

Mingmei nodded and gazed out the windows at downtown Boston.

Satisfied her attorney would protect herself, Nefi stared at her teacup. She appreciated Mingmei's kindness in preparing this exotic drink. She drank the last of it, savoring the scent and flavor.

"Detective Kelly placed a legal hold on the accounts in Richmond. Jane also had a Cayman Island account. You might not get access to them until after the case is closed, but I filed for them to be turned over to you on the grounds you are now the legal owner."

Nefi gazed at Mingmei's back and tried to grasp the news. "A foreign account."

Mingmei turned toward Nefi and nodded.

The ten-million-dollar trust fund had already changed Nefi's life in contrasting ways. The money had made her the target of attempted murder, erased her concerns about being able to pay back her aunt and uncle, and turned her grandparents against her. Would more money bring more strange changes?

Mingmei leaned against the low shelves which lined the glass wall of windows overlooking downtown Boston. The corners of her mouth twitched, and one perfect eyebrow raised. "You haven't asked how much money is in the Cayman Islands account."

"Who is listed on the account?"

Mingmei said, "Jane Wright, Trustee."

Just Jane. Was Jane protecting Ted or excluding him? Mingmei seemed eager to reveal what she'd uncovered, so Nefi asked, "How much?"

"Three million four hundred thousand dollars. Two hundred thousand of the rental income is unaccounted for and probably spent."

Nefi gaped. "How did she move that much money out of the country?"

"Helen and I pieced together that each month Jane paid Jimmy Jones in cash. If the rental income account had been under Jane's name, it would have been reported to the IRS, so she and Jones used an account in Richmond under the name of the Stockton Lofts. Every month she transferred fifty thousand dollars into another account in the name of the trust. As the trustee, she could then do whatever she wanted with it. Individuals can't transfer more than ten thousand dollars in or out of the United States without special permission, but through a trust fund, she could transfer much more money without attracting the government's attention."

"Does that account belong to the trust?"

"The court ordered a freeze on it, which means the funds stay in Grand Cayman until after the trial. In the meantime, we need to prove you are the rightful trustee and remove Jane's access to the account. That should be done in person."

The Cayman Islands were somewhere in the Caribbean, as far as Nefi knew. "When?"

"I've already started the paperwork. Since the account is frozen, we don't have to go right away."

Nefi exhaled a puff of air. "I can manage on eight thousand a month for a long, long time."

Mingmei smiled.

Nefi sighed. It was too late to pick up summer classes, so she felt adrift. Mingmei's knowledge would guide Nefi through her legal problems, but the rest of her life was yet to be determined.

Was Mingmei standing to signal the end of the meeting?

Nefi gathered up her tissues and dropped them in a wastebasket under the desk. She tucked the stack of mail from the renters into her satchel and pulled the strap over her head. In the Amazon, she'd carried a leather satchel for fruit, seeds, flowers, and other childhood treasures. Life had been so simple then.

Her childhood by the Jurua River had been rich and full, though it resembled desperate poverty to the outside world. She was happy when she owned one pair of shoes, a few outfits, a machete, and some books. With the whole wild rainforest to explore, she had an exciting childhood of wonder and freedom.

Life in the United States was stranger and more complex than she had imagined it would be. By the end of the year, God willing, she would be married. Vincent wanted to become part of her family and welcome her into his. Vincent had lost his parents, one to crime and one to cancer. And, when Vincent's brother Oscar married Martina, Nefi would officially become part of Martina's loving, extended family.

Nefi set aside her disappointments and counted her blessings. With no internship this summer, she would have time to read the textbooks for her first semester of graduate school. She would have plenty of time to use Vincent's gift and Blake's. She stood, accidentally bumping the table and rattling her cup on its plate. "What happens now?"

"Jane Wright will stay in jail until next Monday's arraignment hearing. I'll be there on your behalf, but the District Attorney will present the charges. She will enter her plea of guilty or not guilty." Mingmei angled her head. "Would you say she is a sociopath or psychopath?"

"I'm not a psychiatrist."

"Based on your studies and your experience with Jane, what would you say?"

After a moment of gathering her thoughts, Nefi said, "Sociopaths and psychopaths don't think about consequences. Jane carefully planned how to hide her embezzlement."

Mingmei straightened her head. "She seems narcissistic because of her arrogance and attitude of entitlement."

"You've met her?"

"I read the police interviews."

Returning to Mingmei's question, Nefi said, "Psychopaths are narcissistic, but not all narcissists are psychopaths. Psychopaths feel no shame or guilt. In the photo of her arrest, she hides her face. I'd say she's a malignant narcissist. She seeks validation and power through money. When she doesn't get her way, she turns mean."

"Hmm. I thought she'd have to be a psychopath to hire someone to kill a family member."

"Perhaps it's wishful thinking to believe she felt a moment of guilt about trying to kill me. However, she could have hired someone years ago. Why wait seven years? I suspect it took time for evil to grow enough to kill for money."

"What do you mean?"

"Even the worst psychopaths start small. They show anti-social behavior young, such as torturing small animals and bullying. When they get away with it, the behavior escalates." Nefi stopped reciting from her psychology classes and spoke from her heart. "Nothing I've seen suggests a history of torturing small animals or bullying. Not all killers are psychopaths or sociopaths. All it takes to commit a murder is to get caught up in a moment of rage or believe murder is the right thing to do."

"Like vigilante justice."

"Exactly. Becoming evil enough to commit murder is a process. It begins by accepting an evil thought, such as judging a person less valuable or worthy than yourself. When that thought takes root, it's easier to feel justified when saying cruel things to them or about them. People tell themselves rational lies to tamp down guilt and shame when they know what they do is wrong or unjust. Little by little, the conscience gets smothered, and evil becomes a habit. After a while, it's a small step from speaking evil to doing evil."

Mingmei nodded.

Every genocide grew from evil thoughts. Dehumanize a race, a religious group, a political party, or an economic class, and then it doesn't feel wrong to starve, beat, or kill them.

The process of becoming evil was the same for a group and a person. Someone Nefi loved and trusted had chosen that path. Jane had dehumanized her own granddaughter into an obstacle. Nefi couldn't reverse the evil in her grandmother. She searched her own heart. Was it dehumanizing to remove her grandmother from her life? *No.* She was distancing herself from someone who tried to kill her. She had to cut the emotional ties to a toxic, dangerous, and manipulative individual for her own well-being. Time would reveal Ted's true nature.

Lord, guide me.

"While I am looking after your interests," Mingmei said, "I would be remiss if I didn't advise you to consider a pre-nuptial agreement. No matter how unlikely, divorce can happen, and you should not risk your inheritance."

Having trusted an untrustworthy person, Nefi thought Mingmei's suggestion was smart. She could not imagine Vincent becoming untrustworthy. He had proven himself many times. Rather than argue with Mingmei, she said, "I'll think about it."

"Just so you know," Mingmei said, "Mr. Barlow offered to keep an eye on you until the restraining order is activated. He mentioned he needed the practice."

Nefi nodded.

"He's supposed to stay in the background to watch for

other people following you, so don't wave at him or talk with him. Be sure to text him when you go places."

"His nickname is Repo." Nefi headed toward the massive hidden door and noticed it had no knob or handle.

"What an odd name." Mingmei also moved toward the massive wooden door.

"His father repossessed airplanes. Repo specialized in helicopters." Nefi stepped closer to the door in case proximity triggered it to open.

"You know the most interesting people." Mingmei placed her hand on an unmarked area on the wall.

Nefi held the satchel strap that crossed her chest, "That's the truth. Thank you, Mingmei."

Mingmei's driver stood and pocketed his cell phone. The secretary handed Nefi a copy of the contract in a mailing envelope. Nefi thanked her and slid the envelope into her satchel before she followed the driver to the elevator. There, she dug her phone out to send a text message to Arlo, *Hey stalker, Mingmei's driver is taking me home.*

She walked to the curb where the hulking driver parked the black Suburban SUV. She stood beside it and glanced around while he opened the door. Of ten cars parked nearby, only one had someone in the driver's seat. Two women in business suits walked on the sidewalk across the street and stepped into a real estate office. Her phone chimed, so she checked her text messages.

Why do tall women wear heels?

Nefi grinned and climbed into the back seat. Silly Arlo. Her low pumps barely qualified as heels. People often use humor to mask their true feelings. One joker in high school often skewered people with cruel comments, which ended with the all-purpose deflector, "I'm kidding." Though she was confident Arlo's teasing was friendly instead of passive-aggressive, perhaps he felt intimidated by her height. So be it. If God had meant for her to be average in any way, she would be. She embraced her uniqueness.

Her unusual life experiences, skills, and perspective have served her well so far. She was also learning to care less and less about what people thought of her.

She knew who she was, and those who loved her loved her as is. To work in law enforcement, she'd accumulate enemies. Though she never expected to find enemies within her family, this experience prepared her emotionally for her career.

Tonight, she would call Vincent to tell him about being dropped from the summer internship program. He cared about her. What affected her life affected his. Maybe Jimmy Jones would be alive if only she had told Vincent about the trust fund and the embezzlement sooner. She learned two hard lessons.

Vincent had earned her trust, and it was hubris to think she could handle things alone.

It was childish to believe her grandparents loved her simply because she loved them.

Vincent had finalized the airfare, hotels, transfers, and two excursions for the honeymoon with the last payment. He'd kept Nefi in suspense over where they were going until he could confidently tell her the plans. It was a done deal. Everything he'd read about New Zealand convinced him their honeymoon would be memorable. The funny thing was that after Oscar learned where Vincent and Nefi were going, he asked if he and Martina could join them. They would vacation together in the future because Nefi and Martina were best friends. But a shared honeymoon? Exploring the vast wonders of New Zealand would be more fun with his brother. The real question was how Martina and Nefi would feel about sharing their honeymoons.

Within the hour, Oscar had asked Martina, who was thrilled about the plan. She even promised to keep it a secret until Vincent could ask Nefi.

Vincent settled into his sofa and held his cell phone. At that moment, it rang and vibrated in his hand. When he saw the caller ID, the hair on his arms stood up.

How did she know? "Nefi? I was just about to call you."

"Oh, so you heard already?" She sounded sad.

"About what?"

"I'm not going to Quantico this summer."

The pain in her voice alarmed him. "Why not?"

"They withdrew my spot. They said I could apply next summer, but my current legal issues would interrupt my participation."

"Oh, no. I'm so sorry." He bit his lip. The program was demanding. As much as it upset her, it sounded like a reasonable decision. "Would you be at your best with all this stuff hanging over you?"

After a moment of reflection, Nefi answered, "No."

"Are you going to re-apply?"

"Of course." She sniffled. "How could they ignore an application with letters of recommendation like mine?"

"Exactly." Smiling, he leaned back on the sofa cushions and pried off one dress shoe with the tip of the other. "Perhaps this would be a good time to tell you where we're going on our honeymoon." The shoe clunked on the rug.

"I could use good news."

"New Zealand."

After a gasp, she said, "It's perfect! We'll escape winter here to summer there."

What if Nefi didn't want to share her honeymoon? "And there's more news." Kicking off his other shoe, he flexed his sore feet and took a deep breath. "Oscar and Martina want to go with us."

"To New Zealand?"

"Uh-huh." He bit his lower lip and closed his eyes.

"We are so not normal." Nefi laughed.

"Normal is overrated." Vincent nodded. "I was hoping you'd accept the idea. I'll call Oscar to tell him. I bet the travel agent will be surprised to book a group honeymoon package."

Nefi's laughter warmed his soul. Her happiness was his. Two separate people becoming a couple meant sharing the same space, experiences, emotions, and risks. He eagerly anticipated the honeymoon, confident his heart was safe in Nefi's hands. Sure, they'd see their friends at the wedding, but he hoped Nefi would be able to celebrate without feeling the void of who would not be there. Her uncle would walk her down the aisle, and as a twin, he looked like Nefi's father.

After a comfortable silence, he asked, "What are you going to do this summer?"

"It's too late to take summer classes. And I need to hire a manager for the property. Veterans have submitted applications. Many seem overqualified, so I probably need to interview the best candidates. Oh, and Martina started planning a bachelorette getaway."

Dear Lord, please let Nefi's judgment prevail over Martina's. He'd spent so much on the honeymoon he didn't have a lot left for bail.

"I'd like to add Helen Cho to the wedding invitation list. She's dating Mutt, so she might come anyway. Would you mind?"

"As long as she's done punching me." He put his stocking-clad feet on the coffee table. He considered asking about the arrest of Nefi's grandmother but let it go for now. When Nefi was ready to talk about it, she would. "I miss you."

Her soft sigh made him want to fly to Boston to comfort her. Sometimes when she called, they spent minutes listening to each other breathe. He admired Nefi for being comfortable with silence. Though he longed to comfort her in person, he needed to save his remaining vacation days for the wedding and honeymoon. Instead of booking a flight, he brought up something he had been itching for a year to ask. This seemed like an opportune moment. "I've been meaning to ask you about your trip to Brazil last summer. Why did you stay three weeks?"

"The depositions took a few days, and then I visited my godfather."

"Who's your godfather?"

"Alfonso Morales. He went to Harvard with my parents and my uncle. I'll introduce you to him at the wedding. He's the Brazilian Ambassador to the U.S."

"Whoa." That explained why the people at the embassy in Manaus had processed her passport so quickly. All these years, he had attributed the speed to Nefi's uncle, a U.S. Senator.

"He confided in me that the legal system in Brazil is complex and riddled with corruption. An investigation can last years before a trial, and only ten percent of the crimes are cleared."

He could understand a low conviction rate for robberies and other non-violent crimes. "Even murders?"

"The father of a former Brazilian president murdered a man on the floor of the Senate in the nineteen sixties. They arrested him, tried him, found him not guilty, and released him."

Vincent shook his head and thanked God for the United States Constitution. Despite all the flaws of its legal system, it was still the best in the world.

"My parents' murders were among many charges filed. After I visited my godfather, I took a boat to my village. I needed to ask the chief why they were going to send me away."

After hearing Nefi's story about what it meant to be rejected by the tribe, he realized she had been wounded by their rejection. He took a deep breath. Witnessing her parents' killing and then being sent away by the tribe was a double tragedy. "Did you find the village?"

"Yes. A dear woman who used to cook for us was there. Mali has grown nearsighted. She didn't recognize me until she pulled my face close to hers and saw my eyes." Nefi chuckled. "I brought her a cast iron pot and spices. I brought the chief a weatherproof hat to replace the tattered straw thing he wore. Mali was living in our hut. She said she was just taking care of it to keep the ghosts happy." Nefi sighed. "I told her the ghosts were happy, and I prayed over the house."

Vincent waited through the silence for Nefi to reveal why the tribe sent her away. He had carried the pain of his father's death, so he recognized how difficult it was to talk about such things. He was honored she wanted to share it with him.

"Mali invited me to stay. In the morning, I told the chief the house was Mali's, and he announced it to the others. It's not like there was a deed to sign over to her. The tribe doesn't own land. They just build on it."

Vincent recalled when he, Ruis, and Blake found the small collection of huts they called a village. "I saw your house. I also remember meeting an old woman who was cooking something over an open fire. Blake said it smelled like she was cooking something with the fur on."

Nefi laughed. "Mali used the same pot to cook food and to tan leather."

Vincent made a gagging sound.

"That's why I brought her a new pot just for food. Later that day, I asked the chief why he sent me away. He said my parents made him promise to send me back if anything happened to them. It was his duty as chief to do what was best for his tribe, and that was what was best for me." Nefi sniffled. "He pointed to boys playing by the fire and said it would have been unfair to make me wait for them to grow up."

"I absolutely agree!"

"Since women tend to live longer than men, shouldn't women marry younger men?"

"Ouch. And here I finally convinced Oscar I wasn't robbing the cradle."

Nefi chuckled. "Oh, you know I measure all men on a scale of one to Vincent."

Her comment took his breath away because when she said it, he realized he had been measuring all women against her. Even the fourteen-year-old Nefi had more courage, faith, and presence than anyone else he dated. To be loved by Nefi humbled him. "I hope to live up to your expectations."

"You already have."

His heart swelled. "In that case, let's set a date to get the marriage license. In Virginia, we have to apply within sixty days of the wedding."

They agreed on a date. Tapping tones filled the gap in the conversation, which Vincent interpreted as Nefi keying the date into her phone's calendar.

"Since I won't be going to Quantico, I have plenty of time to spend at the range." Nefi sounded like she was smiling.

"There you go." He marveled at her resilience through tragedy and the sudden responsibility of a financial windfall. Nefi remained true to herself and full of faith.

"Oh, Oh! I almost forgot to tell you. I've been accepted at Hunter College, so I can start my master's classes in January."

He leaped from the sofa. "Wait, the college here on Park Avenue?" After she'd been accepted into the master's program at Harvard, Vincent assumed she would live in Boston for a year after the wedding.

"Uh-huh. I applied last spring and ended up on a waiting list. Someone dropped out."

He glanced around his apartment and smiled. "We could move your stuff in before the wedding." He would need to add a bookcase and make room in the bedroom closet. "Then you'd be ready to start classes after the honeymoon."

"My stuff? Yes. But I won't be moving in until we're married."

"Of course," he said. Would she want to change the condo? He was comfortable in this place and this neighborhood. Would she like a bigger place or a house? They hadn't discussed mutual living arrangements in New York City because it was not an option until now.

"When people talk about playing the lottery, why do they believe winning will make their lives better?"

He was beginning to see life through Nefi's eyes. Her question would have sounded odd coming from anyone else, but she was sincere. "I suppose gamblers enjoy playing the odds. People fantasize about being rich. I think the way people handle money reveals their values and who they really are."

"I agree."

Vincent used to believe money could solve problems, but not anymore. In childhood, Nefi was happy with a handful of possessions. In high school, she lived in a mansion with her aunt and uncle and was content. Though she was the niece of a Senator, hers was not a simple, pampered life of privilege. Her joy was not the byproduct of being naïve. She had overcome tragedies to become street smart and wise.

"Mingmei said I should consider getting a pre-nuptial agreement. What do you think?"

He didn't want money to come between them. "I'll sign it." If she wanted to change out the furniture or move into a larger place, he would do it. He knew she wouldn't demand to fill the apartment with pink frilly stuff.

"She hasn't drawn one up. She just suggested it."

"I'll sign it. Let there be no doubt why I love you."

"Let's discuss it with the priest."

"All right." Their pre-marital counseling sessions were

conducted online each week with Vincent's priest. The discussions were challenging and led to homework with scripture research. In their first session, they wrote their honest, most heartfelt stand on how parenthood would fit in their future. They had surprised each other by agreeing they would consider their lives complete if they did not have children. This realization left them feeling relieved and like-minded.

Nefi wrote she wanted to work in law enforcement, which left little time for parenting. She also added she didn't have a pet for the same reason. This week's discussion was on handling finances and stewardship. Though they were not told to reveal the details of their finances, the trust would inevitably come up when they brought up the topic of a pre-nuptial agreement.

The things Nefi valued could not be bought. She wanted people to love, and he was proud to be part of her inner circle, her tribe. Nefi's faith didn't rest on money or her abilities but on a higher power. So far, money had nearly killed her, but it had not changed her.

·28·

Monday, June 7, 2010

A FEMALE SHERIFF's deputy escorted Jane from the restroom into a small conference room at the courthouse. Wearing the clothes she had told Ted to bring, she dropped the hideous jail jumpsuit on a chair. Her pale blue high-neck dress and heels presented a conservative and modest grandmotherly appearance.

The deputy announced they had twenty minutes, and then she stepped outside the only door to the room.

Jane parked herself at the conference table beside Ted and across the table from her attorney. She needed to look presentable for her arraignment, so she used a small mirror to apply makeup. Still seething that the judge had set her bail at five million dollars and taken her passport, she was relieved to face a different judge for today's arraignment. A week in jail was a week too long. She silently thanked Ted for paying her bail to free her from the terrible food and the hostile people who ordered her around day and night. In jail, she couldn't even shower or use the toilet in private. *Barbaric.*

It had taken Ted a whole week to mortgage the house to pay fifteen percent of the five-million-dollar bail required by Virginia law. Ted and the attorney had visited her in jail to sign the mortgage loan. The house was in her name alone. It was, after all, purchased with Jane's inheritance from her father, and Ted had never objected to being left off the deed. Earlier this morning, Ted delivered a check for $750,000 to the bail bondsman.

The two things Jane wanted from today's court appearance were to enter her plea and demand a jury trial. Her attorney would probably recommend a bench trial, but she knew she could convince a jury to see Nefi as a scheming crazy girl and Jones as a dim-witted drunk who felt threatened by Nefi as the new owner.

"Mrs. Wright," the attorney said as he parked himself at the table, "the evidence the prosecutor has is quite considerable for the financial charges, but the more serious aggravated murder charge is the one that worries me." His trim white beard matched the white hair pulled back into a short ponytail at the nape of his neck. He pulled a yellow legal pad from his briefcase and set it on the table before he uncapped his pen.

While he talked about the evidence and read parts of the police report, Jane completed her makeup and brushed her hair.

"Jane." Ted's voice rumbled across the polished table. "Pay attention."

Having finished her hair, Jane put her makeup and compact mirror back into the toilet kit. "I can do two things at once, Ted."

The attorney said, "You are facing a capital murder charge under Virginia Statute 18.2-31."

"I didn't kill anyone." Seriously, did she have to explain the facts to her own attorney? He should be more prepared. She remembered enough from her criminal law classes decades ago to know this much.

The attorney pursed his lips, and after a pause, he said, "The District Attorney charged you with capital murder and felony embezzlement."

"The murder charge is absurd." Jane pushed the makeup bag away. "What is this? Guilt by association? I hired Jones to manage the property."

"Hold on a minute." Ted leaned his forearms on the table. "How can Jane be charged for something Jones did? She was in the restaurant with me."

The attorney shook his head. "Allow me to explain. If anyone dies during the commission of a felony, then those who committed or assisted in committing the felony can be charged with murder. It's known as the felony murder rule."

Ted held both palms toward the attorney. "First of all, Jones committed the felony by shooting Nefi. And secondly, Nefi is alive."

Jane's scalp tingled. The felony murder rule? *No. No. That can't work.* There was no paper trail for those bloodhounds to find.

The attorney folded his hands on the table. "Apparently, the prosecutor intends to prove Jones was working with Jane to kill Nefi."

Ted and Jane spoke at once. Jane stopped talking rather than shout over Ted. They were running out of time before the hearing, and she needed to know what the prosecutor planned to do.

Once Ted stopped talking, the attorney continued, "But, even if I get that evidence blocked, he could try to prove the embezzlement was an ongoing act when Jones tried to kill Nefi. Then all he needs to prove is that Jane committed the embezzlement with the help of Jones and the felony murder rule includes Jane. And though I could argue that it is circumstantial, the trust would become Jane's in the event of Nefi's death, and the prosecutor could guide the jury to connect the dots."

Jane's pulse accelerated. She had taken courses in criminal law even though her focus was on civil law, particularly bankruptcies. From what she remembered, the felony murder rule was intended as a dragnet to catch gang members who assisted others in committing felonies. If the prosecutor could prove the embezzling charge, she'd face the death penalty. She had not factored in this law, but a loophole existed for every law.

Ted shook his head. It looked like he wanted to rattle the information into a meaningful order.

"In light of what we know so far, would you consider a plea deal?" The attorney leaned over the edge of the table toward Jane.

All she had to prove was reasonable doubt. She'd be fine with a smart lawyer and a jury of people of average intelligence. Tying Jones' death to the redirected rent money was a big stretch, and the D.A. would lose the jury with a convoluted explanation. The chances are that the jury would be daydreaming about the money instead of listening. The key was to separate herself from Jones's failed attempt on Nefi. Break that connection, and the felony murder rule stayed out of reach. Then, as a first-time offender, she wouldn't get the full twenty-year sentence even if she were found guilty of embezzlement. "Absolutely not. I will plead not guilty."

"On which charges?" The attorney held his pen over a yellow legal pad.

"Any of them." Jane stared the attorney in the face. "You have tried cases like this before, haven't you?"

"I have tried five murder cases and twenty embezzlement cases."

"How many did you win?"

"I lost one murder case. An immature client got bored during the trial and confessed."

Jane eyed the attorney while trying to recall his name. She'd have to coach him through the trial to win, but he seemed competent.

Ted raised his hands. "Whatever we discuss here is protected by attorney-client privilege, right?"

"Certainly," the attorney said. He capped his pen and set it on his yellow legal pad.

Ted folded his hands on the table and turned his entire upper body toward Jane. "Tell me the truth. Did you hire or encourage Jones in any way to kill Nefi?"

"Whose side are you on?" Jane glared at Ted.

"It's a simple question." His voice came as a whisper.

"Let's not get ahead of ourselves here," the attorney said.

Jane eyed Ted. "I was with you in the restaurant when Nefi got shot, remember?"

"You would benefit from her death by inheriting the trust fund, and you hired the man who shot her. That looks bad," Ted said.

"So what if I'm a beneficiary named in the trust fund? I didn't write my name into the trust. Marta did. I hired Jones to manage an investment property."

Ted rubbed his hand over his mouth and chin. "If you managed the trust on the up and up, then why did you hide bank statements in the freezer?"

Jane crossed her arms and looked away. "The account was in the name of the trust, not my name, so technically, the trust owned it. I bought the rental property with the insurance money. Remember, I told Marta to buy that policy. I knew she'd die in the jungle from something. Why should my eighteen years of sacrifice be for nothing?"

Ted leaned back in his chair. His expression showed how much her comment upset him. She shouldn't have mentioned Marta and death in the same sentence because he was always so sensitive about it. He looked thinner and grayer since last week.

The attorney scowled at his legal pad.

She needed to focus Ted's attention on today's problem in the proper context. "Millions from my family were handed to Marta when Daddy died. Marta was his pride and joy, and Daddy was delighted to become a great grandfather." She tamped down the heat that rose from her soul over the profound injustice of having to share her inheritance. "Marta and Herman showed a little common sense when they set up the trust fund, which prevented the money from being eaten up by inheritance taxes." She sighed heavily. "As trustee, I managed everything until Nefi turned twenty-one. Don't you see? This is a second chance. Since Nefi didn't even know about the trust, I could limit how much of it she could squander. I mean, look, she burned through the first month's eight-thousand dollar payment like pocket change."

Ted looked down at his hands and rubbed them together.

The attorney cleared his throat and dove into the conversation. "We aren't here to try the case. All that happens today is for Jane to enter her plea, then we ask for a bench trial."

"I want a jury trial," Jane said.

The attorney shook his head. "Juries are unpredictable. With a bench trial, we rely on evidence and argument and avoid the public spectacle of the media stirring up interest."

Ted held up his palm to the attorney and faced Jane. "How did you try to limit Nefi's access to the funds?"

Jane squirmed under his direct question. "Let me remind you, the property I bought performed better than the stocks and bonds managed by Attucks, Bird, and Copley. Why are you shaking your head?"

"How did you limit Nefi's access to the funds?"

"Stop shouting at me."

Ted's voice dropped to a harsh whisper as he repeated, "How did you limit Nefi's access to the funds?"

She glanced at her attorney. "Is the account frozen?"

With his elbow on the table, the attorney cradled his forehead in his hand. He raised his head. "Oh, you remembered I'm here. Wonderful. Which account are you asking about?"

"There's more than one account?" Ted gaped at Jane.

Jane said, "The big account."

"Yes, that account is frozen. And, yes, the Stockton Lofts account and the Richmond trust checking account are also frozen. All your personal accounts and assets are likely to be audited until the missing money is accounted for." The attorney glanced at his watch.

Jane explained to Ted, "Most of the rent money is in an account in Grand Cayman."

"Most of it?" Ted's wide-eyed stare accused her.

She had spent a little on travel but refused to tell him about it while he was angry. Poor Ted. Her annual cruise with her society friends wasn't a week in the Bahamas like she told him but in the Mediterranean. He never socialized with her friends, so she didn't have to concern herself with anyone bringing it up in conversation. Her friends were the wives of business leaders and politicians, the invisible second tier of the influential people in Ted's world. As the newspapers declared, she, too, was the *wife of* someone whose name people might recognize. "Why are you attacking me?"

Ted shook his head.

He should have judged her brilliant for managing the trust funds better than the professionals. She'd only spent a fraction of the profits, after all. Why was he so dense? "I should be rewarded for investing well. You know Nefi doesn't even care about money. She wants to be an FBI agent, for pity's sake." Jane realized Ted could not appreciate her years of planning and patience. She muttered, "She's throwing her life away just like Marta. If Nefi doesn't value her life, why should we?"

Ted leaned back in his chair and gripped the armrests.

"Please don't talk like that," the attorney pleaded.

She'd said too much. Ted said he wanted the truth, but he really didn't. He was too sentimental about Marta and Nefi to see the big picture. Why did everyone care so much about lanky, doe-eyed Nefi?

Ted closed his eyes for a full three seconds, and then he opened them. "Did you hire or encourage Jones to kill Nefi?"

Jane turned away from him. "I don't have to answer that."

"You're right. You can invoke the fifth amendment," Ted said. "And I can refuse to be part of this."

Heat radiated through Jane, lifting her to her feet. "You know I meant Nefi didn't value her life because she was throwing it away with a career in the FBI. And you are part of this, Ted, whether you like it or not."

Ted stood. "I don't even recognize you anymore."

The attorney jumped up and spoke softly to Ted, "Please, no matter how upset you are at this moment, you need to be seen standing by your wife at the arraignment and the trial. I shouldn't have to tell you what the media will make of it if you are missing."

"I can't do that. I don't believe anything Jane says," Ted said, clearing his throat. His eyes welled as he spoke to the attorney. "When our only child Marta died, Jane didn't cry. I thought Jane was brave, keeping busy filing insurance claims and handling the funeral. Now it all makes sense. If Nefi had died in the jungle, Jane would have seized control of the fortune she felt she was owed. Her daddy issues have poisoned her soul."

Jane crossed her arms and glared across the room at him. "You know you can't testify against me because we're married."

Ted turned toward the attorney. "When will the trial be?"

"They'll put it on the docket anywhere from six months from now to a year."

Ted walked to the door. "Plenty of time to get a divorce."

Jane's face burned. "You cowardly traitor. The moment being married is inconvenient or embarrassing, you walk away. It's all about you, isn't it? The great publisher Ted Wright can't face being in the news. I can't believe you're going to let Nefi defame me and steal my legacy!"

Ted's shoulders dropped as he opened the door. He turned his head to the side without looking at her. "You defame yourself. Nefi *is* our legacy."

·29·

December 4, 2010

NEFI WORE WHITE sandals, a flowing white beach coverup over her one-piece navy-blue swimsuit, and a white baseball cap with one word embroidered on it in black—BRIDE. On her way through the breezy lobby of the Palm Heights Hotel in Grand Cayman, she spotted the Cho sisters in sheer red caftans and black swimsuits heading to the pool courtyard. She quickly caught up with them.

Mingmei said, "From this moment on, we are here to relax and have fun. Okay?"

Nefi nodded. She didn't want to think about or discuss the horrible things written about her, the embezzlement, or her estranged family members. Most of all, she didn't want to think about the shooting.

Despite the vast ethical difference between murder and killing, the result was the same, and Jones' death felt like a stain on her soul. The stain faded a little over the months, making Nefi wonder when and if she would repair her reputation. The legal system worked at its own pace, with Mingmei leading the way. Though the topic of the crime loomed over her, Nefi would deflect questions and remain positive. *Whatever is true, noble, right, pure, lovely, admirable, excellent, or praiseworthy, think about these things.* Besides, the judge had taken away Jane's passport, so Nefi felt somewhat safer than usual. She vowed to enjoy the three-day bridesmaid's weekend.

An instrumental version of "White Christmas" played softly from speakers disguised as rocks along the concrete path. At a glance, the sand resembled snow.

Helen Cho stopped and hugged Nefi. "Thank you so much for this lovely surprise." She released Nefi and flung an arm around Mingmei. "We haven't had a vacation together in ages."

Mingmei laughed and leaned close to Nefi. "I overheard the bellman tell the manager you and Martina are a couple."

Nefi's face warmed as her mouth fell open. "Wait. What?"

Helen covered her mouth with her hand, which only muffled her laughter. "Two women wearing the same hat..." She hooked her arm through Nefi's and led her toward the courtyard.

Shaking her head, Nefi allowed the sisters to lead her to the beach, where they expected to meet up with the rest of the bridesmaids and Martina. They strolled through a brilliantly sunlit courtyard with a long, vast pool in the center framed by tall queen palm trees, hot pink bougainvillea hedges, and cushioned lounge chairs until they stepped out of the shade onto the bright beach.

Halfway from the hotel to the shore, Terri Pinehurst

Clayton lounged on a chair beside Cassie James under a lemon-yellow beach umbrella. A small table between them held paperback books and tall glasses of rum punch. The ladies were laughing.

Nefi felt joy whenever she saw Terri because she had introduced her to Blake at Ruis's wedding. It was love at first sight. The trial had tested them, but now they had an unshakeable relationship. In her soul, Nefi knew Blake was innocent of the terrible crime. Things were not often what they seemed.

Helen Cho directed her sister to a nearby covered set of lounge chairs with a white towel draped over one chair and a folded towel on the other chair.

"Nefi!" A figure standing on a paddleboard in the water waved. Martina.

Nearby, two other short, curvy women stood on paddleboards looking just as at home in the water as Martina. By their matching smiles and dark ponytails, they were Martina's sisters. The older one, Gloria, had chosen to serve as Nefi's matron of honor after Nefi and Martina agreed that being a bride and maid of honor at the same ceremony complicated things. Gloria was married, and her two darling girls were staying with the Admiral this weekend. The senior Ramos volunteered to watch the children so Gloria's husband could go to work as usual.

Martina's sister Elena, the middle daughter, volunteered to be Martina's maid of honor. Aunt Louise and Martina's mother were planning the entire wedding. Martina's mother had planned Gloria's wedding and Ruis's, so her experience proved valuable. Aunt Louise's contribution to the wedding was calling in favors from caterers and the priest.

Nefi dropped her hat, sandals, and coverup on the empty chair by Martina's. Of course, having two women sitting together on the beach wearing matching BRIDE hats would fuel more rumors, but people would believe whatever they wanted. Nefi walked to the water's edge.

"That one's yours!" Martina pointed to a paddleboard and paddle in the sand. "Put the fin in the water first."

Nefi tossed the paddle into the water and hefted the paddleboard over her head. She waded into the warm turquoise water and set the board in the water fin-first. Hoping they would not paddle out to sea, she climbed onto the board and grabbed the paddle. Next, she stood until she found her footing with the waves. She paddled out to Martina and her sisters.

The three sisters were dry except for a coconut-scented sheen of sunscreen. Seagulls wheeled and squawked overhead.

"Where's Aunt Louise and your mom?" Nefi asked.

Martina wiped her brow with the back of her hand and grinned. "They went to Hell."

"What did you say?" Nefi's paddleboard drifted toward the low-breaking waves.

Gloria said, "It's a place on the northwest side of the island. Nothing grows there on the volcanic rock, and it has its own post office so you can send mail. You know, like, 'Visiting hell, wish you were here.' That sort of thing." She paddled out toward calmer water.

Suspecting a prank, Nefi glanced at Elena, who nodded. "It's legit. I asked them to send a postcard to my ex-boyfriend."

At that, they laughed and paddled into deeper water. Elena was referring to the fool she had dated in college who mocked people who served in the military. Their relationship fell apart the day he met Admiral Ramos. Even retired, Martina's father had the presence and bearing of a Navy Admiral. He didn't tolerate dull-witted or lazy people. The ex-boyfriend was both still living at home in his thirties and proudly proclaiming he was a master over his time. Over dinner, Admiral Ramos told the young man about keelhauling, a usually fatal punishment pirates used at sea. The boyfriend was just smart enough to intuit the message.

The women paddled a mile along Grand Cayman's famous seven-mile beach while Gloria described falling in love with her husband.

"He was a blind date mother arranged. I agreed to the date to stop her matchmaking. One date evolved into a second and a third as we discovered our common interests. We dated a year before he talked privately with the Admiral about proposing. By that time, the whole family adored him, and our families vacationed together on a boat trip to Norfolk, Virginia." Gloria drifted on her paddleboard. "We ate dinner on a rooftop restaurant called Grain, which overlooked Norfolk's Waterside marina. We were lounging around firepits and swapping sea stories when he pulled me away and dropped to a knee. I remember the tiny white lights strung overhead when he proposed."

Gloria asked Nefi about Vincent's proposal.

"We were in North Carolina at a friend's trial."

Gloria bit her lip. "Your friend Terri told me a little about the trial."

Martina and Elena paddled ahead, deep in a separate conversation.

Nefi glanced at Gloria. "It wasn't a romantic evening

like yours. But still, after he asked me to marry him, I was floating in a dream. He fit all the requirements of love. He's patient, kind, humble, and slow to anger. He's my happily-ever-after."

The sun warmed and dried Nefi. She felt beautiful and strong in her swimsuit. An hour a day, either running or working out in the local gym, had transformed her runner's body into a competitive condition. She had greater stamina and strength than ever before. Martina had described the change as 'just shy of being a bodybuilder,' which pleased Nefi. Of course, Nefi wanted to ace the FBI fitness test, but she also wanted to look fabulous naked for Vincent.

Twenty yards ahead, Martina and Elena turned their paddleboards around. Martina announced she was hungry, and the others agreed to return to the hotel.

"So, how did it go at the bank?" Martina tugged down her swimsuit hem in the back.

Nefi turned her paddleboard around. "Mingmei handed them a stack of papers, and we transferred the funds to a new account. I signed everything she told me to." Nefi's childhood fear of the water plucked her nerves. The water was so clear it could easily be deeper than it looked. Sure, she could swim, but she wasn't as comfortable in the water as the Ramos sisters were.

A school of fish, the size of piranhas, darted under Nefi's paddleboard. Reminding herself she was in salt water, she calmed. Just the same, she preferred to keep the paddleboard between her body and the fish.

Elena expertly glided alongside Nefi. "How does it feel to be a millionaire?"

"You wouldn't believe how many people suddenly claim to be relatives."

"That's awkward," Elena said.

"I don't answer my phone unless the caller is on my contact list. My roommates, Cassie and Mutt, sort the mail."

"Protect your personal information. When you move to New York, you could get a post office box to use as your home address." Gloria wiped sweat from her brow.

"Good idea." Nefi paddled slowly on one side of the board, then the other. Her shoulders and face were baking from lack of sunscreen. "I start my master's program in January."

Martina's sisters exchanged a glance. Gloria spoke up. "You are going to live with Vincent after you're married, right? We heard you were accepted to Harvard's graduate program."

Nefi's face tingled. Martina's family treated her as one of their own. Mrs. Ramos had given Nefi a key to their house while Nefi was in high school. The family had shared their lives with her, so it was fair to share her life with them. "I was accepted at CUNY Hunter College."

Martina's sisters continued to stare at Nefi as if she hadn't answered their question.

Nefi added, "In New York City. Vincent's apartment is nearby."

The women looked relieved and resumed paddling.

Gloria eyed Nefi. "Are you ready for your wedding night? I mean, do you have any questions your aunt didn't answer?"

Nefi glanced at Martina.

Elena laughed. "We all know about your pact to stay

virgins until marriage. We are so proud of you! Your husbands will be proud of you, too."

Gloria added, "This is the best present you can give your husband. Something money can't buy."

"Thanks." Nefi squinted against sunlight reflected off the water. She was excited about the honeymoon. "I think I'm ready. I read about it."

"You...what?" Gloria suppressed a grin.

"I read *The Kama Sutra*, a biology textbook, and a lot of steamy romance novels," Nefi said, feeling quite clever.

At that, Gloria and Elena surrendered to laughter punctuated by sputtering gasps for air as they drifted on their paddleboards.

Martina composed herself enough to say, "Good for you. I wish I'd thought of that. Knowledge is power."

Startled by their reaction, Nefi lifted her paddle and spoke to Gloria. "How did you prepare for your honeymoon?"

Gloria stammered and blushed, which made Nefi regret asking. Perhaps Gloria and her husband didn't wait. If only she could suck the words back into her mouth unheard, but she couldn't. The rude question hung in the air like a bad smell.

Gloria's voice whispered across the water, "I got on the pill because we didn't want to have kids right away." Her intimate admission sounded like forgiveness.

In thanks, Nefi said, "Me too. Parenthood scares me."

Gloria smiled so big sunlight sparkled off her teeth. "Raising kids takes more energy and patience than I ever expected. Mom made it look easy."

The others nodded. Gloria and Elena resumed paddling. Nefi and Martina trailed behind. Seagulls wheeled and called above while the surf rumbled and tumbled ashore and dragged itself off the sand with a hiss. Beads of sweat tickled Nefi's back and neck before her swimsuit absorbed them.

Though he'd never said so, and she would never ask, Nefi assumed Vincent was experienced. Unfortunately, experience often trumped knowledge. Nefi wanted to be better than Rose, his ex-girlfriend, a woman who radiated sexuality.

For reasons she could never understand, American culture judged men and women differently. If a man and woman had sex outside of marriage, the man's reputation was enhanced and the woman's ruined. Life was simpler in the jungle.

The ladies paddled closer to the hotel. A little girl in a bright pink swimsuit stood up to her knees in saltwater, pointing toward a beachball bobbing in the waves. Martina batted the ball to the shore, where the little girl hugged it and squealed.

Nefi drifted until her paddleboard bumped into Martina's, and she whispered, "Wasn't there something you wanted to tell your sisters?"

Martina responded with a slight nod and a deep breath. "Glo, Ellie, I want to tell you something. You have to swear not to tell Mom."

Both her sisters paled and froze in place. Their expressions turned slack. All four paddleboards drifted gently on the calm bay waters.

"I want to tell Mom myself—in private, okay?"

The whole family considered Martina the wild child, the one most likely to get a tattoo or do something regrettable. Gloria stared at Martina's belly. Elena bit her bottom lip.

"Don't freak out, but after the wedding, I'm moving with Oscar to Japan. It's only for a few years, and then we're moving back to the States."

Nefi read the sisters' surprise and relief as quickly as reading a billboard, but Martina had utterly missed their stress signals. Nefi snickered.

"You told Nefi?" Gloria asked. The unspoken meaning was 'before us?'

Martina tapped her paddle on the edge of her paddleboard. "Look. Oscar told Vincent. Vincent told her. Brothers can be close, too."

"Why did you laugh?" Gloria asked Nefi.

Nefi countered, "Why did you look at Martina's belly?"

Chagrined, Gloria blushed. "What was I supposed to think when she starts with don't tell Mom?"

Martina slapped her paddle in the water, splashing Gloria. The spray also struck Elena, which triggered a barrage of splashing. While ducking water, Nefi fell off her board but managed to hold onto her paddle. At first, she flailed in the water on her back and smacked herself in the head with the paddle. She spat a mouthful of saltwater and coughed. Fear shot through her, so she forced herself to move purposefully. When she lifted her head above the water the second time, she heard Martina.

"Stand up!"

Nefi tucked her legs, treaded water with one arm, and then stretched out her legs. After she planted her feet on the sand, she discovered the water was shoulder deep. She coughed again and felt foolish for panicking. Saltwater stung the inside of her nose.

The three sisters simultaneously shouted directions for Nefi to climb back onto the paddleboard without flipping it over. It took a few tries, but eventually, she was face down on the board. After lying still and gathering her strength and balance, she eased to her hands and knees and then stood. Sometime during her struggle, she lost her paddle.

Martina retrieved the paddle and handed it back to her. "Pity we didn't record that."

"Sure, laugh," Nefi sputtered, "You didn't grow up by a river teeming with creatures eager to kill you."

They paddled back to the Palm Heights Hotel, where they turned in their boards and paddles and headed to lunch. Helen had reserved outside tables for their group, so they gathered in beach coverups and sundresses. Nefi, Gloria, Elena, and Martina sat on towels instead of seat cushions.

Every table was filled. Families and couples chatted over seafood, fruit, and salads. Caribbean music played softly over the sounds of the surf. A white-haired couple floated in the pool on inflatable chairs.

A young male server delivered drinks and graciously took photos of Martina and Nefi's group with multiple cell phones. He then took out a small notepad and pen. Nefi ordered a fruit salad and nachos. Martina and the bridesmaids ordered salads, while Mingmei and Helen ordered full seafood meals. Apparently, they were not as concerned about fitting into their formal dresses as the rest of the ladies.

"Nefi, where is your cell phone?" Mingmei asked.

"In my room."

Cassie said, "She got lots of calls from unknown long-lost relatives asking for money."

Mingmei unfurled her table napkin onto her lap. "Ah."

Gloria stood and raised her rum punch. "To Martina and Oscar and Nefi and Vincent, best friends marrying brothers, may your wedding lead to happily-ever-after!"

The ladies raised their glasses and voices in salute. Diners at nearby tables paused to watch.

Gloria then sat and leaned over her place setting. "Mother asked me to tell everyone about a special event this evening. An evening swim in Bio Bay." She turned toward Helen and Mingmei.

Bio Bay? Night swimming? Nefi's stomach clenched. Being on the beach in daylight worked well because the water was clear as glass, but swimming at night left her with a sense of dread. Jellyfish, stingrays, crabs, and all kinds of biting creatures crept into her thoughts.

"Helen and Mingmei," Gloria said to the Cho sisters. "This is a gift from Mom and Dad."

Mingmei smiled. "Thank you so much. We would be honored to join you."

Helen nodded. "Is this the place with the big orange starfish?"

Gloria picked up her cell phone from the table and tapped the screen. Next, she handed her phone to Helen, who gasped.

"I didn't know about this place!" Helen held the phone toward Mingmei, who also gasped.

The phone was handed around the table with the same reaction each time. By the time it reached Nefi, she had to tap the screen to refresh it. The photo revealed a person standing in glowing water as if his body had a chemical reaction to the water.

"What is this?" Nefi handed the phone to Gloria. "Is it safe to swim at night?"

Martina bit her bottom lip.

"It's harmless bioluminescent plankton."

The people in the image appeared to be standing in the water, which relieved Nefi enough to marvel at the magical beauty of nature. She welcomed a childhood sense of wonder back into her life. This bridesmaids' vacation was the perfect antidote to the deadly conflict over the trust fund. Though she longed to relax, she knew the turnover of the stolen Cayman Island funds would make her grandmother even more embittered. The fight was not over. Mingmei predicted the trial would take place late next summer or early next autumn. As Nefi had predicted, Jane elected to go to trial.

For a narcissist to accept guilt or a plea deal was as likely as a snowstorm in Grand Cayman. And then there was the libel lawsuit against *The Sentinel-Times*, which had a team of defense lawyers. Nefi had mixed feelings about Ted Wright. He had allowed the front-page smear article, but it didn't seem like him. She couldn't talk to him, according to her attorney. Mingmei had deposed Nefi's high school principal, the track coach, and others who were horrified to discover their comments were twisted out of context. That headline haunted Nefi. She worked toward a career as a protector and was publicly labeled a killer for defending herself.

Using the advice from her Psychiatrist, Dr. Sloan, Nefi changed her self-talk from negative to positive. She had fought for her life and won. She was fighting to hold the newspaper accountable for damaging her reputation. If she won, great. If she lost, she would accept the loss and be at peace for fighting back. The newspaper had to spend money on their panel of attorneys, so even if they won, they lost.

Cassie nudged Nefi. "What are you thinking about?"

Nefi whispered, "The libel lawsuit."

Elena looked up from her food. "It's shameful what that Richmond paper published. That's slander, isn't it?"

Mingmei raised her eyebrows at Nefi.

Nefi said, "You have my permission to talk about it."

Mingmei spoke softly, "Just so you know, slander is spoken, and libel is written. An article written with the intent to damage a private person's reputation by twisting facts and the words of others isn't true journalism, is it?"

The women shook their heads and scowled.

Cassie set her tea down. "Every other news outlet reported the attack on Nefi the way it really happened."

Nefi appreciated the way Cassie spoke up for her. As a witness, Cassie's words carried weight. The reactions of the others at the table showed it. Strains of "Silent Night" played softly during the lull in the conversation.

"I'm going to miss having you around." Cassie forked the last of her fruit salad into her mouth.

"I'll miss you, too." Nefi's boxes of books and clothes were on their way to Vincent's apartment. Her laptop and the rest of her belongings sat in the hotel room closet.

"Mutt and I might have to hire a cleaning lady." Cassie sighed.

Nefi opened her mouth in mock protest. Cassie grinned.

The ladies finished their food and signed the server's bills before they returned to their beach chairs. Nefi moved her lounge chair into the umbrella's shade and stretched out on the cushions.

The group quieted to read and tan themselves while

the surf rumbled. It was in quiet moments like these that Nefi's emotions surfaced. The summer and fall semesters kept her friends in classes while Nefi spent her days shooting at the range, reading next semester's textbooks, and exercising. Having roomed with Cassie and Mutt for four years, they'd formed a bond of friendship and trust. Wherever their careers took them, they would remain part of her tribe. They would always be welcome in her home.

They saved her life.

The process of hiring a property manager was the only real responsibility she'd had over the last few months, and she'd handled it the best way she could—with friends. Martina, Cassie, and Mutt sorted through the hundreds of resumes until they'd narrowed down the list to five final candidates Nefi interviewed in person. She flew the candidates to Richmond one by one to show them the facility. She and three residents of the Stockton Lofts, who were elected by the others, conducted the interviews. All agreed on the third candidate they interviewed.

The Marine served two tours in the Middle East, and though he had a prosthetic foot, he was fully capable of handling repairs and managing the property. He had spent summers in his uncle's construction company building apartment complexes. His confidence and emotional maturity impressed Nefi. His appearance wowed the female residents, and his professionalism won over the male residents. When Nefi offered him the job, he said he would give her an answer in a week because he was also interviewing for a job in another city. Nefi mentioned the ground-floor loft came with the job. A week later, he accepted the offer.

In September, he sent Nefi a wish list of improvements

for the building's gym and a plan to reorganize the room. By October first, the new equipment was installed, and the manager held a meeting with the residents in which he offered to design personal exercise plans and teach the safe use of the equipment and weights. He sent weekly reports to Nefi with itemized expenses, repairs, and receipts. Residents emailed her their thanks.

With that responsibility off her shoulders, Nefi dedicated her time to shooting, taking weekly dance lessons with Vincent, studying, meeting Vincent in Virginia to get their marriage license, shopping for wedding dresses with Martina, and completing the pre-marital counseling with the priest. She believed she could learn something from everyone, but discussing sex with the priest felt absurd. Why would a celibate know more about sex than a virgin?

Soon she would be married and spend a two-week honeymoon with Vincent before launching into her master's studies in psychology. She daydreamed about the honeymoon. Had her research reading been a waste of time?

A beam of sunlight filtered through the umbrella, illuminating her engagement ring with bursts of color. Nefi moved the ring slightly to watch the sparkling colors change. When she looked up, Terri smiled at her and raised her rum punch. Nefi smiled. Marriage did not guarantee happiness or remove challenges. Terri's marriage to Blake proved challenges come to even the best marriages. But, oh, to face life beside someone who loved you through good and bad times! Marriage allowed Nefi to choose who would be in her family. She chose Vincent. He had been with her through the worst days of her life.

Nefi chose to live like she died and came back.

·30·

Saturday, December 18, 2010

THE DOUBLE WEDDING at St. Luke Catholic Church in McLean, Virginia, began in the late afternoon to end near dinnertime. What Vincent remembered of the service was when Nefi entered the sanctuary's threshold with her hand tucked into Senator Jenkin's arm. Nefi was a vision of beauty in a simple, long flowing gown with her face partly hidden under a lace veil. Seeing her stirred his soul. His second thought was—how did she plan to dance in that dress? He had assumed she would wear one with a hem just below the knees.

They had met every weekend in November at a dance studio in the city to practice their first dance. He remembered Nefi dancing with Blake at Ruis's wedding like competitive ballroom dancers. Vincent was raised in a Polish family. Unfortunately, polka wasn't popular, but it was the only dance he knew. He vowed to step out of his comfort zone to dance with Nefi.

When Vincent suggested they make their first dance amazing, Nefi eagerly found teachers in Manhattan to plan and practice a jaw-dropping dance. The instructors were so proud of their choreography that they filmed the last session so Vincent and Nefi could see how they looked together. The dance teachers were coming to the reception to record the performance for their website. They said tall people make dance moves look more dramatic.

When Nefi walked down the aisle with her uncle, Vincent noticed the wedding gown's design. From the hip down, the skirt had layers of overlapping vertical strips of fabric. As Nefi walked, the flowing strips parted to show her ankles and calves. *Simple. Elegant. Ingenious.*

After the long Catholic ceremony, the guests followed the snowplowed path from the church to the school gym for the dinner reception. During the hectic holiday season, they considered themselves blessed to get the gym. It was within walking distance of the sanctuary and large enough to accommodate their reception. The wedding party and assorted family members stayed in the sanctuary for photos for their wedding albums. By the time the wedding party entered the gym, everyone was ready to eat, and some were downing their third drink.

Ruis hired a security crew for the evening. Dressed in black, they vetted the catering staff, the bartenders, the DJ, and even the priests. They patrolled the entrances and exits and politely checked the names and photo IDs of guests against the guest list. Their no-nonsense expressions and military postures brought respect and order.

The unspoken and absent family members cast a shadow over conversations. Guests avoided discussing politics, sex, religion, and the Wrights. After dinner,

Vincent spotted Louise Jenkins sitting alone at the head table, so he sat beside her. "What do you think of Jane and Ted Wright?"

Louise sipped her champagne in silence.

Vincent nodded. "No longer part of your social circle?"

"That, yes, and I taught Nefi, 'if you can't say something nice, say nothing at all.'"

In the comfortable silence that followed, Vincent smiled. After a minute or so of watching people socialize, he said, "I'm glad you and Senator Jenkins took Nefi in."

"We were terrified at first." Louise sighed. "After we lost Jason to drugs, I had no confidence. I was heartbroken and not ready to be a parent again."

"The way I see it, you have done heroic work with Nefi. She has a strong faith, wears shoes, and eats with silverware—"

Louise swatted Vincent's arm as she giggled.

"And now," he said, "I completely understand why she goes by Nefi instead of her given name."

Louise's eyes widened. "Did she finally tell you?"

"I saw her birth certificate when we applied for the marriage license." He couldn't speak the name because he feared being overheard. Her legal name lit up his consciousness like a movie marquee. Nefertiti Olivia Jenkins.

"Marta, bless her soul, had a bit of a bohemian streak." Louise sighed. "I think Herman should have put up a fight for a more traditional name."

Martina gathered up an armload of her lace skirt and parked herself in a chair beside Louise. "What's so funny?"

Vincent said, "I'm trying to imagine Nefi with another name. Susan? Kathy? Ann?" In his mind, none of them suited Nefi.

"A rose by any other name—" Martina offered.

Vincent groaned. He did not want to hear that name at his wedding. It felt like bad luck.

Louise arched one eyebrow and planted a hand on Martina's forearm. "Long ago, your mother gave me permission to spank you if you needed it."

Martina patted Louise's hand, kissed her on the cheek, said, "Time to cut the cake!" and dashed from the table.

Vincent followed her and took his place beside Nefi and their cake. Mr. De Souza posed for the photographer with Nefi and Vincent beside his masterpiece, then he shook Vincent's hand and hugged Nefi. Mr. De Souza whispered something in Nefi's ear and then moved to the far wall by his wife.

Martina and Oscar stood by their three-tier cake and an aunt who had made the cake while the photographer captured the moment. Oscar and Martina cut their cake and fed each other a bite to blinding flashes from phones and digital cameras held by the family, friends, and the hired photographer.

Nefi and Vincent then fed each other a forkful of their cake and headed back to their table to watch Oscar and Martina's first dance. People vacated the dance floor in the center of the gymnasium, and the DJ on the stage introduced Oscar and Martina with all the fanfare of a Vegas boxing match.

Guests returned to their tables which had been arranged to face the dance floor. The room lights dimmed, and spotlights illuminated Oscar and Martina. Their first dance featured a popular romantic ballad which reminded Vincent of a fairytale. They swept across the floor gracefully. Mrs. Ramos and the Admiral grew teary-eyed and held hands throughout the dance.

Vincent knew his parents would have adored Nefi and Martina. Oscar and Vincent fulfilled the promise made at their mother's deathbed to marry for love. If not for cancer, she would have been here dancing. Vincent draped his arm around Nefi's shoulders.

Nefi rested her head on his shoulder. "I just won a bet." An enticing, fresh perfume radiated from her.

"You did?"

"Martina said her mom would cry first. I predicted the Admiral would."

Sure enough, the Admiral was first to raise a handkerchief to his eyes.

Though Nefi's parents were gone, she had many surrogate parents here, Senator and Mrs. Jenkins, godparents Ambassador and Mrs. Morales, and Martina's parents. All held influential positions in government, but to Nefi, they were family. She would have loved them just as fiercely if they were day laborers.

Oscar and Martina ended their dance with a flourish and a bow. Applause and cheers filled the gym, rising to the cloth-draped ceiling and spreading out to the walls. Vincent and Nefi joined others in a standing ovation.

Vincent led Nefi around the head table toward the dance floor. On the way, he passed Blake and Terri. Blake had his hands steepled in front of his chin and his elbows on the table. Though they became friends years ago in basic training, Blake never saw Vincent dance. He suspected Blake was praying for him to get through the dance without crushing Nefi's feet. Vincent expected the result of the secret dance lessons would amaze the wedding guests.

The DJ introduced Vincent and Nefi Gunnerson, who took their places in the center of the dance floor, hand in hand and facing the guests. They took a deep breath in unison, followed by the introductory drumbeat rhythm.

The song "Smooth" came from Santana's Supernatural album. It seemed fitting to Vincent because Nefi was supernatural in her ability to read people. Sadly, she struggled to read people she deeply loved. Like the rest of the population, sometimes she saw what she wanted to see.

The dance started with almost slow-motion movements punctuated with double-time steps and twirls. The Latin rhythm added sex appeal to the choreographed steps. At times they raised their arms, drawing their bodies together, followed by a fast breakaway and then circling as they mirrored each other. At times the dance resembled a tango. To Vincent, it felt like foreplay. Occasionally, Nefi stretched a long leg out from the dress to reveal her athletic form. At one point in the dance, Nefi untied his bowtie. Vincent gently dipped Nefi and eased off her veil. At the end of the dance, Nefi plucked his bowtie free and let it fall. By the time it landed, they were breathing hard and looked a bit unraveled.

The moment after the dance ended, the crowd collectively took a breath and then cheered like Superbowl fans witnessing a winning touchdown. Vincent rescued Nefi's veil from the floor just before the crowd stormed the dance floor, and the DJ fired up a more familiar dance tune that kept people there.

In the crush of gyrating people, Terri leaned toward Vincent and said, "That was incredible!"

Blake added, "I need a cold shower."

Vincent laughed because Blake grew up on a horse-breeding farm. This was high praise.

After Nefi and Vincent visited with guests at each table, the DJ played more slow dance songs. Ruis, Blake, Vincent, Oscar, and Arlo gathered at an empty table near the bartender. Vincent had a ginger ale, and he was glad to be off his feet while Nefi and Martina visited with friends.

Ruis leaned back in his chair. "Nefi tells me you owe me money."

Arlo removed four fifty-dollar bills from his wallet and handed them across the table to Ruis.

Vincent glanced at Blake, who shrugged.

Arlo, the only single man at the table, turned toward Vincent. "Blake said when he met Terri, it was love at first sight. Was it love at first sight for you and Nefi?"

Blake laughed first, followed by Ruis and Oscar.

Vincent rubbed his hand over his mouth.

Oscar, Ruis, and Blake laughed harder every time they exchanged glances. Blake's laugh was infectious and amusing to watch as he leaned back in his chair and waved at the others to make them stop. Ruis shook his head as he laughed. Though Oscar had not been there to witness that first meeting between Nefi and Vincent, he'd heard the story from Vincent and Blake.

First impressions last a lifetime. Images of Nefi armed with a machete and a knife, glaring at him, her face streaked with black and red paint, flashed through his mind. At fourteen years old, she moved so much faster than he expected she could have easily killed him. While his friends laughed out of control, Vincent realized he was still a little scared of her. "She impressed me."

·31·

Friday, August 19, 2011

JANE WRIGHT ENTERED her home, locked the front door, and deactivated the alarm. On her way through the kitchen, she flipped the light switch and headed straight to the nearly empty pantry for a fresh bottle. Exhausted from the day, she needed to unwind.

She kicked off her sensible heels, dropped her purse on the counter, and set the bottle of cheap Amaretto beside it. She would have preferred Kahlua in her coffee, but with the cost of air-conditioning a two-story, ten-thousand-square-foot mansion in August, she couldn't bear drinking anything hot. Opening windows upstairs helped, but she didn't have the energy for the stairs at the moment. She opened the kitchen windows and walked through the half-empty study to open windows for cross-ventilation. The furniture in the study smelled like a wet dog.

She returned to the kitchen, filled a bowl with ice, and jammed the Amaretto bottle and the glass in the bowl. She carried the bowl past the living room and dining room to the Florida room overlooking the garden. The late afternoon was the hottest part of the day, but Jane planned to stay in the room until she could see the stars. The ceiling fan still worked, so she set it on high and settled into a wicker chair where she filled a sizeable cut-glass tumbler with Amaretto.

A long swallow ended with a moan. What a wasted day!

The meeting with her lawyer turned into a long argument because he urged her to take a plea deal weeks ahead of her scheduled court date. He reminded her of the $750,000 bond on her house as if she'd forgotten. She understood the stakes of winning and losing. The attorney then, of course, asked for payment toward his ever-increasing bill.

During the depressing three-hour briefing, he reviewed the state's evidence shared during discovery. The District Attorney named each transfer to the Cayman Islands as a separate act of embezzlement over $1,000. He called it larceny. If found guilty, she could face one to twenty years in prison for each count. Technically, she set up the Cayman account and regularly transferred money into it, but she didn't own the money. The Trust did. She even found the original paperwork in the attic to show she had set up the account legally and properly.

Her lawyer bickered about details, saying the paperwork didn't matter because the funds were not reported to the investment company that managed the trust. As if anything not known to the almighty IRS had to be outright fraud.

For every point she made, he attacked. Truly, the only

money she took was a tiny fraction of the millions safely tucked away in the Cayman account.

She downed her drink and refilled the glass. The money should have been hers all along. If Father had been in his right mind, none of this would have happened.

Movement in the garden caught her attention. It could have been the shadow of a bird flying over the willow tree. She hadn't left a feeder out in months, but birds loved to sing in her garden. An area of green mold on the window partly blocked her view, so she stood and opened the door to the garden. The dark shape crossed the flagstone walkway and stopped beside the bench.

Believing it was a squirrel, she stepped outside and grabbed a metal rake to chase the hole-digging pest away. It turned as she approached. Seeing the creature had a long thin tail instead of a bushy one, Jane jerked to a stop and swung the rake. The rat and the rake bounced off the bench and landed on the stone walkway.

The creature squealed and thrashed while Jane backed away and ran into the house. She shut the door firmly and collapsed into her chair. *A rat! Where did that disgusting thing come from?* She slouched in the chair and hummed, rocking herself until she could breathe normally.

She hadn't been in the garden in weeks. Strands of tea lights hung broken from the willow tree and the far wall. Shriveled forsythia proved how long the irrigation system had been broken. Was the timer broken or the motor? She chided herself for forgetting to call the repairman. Without the gardener, weeds and vines had overtaken the flower beds and crept up the tree trunk.

Without the cleaning lady, the kitchen floors had become sticky, the toilets stunk, and the unused surfaces in the house resembled a light snowfall. Jane drove across town to buy groceries so she wouldn't face questions from nosy neighbors and her old friends. The local pastor regularly called to check on her and invite her to his Sunday service. She was tempted to tell him the believer in the family moved out, but the preacher's calls reminded her she wasn't invisible.

She drank and refilled her glass. It warmed her and helped her sleep. Some nights when she couldn't sleep, she read whatever novels Ted had left in the library. Other nights she watched cable television and drank until her mind quieted.

The neighbors had to notice her coming and going and see lights through the windows, and yet, she felt she was fading away like a color movie changing to black and white. No more juggling social events. When couples divorced, their friends tended to choose sides. Why was it then that her friends disappeared? With Ted gone to his new life in North Carolina, there was no awkwardness about running into him in Richmond.

Were her friends distancing themselves from scandal? She was innocent until proven guilty. Or had her friends already judged her?

Impaired by Amaretto and darkness, she stumbled from the Florida room to the master bedroom upstairs and fell onto the unmade bed.

Everyone expected her to quietly disappear, go to prison, and surrender everything she worked for.

"Go ahead. Underestimate me. We'll see how that turns out."

She sat up, staggered into her half-empty bedroom closet, and found a small, heavy metal lockbox. She carried it across the room. Knocking over makeup and brushes on her vanity, she set the box down. She managed, after three attempts, to enter the correct number code and open the box. She stared into it.

Life is like playing chess. If you play the way everyone expects you to, you lose every time.

·32·

Tuesday, August 23, 2011

AFTER EIGHT MONTHS of marriage, Nefi considered her life blessed. She finished her first semester at CUNY Hunter College on the Dean's List, and Vincent continued to work at the New York Office of the FBI. World events in the news included the March 9.0 magnitude earthquake and tsunami that hit Japan, forcing the shutdown of three nuclear reactors. SEAL Team 6 killed terrorist Osama Bin Laden. The last flight of the United States' 30-year space shuttle program launched from Florida. And a gunman murdered 77 people at a youth camp in Norway. The crimes reinforced Nefi's goal to work at the FBI. The natural disaster in Japan reminded her to count each day as a gift.

Oscar and Martina lived in Nagano, a city in the southwest part of Japan. Though they were well outside the flooded areas, they said they felt the strongest earthquake in the country's history for four minutes, followed by hundreds of aftershocks. Over fifteen thousand people died from the tsunami, which destroyed east coast cities with waves twelve stories high, flooding 217 square miles. Oscar's drones helped search teams locate the missing, injured, and dead. Nefi struggled to imagine such destruction. She was grateful her best friend and Oscar had been spared.

In early August, Mingmei called to say *The Sentinel-Times* agreed to meet a week before the scheduled trial, so Nefi and Vincent flew to Virginia.

It was an overcast Tuesday morning in Richmond, Virginia, on August twenty-third. Outside the Richmond courthouse, Nefi and Vincent met up with Mingmei and her driver.

Vincent looked sexy and uncharacteristically casual in boots, jeans, a t-shirt, and a leather bomber jacket.

Mingmei glanced up at Vincent. "Good to see you again."

Vincent shook hands with her before turning toward the driver. "I'm Vincent Gunnerson."

Mingmei's driver's eyes widened, and he held Vincent's hand in a firm grip. "You are the man who broke Helen's arm?"

Vincent bowed his head and gave a quick nod.

Nefi's back tensed, and she stepped toward the driver.

Mingmei cleared her throat.

He released Vincent's hand. "My name is Hu."

Mingmei spoke softly, "Hu is my cousin and very protective. His name means tiger." To Hu, she said something in Mandarin.

Hu said, "I know it was an accident. I wanted to see his reaction."

Mingmei shook her head and sighed.

Nefi exhaled. The name suited him. He looked calm, like a tiger in the zoo. All the same, Nefi knew Mr. Hu was also a bodyguard by the way he scanned the environment. When a group of businessmen passed by on the sidewalk, Hu's attention went to their hands and torsos as if searching for weapons.

Mingmei's silk top was red, a powerful color in Chinese culture. Her black suit and leather notebook matched her hair with straight, clean lines. She told Vincent and Hu to wait outside the courthouse.

To comply with courthouse rules, Nefi opened her suit jacket and removed her handgun and the holster from the waistband of her pants. When she gave the holstered gun to Vincent, Hu reacted with a flicker of one eyebrow and a half-grin. Nefi's pants hung looser without the holster. She tucked her white shirt back into her black slacks and rebuttoned her black suit jacket.

"Cell phones aren't allowed." Vincent held out his hand.

Nefi grudgingly gave him her cell phone. She squared her shoulders and braced herself for the meeting. With her hair in a loose French braid from her forehead to the middle of her back, she wanted to impress the newspaper representatives as a poised professional.

"How do I look?"

Vincent replied, "Beautiful." He stuck the holstered gun in one pocket of his leather jacket and the cell phone in the other.

Nefi then raised her eyebrows at Mingmei for her opinion.

"Like a federal agent." Mingmei eyed her. "The boots are a nice touch. They put you at eye level with men."

Understated elegance was Nefi's goal, but she was

pleased with the federal agent look. She wore her wedding ring, the diamond stud earrings Martina's brother Ruis had given her as a high school graduation gift, and a gold Seiko watch.

Nefi and Mingmei entered the courthouse and passed through security. During their elevator ride, Mingmei briefed Nefi about rumors of management changes at the paper. The Wrights had finalized their divorce. Jane got the house and an annuity worth half a million. To Nefi, this seemed like a fortune and enough to support a woman in her sixties for the rest of her life.

The elevator doors slid open, and Mingmei led the way down a brightly lit corridor that smelled faintly of paint and bleach to a dark wood-paneled room. Two men stood on one side of a large rectangular oak table. Mingmei and Nefi pulled out chairs across from them.

This was the first time Nefi had seen her grandfather since the shooting. A flicker of childhood longing for family flitted through her, and she reminded herself her grandfather owned the newspaper that smeared her reputation. *They started this.* She could not let it stand unchallenged.

Ted Wright introduced himself and Armand Lightner, the publisher.

Nefi reached across the table to shake hands with the new man in charge. It made sense that the past and present publishers would negotiate a deal.

Mingmei simply nodded at the men and sat. She placed a slim leather-bound notebook on the table and opened it. Her notes were written in Hanzi, a written language from China used for thousands of years.

With the introductions done, Nefi ended eye contact across the table. Everyone opened notebooks and uncapped pens except for Nefi. With a click and a hum, the air-conditioner kicked on. Mingmei reviewed her notes. Nefi sensed the men watching her.

The mediator entered and introduced himself as a retired circuit court judge. He resembled Nefi's high school track coach. A tall man with a receding hairline, he looked fit and healthy. He schooled his face like an expert poker player, smiling at times without showing his teeth or crinkling the wrinkles around his eyes. His one unguarded reaction flashed when he saw Nefi. Surprise.

He took the seat at the end of the table and addressed the opposing parties with his ground rules and procedures. He asked for them to conduct all negotiations in good faith and civil tone to spare everyone the need for a public trial. He invited Mingmei to begin.

Mingmei distributed color handouts and summarized her case against the newspaper with examples of coverage from other major news outlets. She detailed the article, from its inflammatory headline to the article's tone, line by line, as it painted Nefi as a violent, unstable person. Following that, she compared *The Sentinel-Times'* coverage against the same-day coverage from local, regional, and national news companies. Every media source except *The Sentinel-Times* stated that Nefi defended herself from an unprovoked shooting. Point by point, she showed how the Times article was both defamatory and malicious. Considering Nefi's career goals and the loss of the internship at the FBI at a key point in her education, the libel was pointedly damaging to her reputation.

Though Nefi did not have a social media account of any kind, Mingmei directed the men to read the printouts and statistics of the nasty, negative mentions of Nefi

Jenkins in the months following *The Sentinel-Times* front-page story. Most social media comments were linked to the newspaper's social media accounts and website. Like many employers these days, the FBI reviewed an applicant's social media accounts and mentions. Mingmei said she could not accurately measure the responses from the eighty-thousand subscribers and the untold number of readers of the printed newspaper. She asked for a front-page retraction of the story. She did not mention money. She then referred everyone to the last two pages, which listed affidavits of people quoted in the original article who said they'd been egregiously misquoted.

Nefi sat stunned at the volume and hatefulness of the messages documented in the handout. By the fifth page of them, Nefi closed the papers and calmed herself by breathing in four-second stages of inhaling, holding her breath, exhaling, and waiting to inhale. Martina's brother Ruis taught Nefi to do this when she felt emotional. Ruis followed the teachings of the ancient Stoics and applied them to his training as a Navy SEAL.

A few of her favorite stoic rules were to focus on what you can control, control how you respond to things, and don't suffer imagined troubles. She had always embraced the philosophy of valuing time more than money and possessions. These thoughts kept her calm during the arbitration.

Because the trial date fell so close to the last week of the internship, Nefi did not reapply to the FBI's 2011 summer program. The loss felt like a wound. It would have been her third attempt to apply for the program. Were many master's degree students accepted into the internship?

Participation felt like a faraway dream. Another year, another lost opportunity.

Mr. Lightner rose from his chair to present his case, in which he said the paper stood by the accuracy of the profile piece, though the tone of it was regrettable. At that point, Nefi tuned out emotionally and watched as a spectator would watch a high-stakes game of chess. There was nothing she could do to change the outcome of the game, and she trusted Mingmei to counter their moves one by one.

At the end of their presentation, they asked to convene in another room, so the mediator called for a fifteen-minute break and led the men out.

After they left, Mingmei turned toward Nefi. "Thank you for maintaining composure. That must have been hard to hear."

Nefi nodded. "What happens now?"

"They will offer something, and negotiations will go back and forth for hours. This is normal, so be patient. As I told you before, they don't want to admit guilt because libel is a crime, and they are in the information business." Mingmei picked up her pen and wrote on a clean page of her notebook. Her note read: *"When I lean close and whisper, 'what do you think?' that means I recommend the offer."*

Nefi gently took Mingmei's pen and wrote: *"Do you think we are being bugged?"*

Mingmei said, "It has happened before."

Nefi was tempted to search under the table, but she didn't know the size or shape of such a listening device. A retraction or apology on the newspaper's front page would harm its reputation. That was the point. Let them be ashamed of their attack on her reputation.

Mingmei's prediction unfolded over hours of monetary offers and rejections, with the mediator traveling from room to room. Lunch arrived at eleven. Mingmei and Nefi walked together to the ladies' room for breaks.

At noon, the arbitrator said he admonished the publisher's legal team and Mingmei that they would eventually face each other in court if they didn't reach an agreement by 5 p.m. He then returned to the room where Mingmei and Nefi waited, parked himself in a chair on the other side of the table, and faced the women.

"What would be your dream deal?" He addressed his question to Nefi.

"A front-page retraction," Nefi said.

The mediator nodded. "You understand the newspaper doesn't want to admit they committed a crime."

"In a public trial, they would have to explain why their profile on me was so much more personal and slanted than all the other news outlets." Nefi believed a jury would be appalled when the people quoted in the article described how shocked they were to read the article because it did not represent the context of their interviews.

"If you could only have one thing, either a monetary settlement or a retraction, which—"

"A retraction," Nefi said.

The mediator looked at Mingmei as if anticipating her input.

After a moment of silence, Mingmei said, "I told them upfront what we wanted, and they keep offering money. Should we remind them my client has ten million dollars at her disposal?"

The mediator glanced down at his notepad and flipped pages. "You never asked for money," the mediator mumbled as he searched his notes. Finally, he rocked back in his chair and seemed to mull over the revelation. After a single headshake, he said, "Now that money is on the table, do you plan to refuse it?"

Mingmei answered, "Why would we bargain down?"

A raised eyebrow and a flicker of a grin later, he stood and left the room.

Thirty minutes later, he delivered the newspaper's third offer and sat at the table for a response. The monetary offer was a $400,000 lump sum payment and a front-page retraction above the fold. The retraction was worded well and included the facts of the attack on Nefi from the police report. It stated deep regret for the tone of the original article and concluded with the announcement of Ted Wright's resignation. Including the announcement suggested Ted Wright was, in effect, falling on his sword for his lapse of judgment for the sake of the newspaper. The offer stipulated that Nefi would have to agree to drop the defamation lawsuit once and for all.

Nefi expected Mingmei to lean back, but instead, Mingmei spoke to the arbitrator.

"Does Ted Wright have any stock or position with *The Sentinel-Times*?"

The arbitrator left the room and returned minutes later. "Mr. Wright sold all shares upon his divorce. His resignation is complete. He does not serve on the board or in any capacity with the company. His permanent residence is in North Carolina, and he holds no property in Virginia."

"When will the retraction be published?"

"Tomorrow, if all parties agree." He remained standing.

Mingmei leaned in and whispered, "What do you think?"

Nefi whispered, "I am satisfied."

Mingmei said, "Agreed."

By 12:30 p.m., the agreement was signed and witnessed in separate rooms. In the agreement, Mingmei would withdraw the defamation lawsuit and cancel the court date after the publication of the retraction. Upon proof the lawsuit is withdrawn, *The Sentinel-Times* must immediately pay $400,000 to Nefi Gunnerson and record the payment with the court.

On his last trip into their room, the mediator gave Mingmei a sealed envelope addressed to Nefi from Ted Wright along with her copy of the agreement.

"What's this?" Mingmei held the envelope.

"Mr. Wright said it's a personal note for his granddaughter." With that, he walked around the table and shook hands with Mingmei. "It was a pleasure to meet you out of court."

Mingmei gave him a smile and a nod.

Nefi stood to shake the mediator's hand, and as they shook hands, she said, "Thank you, sir."

The mediator left the room. Mingmei handed the envelope to Nefi and placed her papers in her briefcase.

The note from Ted Wright showed Nefi's name in his large loopy handwriting. Nefi stuffed it in her jacket pocket to read later. Eager to share the news with Vincent, she and Mingmei headed to the elevator. With just the two of them in the elevator, Nefi said, "What do I owe you?"

"How about my hourly rate for the time spent in the mediation?"

Mingmei's generous gesture ignored the cost of travel and preparation time, and who knew what other expenses the day cost. "That's very generous, thank you." It didn't matter to Nefi how much it cost because Mingmei helped restore her reputation. Nefi would download a digital version of the apology article to place in her job file along with the recommendations from the past and present heads of the New York City FBI office and her college professors.

They strolled out of the elevator and the courthouse into the sunlight.

∾

Vincent and Hu waited on a bench in the shade to watch the entrance where Mingmei and Nefi had disappeared hours earlier. The bench had concrete molded sides and wooden slats as a backrest and seat, discouraging long-term use. Like any courthouse, this building had public entrances, entrances for lawyers and courthouse employees, and a secured rear entrance for the jail van.

For the first hour, the men didn't talk. Hu played a logic puzzle game on his phone while Vincent watched people. Out of boredom, Vincent entertained himself by remembering classic rock tunes. Hu's name reminded him of a song by a classic rock band, The Who. As the tune played in Vincent's head, the lyrics changed to suit the large cryptic man beside him. *Huuuuu are you? Hu. Hu. Hu. Hu.*

It was okay if Hu didn't trust him. He would feel the same way if their roles were reversed. Helen knew Vincent broke her arm accidentally, and her knowledge mattered more than Hu's opinion.

Vincent's cellphone vibrated in his jacket, so he answered it.

"Hey, hop-a-long."

Vincent stood and stepped away from Hu. "Hey, Oscar."

"When do you get the cast removed?"

His brother and Martina would never let them forget his honeymoon injury. "Last month. How are you?"

"Still waiting for details."

They had hiked, kayaked on the ocean, dived in a cave, gone hang-gliding, horseback riding, and swimming without injury. Getting tangled up in the sheets and falling out of bed with Nefi had sent him to the hospital. "How's Martina?"

"You can tell me anything, brother."

"I'll call you later with news about the mediation." Vincent pocketed his cell phone.

At lunchtime, Vincent strolled to a food truck and brought back food for himself and Hu. The sky changed from overcast to scattered clouds, and a breeze from the west picked up speed.

People rushed into the courthouse with briefcases and coffee. Others paced outside and checked their watches. Officers patrolled the downtown and shooed the homeless away from the building and grounds. Though most of the indigent were males, one pudgy female wandered along the walkway, pushing a rusty stroller loaded with clothes. After the police officer left the courthouse area, a scrawny, wild-eyed homeless man emerged from a hedge and walked toward Vincent and Hu. Vincent was reaching in his pocket for cash when Hu rose to his feet and faced the man. Hu stared until the man pivoted and rushed along the hedge toward the curb.

Hu returned to his spot on the bench and sat with a huff.

Vincent raised his eyebrows.

"Parasites."

"That's harsh."

Hu grunted. "They get fleas and lice from sleeping on the ground. I itch thinking about such things. I have many places I cannot reach to scratch."

Vincent laughed, which made Hu laugh. Vincent feared Hu would burst the seams of his suit, which made him laugh even more.

"Thank you for avoiding small talk." Hu looked directly at Vincent. "It is tiresome to chat about weather and politics and sports. Some people are uncomfortable with silence. Others talk to hear their own voices."

"You'd get along well with Nefi."

Hu straightened his back. "A woman of few words?"

"She told me silence makes words meaningful."

"A wise young woman." Hu slapped his knees.

After lunch, the tree canopy no longer shaded Vincent's half of the cement bench, so he opened his bomber jacket to cool off. Hu looked up from his phone and pocketed it. Next, he stood and waved for Vincent to get up. Hu then squatted, lifted the cement and wood-slat bench, side-stepped into the shade, and set it down. Without a word, he sat back down and resumed the game on his phone while Vincent wondered how much the bench weighed.

After a few moments, Hu glanced up.

"Thank you." Intimidated, Vincent returned to his half of the bench to enjoy the shade.

At noon thirty, Mingmei and Nefi strolled out of the courthouse. The ladies were smiling in animated conversation. Vincent stood, which caused Hu to look up and stand as well.

Mingmei stopped in front of Vincent. "One case down, one to go. Do you have the September court date on your calendar?"

"Yes, ma'am." Vincent appreciated having this formidable lawyer representing Nefi. He saw a strong resemblance between Mingmei Cho and her sister Helen. Together the sisters championed Nefi's best interests despite whatever grudge they still held toward him.

"I will see you both then." She smiled at Hu, and they continued down the walkway toward the road. Hu's Towncar was parked at the curb under a large oak tree.

Nefi hugged Vincent and spoke into his ear. "The newspaper is publishing a front-page retraction tomorrow and a lump sum settlement of four-hundred-thousand."

"Congratulations."

As their embrace loosened, he slipped her holster from his pocket and held it close to her stomach. When she took it, he opened his jacket to hide her while she secured the holster to the waistband of her pants, appendix-carry style. He preferred to keep his weapon under his armpit for easy reach. Appendix-carry bothered him because he had read about men shooting off vital parts while drawing their guns. One slip near the trigger and, bang, eunuch time. He dreaded that more than a shot to the femoral artery in the thigh.

"Mingmei said Mutt and Helen are engaged."

The thought of that unlikely pairing made him smile. "Have they set a date?" He handed Nefi her cell phone.

Without glancing at it, Nefi stuffed it in her jacket pocket. "Sometime after Mutt graduates next summer. He and Cassie are a semester ahead of me because they took summer classes." She had a wistful look as she reached her left hand around his arm.

He bent his right arm and escorted her toward the parking garage the way his father had taught him. A gentleman walked closer to the road as if to shield a lady from harm or splashing mud. He knew Nefi didn't want to stay in Richmond any longer than necessary. His watch read 1:50 p.m. "Do you want to see if we can catch an earlier flight—"

Dogs started barking, and birds burst from trees around the courthouse square. It spooked Vincent so much that he stopped walking. The moment reminded him of a time in the jungle years ago. An eerie quiet fell before a jaguar appeared at the riverbank. Monkeys, birds, and even insects stilled in the presence of danger.

"What's happening?" Nefi's attention followed the flight of an owl overhead. She let go of Vincent's arm.

BANG. Something sharp slammed into Vincent's right thigh, knocking him down on his knee in burning pain. "Gun!"

Nefi gasped.

People screamed and scattered. Vincent dropped to his right side and rolled to a sitting position on the sidewalk while he yanked his gun from the holster. He secured both hands on his Glock 21 service handgun and scanned for the threat.

A homeless woman stood beside a fallen stroller. Was she frozen in shock? She was fumbling with something shiny in her hands.

Nefi roared a powerful, primal sound of rage. "Noooo!"

Nefi's voice raised the hair on Vincent's arms, then the ground shook. Car alarms squealed, and a store window shattered. Bomb blast? The shaking continued. The home-less woman raised the object in her hands. A revolver? Vincent aimed his Glock at her while she aimed high and to the left, where Nefi stood.

The world fell into a vacuum of silence, and seconds stretched into slow motion, full of detail. The homeless woman's face contorted into fury. The revolver muzzle flashed, and the woman closed her eyes at the sound of the blast and the recoil. Vincent aimed for the woman's center of mass—heart, lungs, and spine—and gently squeezed the trigger, reset aim, squeezed, reset aim, and squeezed. His hands and arms vibrated with each firing against his tight grip on the gun. Sunlight flashed on the brass car-tridges ejecting to his right. The homeless woman jerked backward from the impact of each bullet to the chest, which sent fabric flying.

A fourth bullet struck her between her eyebrows, snap-ping her head back. *Kill shot.* The revolver fell. Her arms and torso landed on the concrete and bounced. Then she was still.

Vincent looked up to confirm the kill shot came from Nefi, but she was falling away from him, her braid flying until she dropped to her hands and knees on the grass. The world stopped shaking. Car alarms and screams filled the air. One of the voices was his.

"Noooo!" He holstered his gun and scrambled on his knees to Nefi. His hands shook as he reached for her shoulder.

She dropped to her hip and sat facing the body on the sidewalk. She blinked and grimaced and looked around as if to get her bearings. When her face turned toward him, she rose to her knees. She withdrew her finger from the trigger and wrapped it around the grip.

Over the noise and commotion around them and the ringing in their ears, they panted, staring at one another.

Vincent's leg stung like he'd been struck by a line drive. He needed to see what caused Nefi to fall. On his knees, he pressed his left hand on his thigh where it hurt, and warm blood seeped through his fingers.

Nefi gasped and leaned toward him to press the wound.

That was when he noticed blood dripping on her white shirt. A chorus of discordant car alarms wailed.

A police officer ran toward them with his right hand on his holster and his left hand pointing to the ground. Vincent raised his hands. Nefi turned to face the officer and set down her gun near the officer's feet. Vincent pulled back the lapel of his leather jacket to show his holstered weapon, and he slowly withdrew it, barrel down, and laid it on the sidewalk.

The officer nudged the handguns away from Vincent and Nefi while he spoke into a walkie-talkie on his shoulder. Between the car alarms and the ringing in his ears, Vincent strained to hear the officer. The officer mouthed a series of police code numbers Vincent interpreted as 'shooting' and 'ambulance needed.'

Nefi once again pressed her hands over his wound.

Gently, Vincent held Nefi's chin and turned her head. A line of blood ran along her cheek to her ear. A notch of her ear tissue was missing. He flung his arms around her and thanked God the bullet only grazed her.

"You're bleeding," Nefi spoke into his ear.

"So are you, my love. I need to slow the bleeding." He leaned his back on the grass and reached for his belt.

He hoped for a through and through and that the bullet missed the artery and bone.

Two large, meaty hands suddenly clamped onto Vincent's thigh like a vise. Vincent groaned at the fresh pain. The burning sensation was almost as painful as the pressure.

"An ambulance is on the way, Mr. Gunnerson." Hu knelt beside him.

Through gritted teeth, Vincent said, "Call me Vincent."

Hu nodded. "We heard shots before the earthquake."

Earthquake? He recalled how the dogs and birds behaved before the eerie silence. "An earthquake in Virginia?"

"I grew up in California," Hu shouted. "That was an earthquake."

Mingmei pressed a lacy handkerchief on Nefi's ear.

Two crowds gathered, one around the body, the other around Vincent and Nefi.

"That woman shot Vincent," Nefi told Mingmei over the car alarms.

A heartbreaking percentage of the homeless have a mental illness or drug addiction. Perhaps the woman was having an episode of some kind. Something about the shooter seemed odd because her actions were focused and purposeful though it didn't look like she knew how to handle the weapon.

Mingmei blinked twice and inhaled before she said, "I believe she was aiming for you."

Nefi resembled the lost, frightened teenager he'd met in the Amazon for a moment. She didn't seem to understand or hear what Mingmei said because she did not react.

The threat was gone, but the damage would last. Vincent reached for Nefi's hands and held them over his heart.

Nefi looked at him with blood streaming down her worried face. Words would not comfort her now as much as the touch of someone she loved, someone who loved her more than he could express.

·33·

An **emergency medical** team loaded Vincent into an ambulance while Nefi held Mingmei's handkerchief to her face. A piece of her ear was missing, and she knew she'd have a scar, but she thought about it in an abstract way, as if assessing someone else's injury. Flashing lights, noise, and pain anchored Nefi in place. Police cruisers screeched to a stop along the road. She remained aware of her surroundings, but her body moved as if by remote control. One moment kneeling in front of Vincent, the next standing by Mingmei, and she couldn't remember getting up from the grass or how long she'd been standing.

The police officer who took Vincent's gun was bagging Nefi's, then Nefi turned toward the body on the sidewalk. A homeless woman with a gun caused all this chaos. Nefi took a step toward the heap.

Mingmei grabbed her arm. "Don't."

Out of trust, Nefi stopped. She remembered drawing her weapon and wondering if her legs were shaking or the ground was moving. After the homeless woman raised her gun, the muzzle flashed, and something scraped Nefi's face while she took aim, held her breath, and gently squeezed the trigger. Muscle memory from months of daily practice overcame emotion. The ten-yard shot was true—between the eyebrows.

Officers gathered to stake off the crime scene with wide yellow plastic tape as news vans arrived. Voices shouted over the car alarms, and a crowd gathered at the edge of the flimsy taped perimeter. Bystanders held up their cell phones toward Nefi and the body.

A crime scene van pulled to the curb between squad cars, and people in white jumpsuits spilled out. One of the technicians draped a plastic cloth over the body.

Where did all these people come from?

Among the onlookers was a familiar face. Nefi spotted Ted Wright and stared across the crime scene at him. Had he witnessed the shooting? Even in self-defense and to protect Vincent, the act of killing weighed on her. She had taken a life. Again.

Ted pushed through the crowd to look at the homeless woman. His curiosity turned to horror, sorrow, and recognition.

Nefi gasped. "Is that—?"

Mingmei pursed her lips and nodded. She and Hu flanked Nefi as they walked toward the uncovered body. Nefi willed her legs to move step by step. *No. No.* Someone shot Vincent and had to be stopped from shooting him again. Nefi had stopped the threat. *It couldn't be her! Jane lived in a mansion.*

A bald man in a dark gray suit blocked Nefi's path. With a latex-gloved hand, he pulled back his suit jacket to show a metal badge clipped to his waistband. "Do you remember me? I'm Detective Avery. Miss Jenkins, I need to ask you to come to the—" he tilted his head. "Are you hurt?"

Nefi peeled the handkerchief off for a moment to show him. "I'm Nefi Gunnerson now." The body wasn't going anywhere, but Nefi needed to see it.

Avery glanced at the departing ambulance, and his expression softened.

Nefi opened her right hand toward her friends, "My attorney, Mingmei Cho, and her driver, Hu."

All but the detective had blood evidence on their hands. Mingmei and Hu nodded at Detective Avery and held their positions. Avery glanced at his notepad and pen before jamming them in his jacket pocket.

"If that's who I think it is," Nefi said, opening her hand at the body, "I want closure. I won't go to the funeral."

Avery stared at Nefi's face. After a moment, his shoulders relaxed, and he said, "I can take you to identify the deceased."

Nefi followed the detective, leaving Mingmei and Hu behind. Officers moved out of his way, and he stopped four feet from the body. Detective Avery nodded to a crime scene technician, who then lifted the plastic blanket and held it like a curtain to block the view of one side of the crowd.

Unseeing eyes stared at the sky. The body wore loose, bulky layers of clothing topped with an unbelted beige raincoat. A silver revolver with a black grip rested on one side, and on the other side, a stroller dumped clothing toward the curb. Without makeup, the woman appeared faded and ten years older. Her face looked gaunt and angular instead of slender. The roundness of her torso seemed out of proportion to her bony face and hands. Nonetheless, this was the body of a person Nefi had loved from afar throughout her childhood. The body remained without the soul.

No longer angry or greedy or a narcissist, no longer a thief or a wife or a grandmother, Jane Wright was gone. Without the soul, it was simply a corpse.

This didn't have to happen. Nefi looked up and saw her grandfather's face contorted in grief. He turned and disappeared into the crowd.

"Can you positively identify this person?" Avery's voice brought Nefi back to his reason for allowing her this close.

"Jane Wright." Nefi wiped her eyes with the back of her right hand. With her left hand, she held Mingmei's handkerchief against her ear.

Nefi looked down where blood pooled from the head, but not the torso. Oddly, Vincent's shots were not marked with red stains. She asked Detective Avery, "Is she wearing body armor?"

Avery grunted. "Looks like she took shots to the chest," he spoke as if thinking out loud.

"Three from Vincent."

The technician re-draped the plastic blanket over the body.

Avery leaned close to Nefi. "I must advise you that whatever you say will be in my report."

Nefi spoke softly to Avery, "She shot Vincent from behind. We returned fire." *Let him investigate.* Ballistics will match the shots with the weapon and the shooters. Let him interview witnesses and gather recordings from security cameras. *The facts will speak.* She had questions, too.

A woman in a white jumpsuit approached. "Hold out your hands, please."

Nefi held out her hands, which the woman swabbed, avoiding the blood. She put the swabs in small evidence bags and labeled them. Next, the technician swabbed blood from Nefi's hands, placing each swab in a separate evidence bag and labeling them. Nefi handed Mingmei's lace-trimmed handkerchief to the technician, who stuck it into a separate evidence bag.

A businessman dashed to a luxury sedan parked nearby and turned off its alarm. Police officers and a few bystanders applauded. Other car alarms rang in the distance.

People who had run for cover were back to record the aftermath on their cell phones. Nefi believed they would post messages on social media about how close they came to danger.

Nefi's face hurt worse than her ear. She wasn't sure pressure slowed the bleeding much, but it seemed the proper thing to do. As her emotions calmed, she looked around. Somewhere inside the taped-off crime scene, she left a spent 9mm shell casing and a piece of her ear.

Avery motioned to a paramedic, who cleaned and bandaged Nefi's face and ear. After the paramedic left, Avery introduced Nefi to a uniformed police officer and explained the officer would accompany her to the precinct for her statement. Avery placed his business card in Nefi's right hand. To the officer, he said, "Put her in the front seat."

"The front?" the officer asked.

"We have a statement from a courthouse officer who saw the shooting," Detective Avery said. "You are escorting Mrs. Gunnerson to the precinct for a victim statement."

On the way to the officer's car, Nefi handed the card to Mingmei. "We're going to the police precinct."

Mingmei held the card and nodded.

Nefi kept pace with the young officer who guided her under the tape barrier to his car, placing her in the front seat while cameras pointed at her and reporters shouted into microphones over the car alarms.

Once inside the car, Nefi said, "Which hospital was Vincent Gunnerson taken to?"

"He's the big guy who got shot in the leg?"

"Yes. My husband." She thanked God for the ambulance's quick response.

The officer started up his squad car. "I'll find out." He drove around shards of glass from a storefront. Along the way, clusters of people stood on the sidewalk in animated conversations. Nefi's cell phone rang and rang, vibrating her jacket. *Bad news travels fast.*

Once again, she'd be front-page news in the media's feeding frenzy. Of course, the retraction would share the front page with the shooting and earthquake, which were bigger news than the promised retraction, but a contract was a contract.

The television news teams and bystanders would spread the word about the shooting and the earthquake far and wide from their point of view, driven more by the desire to be the first to report than to be factually accurate.

The police radio blared calls and responses from units about power outages, lost traffic lights, people stuck in elevators, and other pleas for help.

"I've lived here all my life," the officer said. "This is my first earthquake. I heard on the radio it registered five-point-eight on the Richter scale."

Nefi turned toward him to let him know she was listening.

He glanced at her. "We're almost there. How are you doing?"

"I appreciate riding in the front."

He chuckled. "Have you been in a police cruiser before?"

Nefi nodded and looked away.

"Oh. Okay."

The more she tried to avoid thinking about her last ride in police custody, the more the memories flashed through her mind. After a deep breath, she thanked God she was alive and prayed Vincent would recover quickly. The rest of the ride was quiet except for radio transmissions and the ringing of her cell phone. As soon as she could, she'd call her friends and family to report her status and Vincent's. She believed one of the unanswered calls came from Martina. Martina's addiction to social media had waned since her kidnapping, but she would see the trending news from Richmond, Virginia, and worry.

She dug into her pocket for her phone.

"Do you have any weapons?" the officer's voice was firm.

"No. I'm looking for my phone." She pulled it out, and the envelope from her grandfather fell onto her lap. This was as good a time as any to read the message, so she opened the envelope. When she unfolded the handwritten letter, a photo dropped out. It showed a smiling, balding man cradling a baby who stared up at him while Marta looked over the man's shoulder.

"Dear Nefi,

I've thought about calling you a hundred times but could not because of the pending libel case. Please forgive me. It seems Jane used the newspaper to deflect attention from her own crimes. When I saw the evidence against her, I realized she was not the person I loved and trusted.

When Jane's trial comes, I will testify for the prosecution.

I am proud of you. You have overcome tragedy and flourished under the care of Louise and Hamilton.

You were one month old when Marta brought you to see Jane's father.

If you ever choose to speak to me again, you can reach me at my phone number and address below. If you choose not to, then the loss is all mine.

Ted Wright"

Nefi patted the photo of her great-grandfather. Having studied Maslow's Hierarchy of Need, Nefi understood after people's basic needs of food, clothing, and shelter were met, they wanted their lives to matter. In their search for meaning, some seek immortality through foundations, monuments, applause, popularity, and children.

In the end, everyone gets the same size coffin.

Just like her great-grandfather, her grandfather suffered losses. Ted had lost his company, his marriage, and his only child. As the only other member of his family, Nefi decided to respond to the letter later.

She wanted her legacy to be one of love and service to others. She could not fix the broken like her grandfather, but she could forgive him. She could not fix the empty-hearted like her grandmother, who chose evil instead of love, self instead of God, and the temporary instead of the eternal. Nefi could forgive.

Under her grandfather's signature were his phone number, his new address, and a postscript that read, *"P.S. I have lost track of an old revolver. It is a Smith & Wesson 9mm Luger, Model 940. Perhaps it's in one of my unpacked boxes. At today's hearing, I will mention it to my attorney. If I find it, would you like it?"*

Nefi laughed.

·34·

VINCENT TOOK A deep breath as he stepped out of his car. He had not been back since the graduation dinner years ago, and being at Modelo's Café again raised painful memories. They were here to celebrate Nefi's graduation from FBI training. He exhaled slowly on his way around the car to open the passenger door for Nefi.

She climbed out of the car and hugged him hard as if sensing his unease.

"I still don't understand why you want to celebrate here."

Nefi released him and said, "I didn't get dessert last time."

He grunted and followed her, shaking his head. This time, he would stay by her side or keep her in sight all evening. He took long strides to open the door for her.

She smiled and dragged her fingers across his chest as she passed him.

Her gesture completely changed his mood.

Vincent drew in a deep breath and exhaled quickly before following her into the bakery section of the building. He'd read somewhere how scent triggered memories. It was true. Modelo's Market Café smelled like fresh-baked bread, buttery sweetness, coffee, pork roast, and spices favored in Brazilian food. Though the scents enticed him, they also elicited visions of red and blue strobe lights, blood, and Nefi lying face-up on the road, struggling to breathe.

Sounds also triggered memories. As he and Nefi passed through the shopping aisles to the restaurant in the back, he recognized Mutt's laugh mingled with Senator Hamilton's voice over the din of multiple conversations.

Let tonight be joyful. No drama. No gunshots. No blood.

When Nefi crossed the threshold between the shop and the restaurant, friends and family cheered. Nefi rushed to embrace her aunt and uncle, then the Brazilian Ambassador and his wife. Hu's bulk framed petite Mingmei Cho. Mutt had his arm around Helen Cho's shoulders. Ruis and Sofia Ramos were huddled in conversation with Blake and Terri. Vincent found himself following Nefi with handshakes and hugs as if they were working the room at their wedding. Blake weaved around the tables, which formed a large U shape with the open end facing the kitchen.

Blake held a champagne flute while he greeted Vincent with a manly one-armed, back-slapping hug. "How does it feel to be married to an FBI Agent?"

"I'm a little intimidated." Vincent stole a glance at his beautiful soul mate. She was among friends and family, and she was armed.

Ruis handed Vincent a flute of bubbling champagne.

The three men raised their glasses in salute. Blake and Vincent had first met Ruis on the mission to rescue Nefi in the Amazon rainforest over seven years ago. This day felt like the culmination of their mission. Nefi had survived and flourished in the United States despite her meager command of English and the enormous cultural chasm between a childhood in the rainforest and high school life among the rich and powerful families of Washington, D.C.

After they all took a sip, Ruis asked Blake. "How's Atlanta?"

"We love the suburbs. Buckhead has welcomed us. Our house is in a great neighborhood, and Terri makes house calls for a farming co-op." He set down his glass. "Pray for me. She takes me to fly-ins on weekends. I own stock in air-sickness bags."

"Why don't you take flying lessons?" Ruis aimed his glass toward Arlo "Repo" Barlow, the private investigator and helicopter pilot. "You know, share her passion?"

Arlo and Terri were in an animated discussion involving sweeping hand movements as if simulating aerobatic flight. Vincent smiled. As if it weren't challenging enough to be a veterinarian, Terri was also an instrument-rated private pilot. Pity Blake was afraid of flying.

Blake scowled. "I suppose if he can do it, I can."

Ruis elbowed Blake. "I happen to know Repo is afraid of horses."

Blake grinned. "Thanks. I needed that."

The men watched Terri and Arlo.

A young male server carried a tray of filled glasses around the room. Terri took a glass of tea. Arlo held a soft drink. The server paused near Nefi long enough to get a hug before handing her a soda. *The server must be Carlos, the young man who felt guilty about not walking Nefi to the car that night.*

Blake sighed. "Terri's not going to give up flying, so I might as well learn how."

Across the room, Nefi handed her credentials to Cassie, who opened up the leather wallet displaying a metal badge and government-issued identification.

Vincent spoke just loud enough for Blake and Ruis to hear. "Do you know what Nefi's training class called her?"

"The Amazon?" Blake said.

Vincent shook his head.

"Mrs. Gunnerson?" Ruis said.

Vincent leaned toward his friends. "The Beast. Apparently, she broke a few training records."

Ruis and Blake spoke in unison. "I'm not surprised."

Blake, being Blake, turned away and waved, "Hey, Helen, look who's here!" He pointed at Vincent.

Helen Cho immediately abandoned a conversation with her sister and marched toward Vincent, with Hu following in her wake.

Blake paled and whispered, "Who's the giant?"

"Hu," Vincent said.

"Who? The one headed toward us," Blake whispered.

Helen hugged Vincent. "We are all so proud of Nefi." She then turned toward Blake. "This is my cousin, Hu. Hu, meet Blake Clayton, Terri's husband."

Blake exhaled and stuck out his hand.

"Hu kept me from bleeding out at the courthouse," Vincent said.

"Ah, you're the man with the vise grip," Blake said, shaking Hu's hand.

Hu nodded.

The restaurant owner, Joe De Souza, announced dinner was about to be served, so people searched for their names on tented cards. Nefi pointed to the center of the tables arranged in a U. Vincent found his name written in calligraphy beside Nefi's place setting. He pulled out her chair, which earned him smiles from Nefi and Mrs. Louise Jenkins seated on the corner beyond Nefi.

Vincent knew everyone in the restaurant except one well-dressed couple seated between Senator Jenkins and Cassie. Was he a local congressman? Once seated, Vincent leaned close to Nefi. "Who is sitting beside Cassie?"

"Ronald Lancaster and his wife May. He's an investment advisor with Attucks, Bird, and Copley. He just became a full partner."

"Nice." Vincent recognized the name from the wedding guest list. He suspected Nefi had helped the man secure a partnership position. As of last quarter, her trust fund was valued at $13.8 million. So far, her biggest purchase was a desk and two bookcases for the study. She had fewer clothes in the closet than Vincent did, which amused Martina and Oscar.

Vincent could not imagine his life without Nefi. By the grace of God, Nefi had dodged a bullet. A renowned plastic surgeon reduced the scar on her cheek to a fine smooth line but couldn't patch the missing chunk of the ear, so the surgeon trimmed the ear's edge to minimize the gap of the missing part.

While dinner was served, Vincent ran his fingertips along the scar on his thigh. Nefi treated him as though he'd thrown himself like a human shield to stop the bullet meant for her. The truth was, he didn't see it coming. Having reviewed the surveillance recordings of the shooting and the police reports, he learned Jane had no experience firing a weapon. He concluded the weight and recoil of the short-barreled, double-action revolver was too much for the petite older woman to handle, so she jerked the trigger, which pulled the barrel down and to the left—where he was. Had it been a .357 revolver, he would have lost his leg.

Vincent considered Nefi to be the hero of the day. Her quick reaction and expert aim ended the threat with one shot while his three rounds staggered but did not stop Jane. Days later, when Vincent and Nefi settled into bed together, bandaged and sore, he asked why she aimed for the head. Was it easier to see the laser's green dot on the skin? Nefi said when she aimed, the forehead appeared larger than life-size as though guiding her where to fire.

Detective Kelly's report showed Jane was wearing an old Army surplus vest under layers of her homeless disguise. Clever, but not clever enough.

Tonight, their friends and family gathered to celebrate FBI Agent Nefi. Vincent was so proud of her that it sometimes staggered him. Nefi had grown into a formidable woman. She had the skills, the authority, the love, and most of all, the faith to live a life that mattered. Nefi Gunnerson understood the world was dangerous.

So was she.

The End

Thank you for buying this book!
Please take a moment to leave a quick review, just
a sentence or two, to let other readers know about
it. Your review is vital to the success of this book.

ABOUT THE AUTHOR

After working decades in journalism, **Joni M. Fisher** turned to crime. Her Compass Crimes series has garnered attention in *Publisher's Weekly* and the *US Review*. Her books have won or finaled in the Kindle Book Awards, the Clue Book Awards, The Next Generation Indie Book Awards, the National Indie Excellence Awards, the Royal Palm Literary Awards, and others. She is a member of Sisters in Crime, the American Christian Fiction Writers (ACFW), and a lifetime member of the Florida Writers Association. She served on the Arts and Humanities Advisory Board for Southeastern University. Her fingerprints are on file with the FBI.

Visit her online at JoniMFisher.com or
sign up for email updates at *http://eepurl.com/dNTVCA*

Instagram: authorjonimfisher
Twitter: @JoniMFisher
Facebook.com/AuthorJoniMFisher

Thank you for buying this book. To receive special offers, bonus content, and info on new releases and other great reads, sign up for our newsletter *http://eepurl.com/dNTVCA.*